CW00696943

SCARLET
LETTERS

Also edited by Eleanor Sullivan and available from Carroll & Graf:

Fifty Years of the Best from *Ellery Queen's Mystery Magazine*

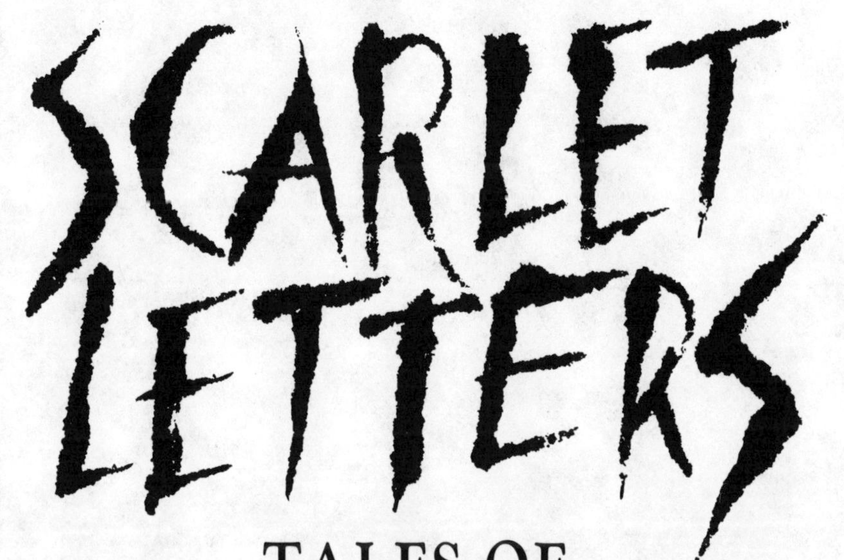

SCARLET LETTERS

TALES OF ADULTERY FROM ELLERY QUEEN'S MYSTERY MAGAZINE

EDITED BY ELEANOR SULLIVAN

Carroll & Graf Publishers, Inc.
New York

First Carroll & Graf edition 1991

Carroll & Graf Publishers, Inc.
260 Fifth Avenue
New York, NY 10001

Library of Congress Cataloging-in-Publication Data
Scarlet letters : tales of adultery from Ellery Queen's mystery magazine / edited by Eleanor Sullivan.
p. cm.
ISBN 0-88184-684-8
1. Detective and mystery stories, American. 2. Adultery—Fiction.
I. Sullivan, Eleanor. II. Ellery Queen's mystery magazine.
PS648.D4S28 1991
813'.087208353—dc20 91-12565
CIP

Manufactured in the United States of America

CONTENTS

ACKNOWLEDGMENTS

Grateful acknowledgment is made to the following for their permission to use their copyrighted material.

"Happiness You Can Count On" by William Bankier, Copyright © 1980 by Davis Publications, Inc. Reprinted by permission of Curtis Brown, Ltd.

"Breakfast Television" by Robert Barnard, Copyright © 1986 by Davis Publications, Inc. Reprinted by permission of the author.

"As Good as a Rest" by Lawrence Block, Copyright © 1986 by Davis Publications, Inc. Reprinted by permission of Knox Burger Associates, Ltd.

"Count Your Blessings" by Simon Brett, Copyright © 1980 by Davis Publications, Inc. Reprinted by permission of JCA Literary Agency, Inc.

"The Three Musketeers" by Jeremiah Healy, Copyright © 1990 by Davis Publications, Inc. Reprinted by permission of Jed Mattes, Inc.

"High Noon at Mach Seven" by Clark Howard, Copyright © 1986 by Davis Publications, Inc. Reprinted by permission of the author.

"The Last Time" by Andrew Klavan, Copyright © 1988 by Davis Publications, Inc. Reprinted by permission of the author.

"In The Clear" by Patricia McGerr, Copyright © 1978 by Davis Publications, Inc. Reprinted by permission of Curtis Brown, Ltd.

"Widow?" by Florence V. Mayberry, Copyright © 1985 by Davis Publications, Inc. Reprinted by permission of the author.

"Web of Circumstance" by Donald Olson, Copyright © 1980 by Davis Publications, Inc. Reprinted by permission of Blanch C. Gregory, Inc.

"A Taste for Foxglove" by Sharon Pisacreta, Copyright © 1989 by Davis Publications, Inc. Reprinted by permission of the author.

INTRODUCTION

Reflecting on this anthology of stories about adultery, it occurred to me that the reader might enjoy the challenge of trying to guess from a blind excerpt from several stories which one it is from. If you choose to do this after reading the stories, you will of course have an edge. And if you are familiar with the work of the authors, that should also give you an edge. There is no prize for correctly matching the story and author aside from the fun of doing it, but that I hope will be considerable. Happy sleuthing!

Brenda looked at the still water in the tub and fiddled with her neat little chin, pondering. Who would have come sneaking in and stabbed Roy? Frank?

No, Frank had no call to get drastic—Roy was away on business trips most of the time. He hardly got in the way of Brenda and Frank's long-running affair.

Who then? *Someone* had finished him, that was for sure.

A smile touched her pretty if somewhat sharp-featured face. Things work out, sometimes.

Autumn tried to force her paralyzed body into action, to cry out for help—beg Chris to lift her, put her feet on the floor, walk her back to life.

But he only stood there, not touching her. Chill emanated from him. He has wandered too long in the cold, she thought. "You found out," he said, his voice tired and flat. "And that killed me."

"Oh, look, his tie's gone askew," Caroline would say, or, "You know, Ben's much balder than he was twelve months ago—I've never noticed it in the flesh." Michael seldom managed to assent to such propositions with any easy grace. He was much too conscious of balding, genial, avuncular Ben grinning out from the television screen as he tried to wring from some graceless pop star three words strung together consecutively that actually made sense. "I think he's getting fatter in the face," said Caroline, licking marmalade off her fingers.

Cruft picked up the money the next day, his bags packed, his hotel bill paid, the plane ticket in his pocket. Fergie and Rita did not offer him a drink. They did not ask him to sit down. He took the envelope and went away with his face burning, knowing they had paid him off just to be rid of him. The word "blackmail" had not been mentioned.

Well, damnit, they were getting away with murder, or something akin to it. By cheating, they had arranged happiness for themselves. Why should he not have his share?

Lying awake in the night, Tricia thought of what leaving Ford would mean—going back to live with her mother while he went to Marguerite. Ford wasn't asleep, either. She could hear the sound of his irregular wakeful breathing. She heard the bed creak as he moved in it restlessly, the air conditioner grinding, the whine of a mosquito.

Andrew and Elaine and Harry and Sue "did" six countries in twenty-two days, but what they did in each, and where and with whom, was strictly up to them.

Donna grunted. "Do you know how much Harvey makes for doing the same thing? Sixty-two thousand a year."

"Yeah, but he gets to wear those snappy uniforms and have all the peasants salute him."

"Big deal."

"I *never* get saluted."

"Poor baby. Want me to salute you?"

Buddy looked over and smiled. "I'd rather salute you."

Donna returned his look knowingly. "Better get in the water, Briscoe, and cool off."

When it was done it was the prettiest thing Lucy had ever baked.

She served it for dessert that night.

Ray began to eat the cake and to savor it and to say extravagant things to her, and when he finished the first slice he said, Lucyhon, may I have another piece, a big one, please.

Why, Ray, it's all yours to eat as you like, she said.

Although a moderate gambler, Frank Crawford did not bet more than he could afford to lose, seldom backed a long shot, and never drew to an inside straight. When his marriage at last became intolerable, he studied his alternatives with the same cautious deliberation that he gave a sales campaign for his appliance company.

"I'll go along with whatever lie you've told these doctors," Anne went on. "I'll tell them about mixing up my medication or whatever *merde* you've handed them. What *did* you tell them, by the way?"

"That you like to make new herbal teas," said Lucien, "and you accidentally picked the wrong herb."

Just before leaving, Edward came lugging his old suitcase downstairs.

"Oh, you found it," Cecile said. "Was it in the attic?"

"No. In the closet."

Even then nothing registered, and it was only after he'd driven away that the thought struck her: the closet! Good heavens, that's where she kept the diary hidden. She rushed upstairs and pulled on the light. An oblong space in the film of dust showed where the old suitcase had been sitting, directly beneath the shelf where she kept the diary.

"I have come tonight to plead for romance in the world of crime," Oliver said, "for the locked-room murder, the impossible theft, the crime committed by the invisible man. I have come to plead that you should bring wit and style and complexity to your writings about crime, that you should remember Stevenson's view that life is a bazaar of dangerous and smiling chances, and the remark of Thomas Griffiths Wainewright when he confessed to poisoning his pretty sister-in-law: 'It was a terrible thing to do, but she had thick ankles.' "

That's it. Have a wonderful read. Good luck with your score. And don't take it to heart if I wish you a red-letter day, all right?

—Eleanor Sullivan

SCARLET LETTERS

HAPPINESS YOU CAN COUNT ON

by WILLIAM BANKIER

Corey Telford first came from Canada to London in search of fame and fortune. He settled for a good living as a correspondent sending back voice reports of European news stories to the Canadian Broadcasting Corporation in Montreal. Thirty years old, a handsome bachelor, articulate in four languages, Telford indulged himself for the first year, going where he chose, doing what he liked. Then he fell in love with Stephanie Robson.

They met at a publicity reception for a West End play. Telford was freeloading on his press pass. Stephanie was there because one of the actors had worked recently at the Richmond Theatre where she was assistant stage manager. They drank a lot of white wine together and Telford drove her home to suburban Surrey on a June evening with the sky red and pale-green after ten o'clock.

She was absolutely made for Telford. He liked strong women. Stephanie was solidly built, her chestnut hair shorn shoulder-length and scented with whatever she used to keep it shiny. In repose, her face—slightly protruding upper lip, heavy eyebrows, high cheekbones, slanting eyes—could be called fierce. When she smiled, a magnetic delight radiated from her. Telford knew a lot of men would think her "butch." But she was exactly his cup of tea, not to say his roast-beef sandwich.

The attraction was mutual. Saying goodbye with false dawn in the sky, Stephanie stood in the semi-basement doorway of her bedsitter on Richmond Hill and frowned at him. "Are you sure you weren't just released from prison?" she said.

"I'll never be a free man again," Telford countered happily. He walked along the Royal Terrace to where he had parked his car. The Thames curved like spilled silver far below between dark trees.

To be closer to Stephanie on a daily basis, Telford moved out of his flat in Chelsea and into rooms which were part of one of the big white houses overlooking the cricket pitch on Richmond Green. His landlord was a friendly businessman named Ferguson Cruft. Cruft owned the largest Ford dealership in Surrey, purchased by him years before with inherited money when a pound was worth over three dollars; he was a wealthy man.

"Have a housewarming drink," he said on the first day, appearing in the rose-festooned kitchen doorway to catch Telford as he emerged from his private entrance at the back of the house.

"I won't say no."

Telford followed his host into the kitchen and on through into a small room where most of a precious oriental rug was hidden under Jacobean furniture. Crystal gleamed behind cabinet doors and there were family photographs in oval silver frames. Dark beams crossed the ceiling.

Cruft poured whisky into squat tumblers. He raised his eyebrows and the water carafe at the same time. Telford nodded in silence, inhaling the dry smell of security, grateful to share some of it, not envious. After all, he had Stephanie—let Ferguson Cruft top that.

They were standing drinking, an English custom, when Beryl Cruft came into the room. She smiled at Telford but not before he caught the disapproving glance she gave the whisky bottle. Her husband escaped censure—the bottle took the blame.

"All settled in, then?" she said. "No thank you, Fergie, much too early for me. Will you have some supper with us, Mr. Telford? You'll be too tired to prepare your own."

"Thank you, another time. I'm meeting my friend. She works at the theater down the road."

"Ah. Very nice." Cruft beamed down at his wife. He was a substantial cedar tree of a man, rusty-haired with massive trunk and spreading arms which he liked to drape companionably over family or friends or customers. Anyone within arm's reach of Fergie Cruft might at any moment be drawn against him and smiled down upon. Beryl Hees-Cruft, as she was addressed on her copious daily post, was one of those alert, grey, bird-women who park their tiny cars on English high streets and run in and out of shops. Her tweed skirt stopped at the knees, leaving sinewy legs to extend into flat shoes. Telford looked away.

"Feel free to entertain your friends when you like," Cruft said. "The only house rule is be happy."

"Is she an actress?" Beryl inquired.

The summer was such perfection that when a wasp stung Telford on the neck in September it seemed no more than an adjustment of the balance of his life toward a more realistic alignment. He had been active for weeks with Stephanie. On a bright Saturday they went walking in Richmond Park, where herds of deer browsing in tall grass and the persistent clouds of black flies filled Telford's imagination with thoughts of the African savannah. On a rainy Sunday they drove to Teddington and enjoyed a lavish cream tea in a cottage named after the Eighteenth Century actress Peg Woffington who was said to have lived there.

On a late evening in July the young couple entered a roadhouse outside Twickenham and came upon Ferguson Cruft and a dark-haired woman at a table near the back door. They were head-to-head over empty glasses, his hand touching hers.

"Where are we going?" Stephanie asked as Telford steered her abruptly into another room.

"That looks like my landlord," he said. "But it doesn't look like my landlord's wife."

"Shocking." She bit him on the cheek. "That house will be a wicked influence on you."

"Is there such a thing as contributing to the delinquency of a pervert?"

"Guilty, your honor. And proud of it."

When Cruft led his woman outside, Telford had a better look at her through a window. She was pleasantly heavy with shiny black hair braided and pinned. Unfastened, it would make a spectacular display. Her eyes were dark and intelligent. The pair of them floated to Cruft's car as if they had been drinking for some time.

The wasp that got Telford found him when he was fishing for his front-door key late one afternoon. The insects were everywhere these days, one per flower and enough left over to make you think twice before reaching into the window of a pastry shop for a couple of jam tarts. The locals said they were "dozey" at this time. As he took out his key, Telford felt a movement on the back of his neck, brushed at it, and experienced a sharp pain. The wasp fell to the pavement where Telford mashed it under his shoe.

Two days later, he mentioned to his landlord that he was still feeling pain in the swelling on his neck and a bit of discomfort under his right arm. "Some people are allergic to stings," Cruft said. "Let me telephone Dr. Hathaway for you." As he made the appointment, Fergie draped a reassuring arm over Telford's shoulder.

The doctor's surgery was within walking distance. Telford went there, surprised that the health service would see him so promptly for such a non-emergency. When he was greeted at the door by Dr. Hathaway, he was surprised again. She was the dark woman from Cruft's roadhouse rendezvous.

A short course of antibiotics was prescribed. The doctor seemed to think Telford's place of residence made him a favored patient. She said her name was Rita. "I've been the Crufts' family doctor for a long time. He's a marvelous man."

"Yes, I like Fergie very much."

"He never thinks of himself. He's the sort of man who can keep something hidden for years, just to spare others."

Telford wondered if Rita Hathaway was referring to Cruft's relationship with her. It seemed she was not. "I suggested he at least tell his son," the doctor said cryptically as she handed over a scribbled prescription. "Sebastian's stock in trade is, after all, secrets. What about the confessional? But Fergie said no."

"Sebastian?"

"Their only son. You must have seen his picture on the mantelpiece."

"The priest?"

"Yes. Sebastian converted to Catholicism years ago. His parish is in Yorkshire."

Telford went away with a confused mind. The Crufts had a son in the Catholic clergy. Fergie had a secret that he was concealing from his family but not from his doctor. What was going on?

Telford's wasp-sting responded quickly to the antibiotic. This was a good thing because his swollen neck was inhibiting Stephanie's embrace. They celebrated with an evening at her bedsitter on the hill. When he arrived back down at the house on the Green, tousled and spent, Telford was surprised to find the lights on and the side door open. Fergie heard him walking by and called him in. It was a full family conference, plus physician.

"Meet my son, Sebastian. Mr. Telford is a famous voice in Canada. He's on the radio from London more than Ed Murrow used to be."

The young priest was a sober individual. He was his father with all the love of life drained out of him. His chin showed a couple of shaving cuts and his eyes suggested he might have enjoyed inflicting them. He gave Telford a tentative handshake and sat back down. Rita Hathaway sat in a deep chair holding a whisky glass with both hands in a dramatic pose, all eyes and pouting lips. She might have been about to bless sacramental wine. Fergie was drinking too. Mother and son were dry.

"We're digesting some bad news," Beryl said in a scolding tone. "The family is deciding what to do."

"I have already decided," Cruft said. "And it isn't bad news. How many men receive the sort of warning given to me? Without it, I might have refused my competitor's offer to buy my business. I might have gone on and on until—who knows?"

After a silence, Dr. Hathaway explained: "Fergie and I have done some tests. He's been experiencing symptoms for quite a while. The fact is, his heart will not let him pursue an active life any longer."

"It's all the drinking," Beryl said to her son.

"Drinking makes me happy," Cruft said. He turned to Telford. "Here's the plan. I've accepted a huge offer—not a king's ransom but a couple of princes' ransoms—to buy my business. When the deal goes through, I'm off to Canada, just me, to visit my old haunts."

Sebastian glanced at his father with a glitter of respect in his china eyes. "Father was an instructor with the Commonwealth Air-Training Plan during the war," he said. "He spent four years at Trenton in Ontario."

"I don't expect to see a lot of the old people," Cruft said. "Perhaps a few, and some of the familiar places." He sighed and raised his glass in Rita's direction. She toasted him silently.

A few weeks later, Ferguson Cruft purchased a round-trip ticket from Air Canada. As it turned out, the airline had to refund half the fare because Fergie ended up coming home in Rita Hathaway's suitcase. Telford explained the circumstances to Stephanie during the interval at the Aldwych Theatre where they had gone to see the Royal Shakespeare Company production of Marlowe's *Dr. Faustus.*

"Fergie was a unique man," Telford said, sipping tepid gin in the Circle Bar. "So open. On the day I met him, he made me feel I'd known him for years."

"I'm sorry he died."

"All alone over in Canada." Telford sighed. "I suppose it was what he wanted. He knew he was going. His doctor told me the symptoms were present for years but he told nobody till near the end."

While Stephanie pretended not to be bored, Telford related the details of Cruft's death in Trenton. It had been sudden. A local doctor had wired Rita Hathaway the news, following instructions on a card Cruft carried with him. Rita volunteered to fly out and claim the body and bring it home. Beryl accepted this arrangement because both women knew Rita would make a better job of it.

Unfortunately, there was a misunderstanding on the part of the Trenton undertaker. When Dr. Hathaway arrived, she discovered that Fergie's body had been cremated. After the initial shock, she saw the event as a convenience and she was able to put this point of view across successfully in a transatlantic call to Beryl. Next day she flew home with Fergie's ashes in a small sky-blue urn which rested now on the Richmond mantelpiece beside the photograph of Father Sebastian Cruft.

This macabre story almost spoiled the evening for Stephanie. Her mood was restored only by the sight of a half naked, screaming actor slithering through a crevice in the stage into smoke and realistic flames. She was nice to Telford when they went to his place later that night but she let it be understood she wanted to hear no more about the late Ferguson Cruft.

The way things turned out, Stephanie was soon in danger of hearing very little more from Telford about anything. His CBC employers summoned him back to Montreal for discussions about his future status. The ominous words "budgetary considerations" were mentioned.

Saying his farewells, hoping to be back soon, Telford dropped around to take his leave of Dr. Hathaway. She was gone. Her replacement explained that Rita had finally become fed up with the bureaucracy of the National Health Service. She had been hanging on only because of connections with certain private patients. That situation had changed with Cruft's death and she had taken off for Montreal.

During the week of his departure, Telford was trapped into a conversation with the widow Beryl. He had been avoiding her. While her husband was alive, she had existed as a dim figure in the shadow of his larger-than-life personality. Now that Fergie had been cut down, she stood alone in the foreground of Telford's awareness, a forlorn woman but somehow demanding and vaguely dangerous.

On this day, she maneuvered him into the sitting room and poured two whiskies. The guest's drink was not large but her own was barely a stain on the bottom of the glass. "You will be back, won't you?" she asked. "I'd like to know how to think of the apartment."

A week ago, shocked by his summons back to Montreal, Telford had blurted out the risk of losing his job. "I hope so," he said. "If the news is bad, I'll let you know in time to rent the apartment."

"It isn't the rent. Ferguson left me the house free and clear and most of the proceeds from the sale of the business. He also did well by Sebastian. No, we're fine." She dampened her lower lip with whisky. "It's a matter of missing you. I've become quite used to having you in the house, Corey."

He returned her smile with an effort. She had aged after her husband's death. There was a brittle look about her hair and the backs of her hands gleamed like wax. Telford began to suspect, irrationally, that the breath she was exhaling might be poisonous. He excused himself and, as an antidote, hurried to see Stephanie.

Back in Montreal, his worst fears were realized. Hébert, the director, was diplomatic and apologetic but the decision had been made. The Corporation would buy reports when needed from Europeans on the scene. Telford was to come home where some sort of work would be found for him.

"Bien, c'est pas mal," Hébert said. "You had a good run, eh? Now you come back to Montreal."

"I suppose so," Telford said. Were it not for Stephanie, he might have come back willingly. But he could not leave her.

It was out of the question. There had to be a way for him to go on living in London.

"Cheer up." Hébert took something from a drawer in his desk. "Here's a spare ticket for the Expos game. Go and enjoy yourself."

Telford went to the Rainbow Bar, where he stuffed himself with spinach pie and made himself fairly drunk on the bourbon he could seldom find in English pubs. Then he rode the gleaming new Metro line to the Olympic Stadium. The place was crowded. The Expos, for the first time in their brief history, were making a run at the National League pennant. Stargell and his accomplices were in town from Pittsburgh to show the locals that the good experienced team will always beat the good young one.

The game was exciting and Telford managed to lose himself in it. During the seventh-inning stretch, he stood and looked around, comparing the spectacular stadium with the bandbox intimacy of the old Jarry Park.

That was when he saw Fergie Cruft sitting four rows behind him, drinking from a large carton of beer. Rita Hathaway was doing the same. They were flushed and fat and smugly alive. Telford sat down and divided his attention between the game and the ghost behind him. When the last Expo was out and the crowd moved to the exits, he kept the pair in sight, overtaking them in the parking lot.

"I don't believe this, Fergie," he said.

"Hello there, Corey. Wasn't that a great game? Baseball is one of the things I missed when I went back to England in 1946." Cruft seemed unembarrassed. His massive arm encircled Telford and steered him into the back seat of the sedan. He followed the puzzled broadcaster inside while Rita slid behind the wheel and drove downtown, glancing anxiously from time to time in the rearview mirror.

Telford held his tongue until they arrived at a house in Westmount near the park. It was not as grand as the residence in Richmond, but inside it showed the confident disarray of rooms that are happily lived in. An obvious difference in Fergie's new life style was the size and prominence of his liquor cabinet. When they were seated with full glasses, Telford got to the point.

"I won't say I'm not happy to see you alive and kicking," he said, "but what's the story?"

"A hoax, of course. I had to get away from Beryl. I had to be able to settle down with Rita."

"So you faked the whole thing?"

"That's right," Rita said. She was sharing the sofa with her man, the two of them thigh to thigh, close as animals in a burrow. The couple adored each other and Telford was reminded of himself and Stephanie. "Even the symptoms I told you about. We worked it all out. Fergie is perfectly healthy. But we told Beryl and Sebastian he had been keeping his heart condition a secret for years. Then it worsened, we said, and the trip to wartime haunts became now or never."

"But how did you get a Canadian doctor to go along with you?"

"There was no Canadian doctor. Fergie simply sent me a wire with the bad news, signed by a phony name. I showed Beryl and convinced her I should come over. I flew to Montreal, picked up an urn from an undertaker's supply shop, and flew back. The ashes I collected from my fireplace."

"It's too easy," Telford protested. "It could never work."

"Why not?" Fergie asked, generously refilling glasses. "Nobody had any reason to query the situation. My family doctor said I was terminal. She brought back the remains. My wife and son were both bequeathed a great deal of money and property." He smiled. "The only people who probe deaths are insurance investigators. But I had no insurance. My money was in negotiable securities."

"Not all of it," Rita said. "For a few years, Fergie has been taking cash out of the business and buying diamonds. When he came away, he brought them with him. We're living on them now, and on my savings."

"But why go to all this trouble? Couldn't you have divorced Beryl and remarried in England?"

"With my son a Roman Catholic priest? Impossible."

"It still seems like a complicated business just to unload an unwanted wife."

"Not very. It was exciting, in fact. Never forget, people feed on excitement. Boredom is what grinds us down." Fergie put his arm around Rita's shoulders and they sat there radiating satisfaction.

"Besides," he went on, "Beryl wouldn't let me drink. That may sound ridiculous—she couldn't stop me—What I mean is she took the fun out of it. Is alcohol that important? To me it is. Rita and I have a whole range of places we go to—hotel lounges, hole-in-the-wall bars, brasseries—and we have this place. There's always warmth and music and conversation. Dreams. Memories." He raised his glass. "And this. It's happiness I can count on. I turn it on every day, like lighting the fire." His face became a little sad. "Back home it was denied me. Rita and I had to steal a few hours here and there. Poor Beryl—she can't help thinking there's something wicked about it."

Telford went back to his hotel bemused by the story—not critical of the devious couple, but feeling their situation had some significance for him.

He awoke in the morning knowing what it was.

"It's me, Fergie," he said on the telephone after breakfast. "We talked so much about you two last night I hadn't a chance to mention *my* problem."

He went on to describe his loss of London employment and his conviction that without Stephanie he wouldn't survive. "So I don't know what to do," he concluded. "I've got to get my hands on a chunk of money to keep me in Richmond at least until I can—" He stopped.

Cruft let silence accumulate. When he spoke there was only a hint of annoyance in his voice. "I understand your wish to stay with the woman you love. You and me and Edward the Eighth. I can let you have some money. Shall we say five thousand dollars?"

"In cash, please, Fergie."

He picked up the money the next day, his bags packed, his hotel bill paid, the plane ticket in his pocket. Fergie and Rita did not offer him a drink. They did not ask him to sit down. He took the envelope and went away with his face burning, knowing they had paid him off just to be rid of him. The word "blackmail" had not been mentioned.

Well, damnit, they were getting away with murder, or something akin to it. By cheating, they had arranged happiness for themselves. Why should he not have his share?

The trouble was that five thousand dollars, converted to pounds, did not last Telford long. Alone in the big house with Beryl—albeit in his separate apartment—he was continually aware of her presence. She called on him to adjust the television picture or help move a table. Her manner was grotesquely flirtatious.

To escape her attentions, he avoided the house, feeding Stephanie nightly in restaurants. "You aren't working," she commented. "Where is all the money coming from?"

"Savings," he said. "Don't worry, I'm all right." Then he made a suggestion he'd been mulling over. Would Stephanie consider moving to Canada where his CBC future would be assured?

Stephanie would consider no such thing. Her intention was to move her career ahead in a straight line from Richmond to London's West End. There was no alternative.

Telford's financial situation went from bad to worse. He was selling an occasional article to *The Listener,* and once he picked up a fee for phoning in a few reports to a private Canadian station. But these sums were insignificant. With no income from the Corporation as long as he remained on this side of the Atlantic, Telford could see the day approaching when he would be stoney broke.

He didn't want to approach Fergie again. But he made up his mind to do it as he walked home early on a frosty morning after the sweetest of all nights in Stephanie's arms. Her attraction for him was not fading; he was more committed to the relationship than ever.

Next day, he telephoned Montreal. Fergie did not seem all that surprised to hear from him. "You lasted longer than we expected," he said.

"I need money. I'm sorry. I hope to get reestablished—"

"Why do you imagine we should pay you again?"

"Because I can make things difficult for you." There it was —out at last. Blackmail was clearly implied.

"Difficult in what way?"

"You spirited money out of England. You've infringed the currency regulations."

"Believe me, there's no evidence. I was extremely careful. You'd have trouble proving anything."

"You faked your own death. That can't be legal."

"Rita forged a death certificate so that Beryl could inherit, I'll grant you that. Are you desperate enough to get her in trouble?"

"Your wife, then. I'll tell Beryl. She'll bring the two of you back to earth."

"Do what you think you must," Cruft said, and he did Telford a favor by terminating the expensive telephone call.

In the days that followed, Telford made a further effort to convince Stephanie she would learn to like living in Canada. If only he could persuade her to move back home with him he would be happy. "I'm telling you for the last time," she stated, erasing that possibility forever. "The English theater is London. Period. *J'y suis et j'y reste!*"

"That sounds like the French theater," he ventured. "Sounds like Montreal."

She did not laugh. The subject was well and truly closed.

Yet another avenue to survival was denied Telford a week later with the news from Yorkshire of Sebastian Cruft's unexpected death. The priest was on his way home from a visit to a parish family trying to cope with the problem of a runaway daughter. Crossing a normally quiet road at night, camouflaged in his black cassock, he was struck down by a speeding car. The only comfort Beryl Hees-Cruft could take with her on the desolate trip north was the realization that her son had died instantly. The burial took place, as Sebastian had ordained, in his own churchyard.

Within four days it was all over and Beryl had returned to Richmond.

Now Telford asked himself if he would have gone so far as

to blackmail Beryl? Would he have said to her, "Support me here in England or I'll tell your son his father's living in sin with Rita Hathaway in Montreal" ? Yes, he had been on the verge of doing that very thing.

Beryl was potting plants at a table by the side of the house when Telford emerged from his apartment in a destructive mood on an afternoon of alternating sunshine and shade. She must have read something in his eyes. "Is anything wrong?" she asked him.

"Nothing serious." He looked at her and saw the hickory face, the fringe of grey hair under the kerchief she had knotted on her head, and he thought, Why not fix Fergie? If he, Telford, was going to be forced home, leaving Stephanie here, then let Cruft come back and face his responsibilities. "Actually, there is. A while back when I was in Montreal, I had this incredible experience."

"Come in and have a cup of tea. Tell me all about it." She took his arm and drew him through the rose-framed doorway.

While the kettle whistled and Beryl made tea, Telford went through the whole improbable story. At the end, she remained calm. "I know," she said. "I agreed to let them go."

Telford was stunned. "But if you knew—"

"Sebastian didn't know. That was the agreement. Ferguson could fade away and die as long as my security was assured and Sebastian was spared the shock of knowing that his father was living with another woman. It doesn't matter any more." She sipped tea. "Poor Corey, you look shattered. You must have thought you could go on getting money from him."

"Don't tease me, Beryl. I'm in love with Stephanie—I can't tell you how much. I must stay in Richmond. But I can't earn my living here."

"That's the first time you've called me Beryl." She got up to carry her cup to the sink and paused behind his chair. "I have a suggestion."

He waited, knowing what was coming.

"I have plenty of money. More than enough for both of us. I'm lonelier than ever now that Sebastian is gone. Surely you'd prefer to move out of that cramped apartment into the main house with me." She paused, then went on. "I've no objections to your seeing Stephanie. You're a strong young man, full of love. There's no reason why you shouldn't continue living here with no money worries whatever. As long as you don't mind sharing . . ."

When Telford showed up at Stephanie's bedsitter that evening she was surprised that he immediately took a shower. Later, he seemed subdued. She had to work hard at enticing a response from him. It was as if, for him, the act of love had turned into a terrible duty.

BREAKFAST TELEVISION

by ROBERT BARNARD

The coming of breakfast television has been a great boon to the British.

Caroline Worsley thought so anyway, as she sat in bed eating toast and sipping tea, the flesh of her arm companionably warm against the flesh of Michael's arm. Soon they would make love again, perhaps while the consumer lady had her spot about dangerous toys, or during the review of the papers, or the resident doctor's phone-in on acne. They would do it when and how the fancy took them—or as Michael's fancy took him, for he was very imperative at times—and this implied no dislike or disrespect for the breakfast-time performer concerned. For Caroline liked them all, and could lie there quite happily watching any one of them—David, the doctor; Jason, the pop-chart commentator; Selma, the fashion expert; Jemima, the problems expert; Reg, the sports-roundup man; and Maria, the linkup lady. And of course Ben, the linkup man.

Ben—her husband.

It had all worked out very nicely indeed. Ben was called for by the studio at four-thirty. Michael always waited for half an hour after that, in case Ben had forgotten something and made a sudden dash back to the flat for it. Michael was a serious, slightly gauche young man, who would hate to be caught out in a situation both compromising and ridiculous. Michael was that rare thing, a studious student—though very well built, too, Caroline told herself appreciatively. His interests were work, athletics, and sex.

It was Caroline who had initiated him into the pleasures of regular sex. At five o'clock, his alarm clock went off—though, as he told Caroline, it was rarely necessary. His parents were away in Africa, dispensing aid, know-how, and Oxfam beatitudes in some Godforsaken part of Africa, so he was alone in their flat. He put his clothes on so that in the unlikely event of his being seen in the corridor he could pretend to be going out. But he never had been. By five past, he was in Caroline's flat, and in the bedroom she shared with Ben. They had almost an hour and a half of sleeping and lovemaking before breakfast television began.

Not that Michael watched it with the enthusiasm of Caroline. Sometimes he took a book along and read it while Caroline was drawing in her breath in horror at combustible toys, or tut-tutting at some defaulting businessman who had left his customers in the lurch.

He would lie there immersed in *The Mechanics of the Money Supply* or *Some Problems of Exchange-Rate Theory*—something reasonably straightforward, anyway, because he had to read against the voice from the set, and from time to time he was conscious of Ben looking directly at him. He never quite got used to that.

It didn't bother Caroline at all.

"Oh, look, his tie's gone askew," she would say, or, "You know, Ben's much balder than he was twelve months ago—I've never noticed it in the flesh." Michael seldom managed to assent to such propositions with any easy grace. He was much too conscious of balding, genial, avuncular Ben grinning out from the television screen as he tried to wring from some graceless pop-star three words strung together consecutively that actually made sense. "I think he's getting fatter in the face," said Caroline, licking marmalade off her fingers . . .

"I am not getting fatter in the face!" shouted Ben.

"Balder, yes, fatter in the face definitely not!" He added in a voice soaked in vitriol: "Bitch."

He was watching a video of yesterday's lovemaking on a set in his dressing-room, after the morning's television session had ended. His friend Frank, from the technical staff, had rigged up the camera in the cupboard of his study, next door to the bedroom. The small hole that was necessary in the wall had been expertly disguised. Luckily, Caroline was a deplorable housewife. Eventually she might have discovered the sound apparatus under the double bed, but even then she would probably have assumed it was some junk of Ben's that he had shoved there out of harm's way.

"Hypocritical swine!" yelled Ben, as he heard Caroline laughing with Michael that the Shadow Foreign Secretary had really wiped the floor with him in that interview. "She told me when I got home yesterday how well I'd handled it!"

As the shadowy figures on the screen turned to each other again, their bare flesh glistening dully in the dim light, Ben growled. "Whore!"

The makeup girl concentrated on removing the traces of powder from his neck and shirt-collar, and studiously avoided comment.

"I suppose you think this is sick, don't you?" demanded Ben.

"It's none of my business," she said, but added: "If she is carrying on, it's not surprising, is it? Not with the hours we work."

"Not surprising? I tell you, I was bloody surprised! Just think how you'd feel if your husband, or bloke, was two-timing you while you were at the studio."

"He is," said the girl. But Ben hadn't heard. He frequently didn't hear other people when he was off camera. His comfortable, sympathetic-daddy image was something that seldom spilled over into his private life. Indeed, at his worst, he could slip up even on camera: he could be leaned forward, listening to his interviewees with every appearance of the warmest interest, then reveal by his next question that he hadn't heard a word they were saying. But that happened very infrequently, and only when he was extremely preoccupied. Ben was very good at his job.

"Now they'll have tea," he said. "Everyone needs a teabreak in their working morning."

Tea—

Shortly after this, there was a break in Caroline's delicious early-morning routine: her son Malcolm came home for a long weekend from school. Michael became no more than the neighbor's son at whom she smiled in the corridor. She and Malcolm had breakfast round the kitchen table. It was on Tuesday morning, when Malcolm was due to depart later in the day, that Ben made one of his little slips.

He was interviewing Cassy Le Beau from the long-running pop group The Crunch, and as he leaned forward to introduce a clip from the video of their latest musical crime he said:

"Now, this is going to interest Caroline and Michael, watching at home—"

"Why did he say Michael?" asked Caroline aloud, before she could stop herself.

"He meant Malcolm," said their son. "Anyway, it's bloody insulting, him thinking I'd be interested in The Crunch."

Because Malcolm was currently rehearsing Elgar's Second with the London Youth Orchestra. Ben was about two years out of date with his interests.

"Did you see that yesterday morning?" Caroline asked Michael the next day.

"What?"

"Ben's slip on *Wake Up, Britain* yesterday."

"I don't watch breakfast telly when I'm not with you."

"Well, he did one of those 'little messages home' that he does. You probably don't remember, but there was all this focus about families when *Wake Up, Britain* started, and Ben got into the habit of putting little messages to Malcolm and me into the program. Ever so cosy and ever so bogus. Anyway, he did one yesterday, as Malcolm was home—only he said 'Caroline and Michael.' Not Malcolm, but Michael."

Michael shrugged.

"Just a slip of the tongue."

"But his own *son!* And for the slip to come out as *Michael!*"

"These things happen," said Michael, putting his arm around her and pushing her head back onto the pillow. "Was there a Michael on the show yesterday?"

"There was Michael Heseltine on, as usual."

"There you are, you see."

"But Heseltine's an ex-cabinet minister. He would *never* call him Michael."

"But the name was in his head. These things happen. Remember, Ben's getting old."

"True," said Caroline, who was two years younger than her husband.

"Old!" shouted Ben, dabbing at his artificially darkened eyebrows, one eye on the screen. "You think I'm old? I'll show you I've still got some bolts left in my locker!"

He had dispensed with the services of the makeup girl. He had been the only regular on *Wake Up, Britain* to demand one anyway, and the studio was surprised but pleased when Ben decided she was no longer required. Now he could watch the previous evening's cavortings without the damper of her adolescent disapproval from behind his shoulder.

And now he could plan.

One of the factors that just had to be turned to his advantage was Caroline's deplorable housekeeping. All the table tops of their kitchen were littered with bits of this and that—herbs, spices, sauces, old margarine-tubs, bits of jam on dishes. The fridge was like the basement of the Victoria and Albert Museum, and the freezer was a record of their married life. And on the window-ledge in the kitchen were the things he used to do his little bit of gardening—

Ben and Caroline inhabited one of twenty modern service flats in a block. Most of the gardening was done by employees of the landlords, yet some little patches were alloted to tenants who expressed an interest. Ben had always kept up his patch, though—as was the way of such things—it was more productive of self-satisfaction than of fruit or veg. “From our own garden,” he would say as he served his guests horrid little bowls of red currants.

Already on the window-ledge in the kitchen there was a little bottle of paraquat.

That afternoon, he pottered around in his moldy little patch. By the time he had finished and washed his hands under the kitchen tap, the paraquat had found its way next to the box of teabags standing by the kettle. The top of the paraquat was loose, having been screwed only about half-way round.

“Does you good to get out on your own patch of earth,” Ben observed to Caroline as he went through to his study.

The next question that presented itself was: when?

There were all sorts of possibilities—including that the police would immediately arrest him for murder, he was reconciled to that—but he thought that on the whole it would be best to do it on the morning when he was latest home. Paraquat could be a long time in taking effect, he knew, but there was always a chance that they would not decide to call medical help until it was too late. If he was to come home to a poisoned wife and lover in the flat, he wanted them to be well and truly dead. Wednesday was the day when all the breakfast-TV team met in committee to hear what was planned for the next week—which aging star would be plugging her memoirs, which singer plugging his forthcoming British tour. Wednesdays Ben often didn’t get home till early afternoon.

Wednesday it was.

Tentatively in his mental engagements-book he pencilled in Wednesday the fifteenth of May.

Whether the paraquat would be in the teapot of the Teas-made, or in the teabag, or how it would be administered was a minor matter that he could settle long before the crucial Tuesday night when the tea things for the morning had to be got ready. The main thing was that everything was decided.

The fifteenth of May—undoubtedly a turning-point in her life—began badly for Caroline. First of all, Ben kissed her goodbye before he set off for the studio, something he hadn't done since the early days of his engagement on breakfast television. Michael had come in at five o'clock as usual, but his lovemaking was forced, lacking in tenderness. Caroline lay for an hour in his arms afterwards, wondering if something was worrying him. He didn't say anything for some time—not till the television was switched on. Probably he relied on the bromides and the plugs to distract Caroline's attention from what he was going to say.

He had taken up his textbook and the kettle of the Teasmade was beginning to hum when he said, in his gruff, teenage way:

"Won't be much more of this."

Caroline was watching clips from a Frank Bruno fight and not giving him her full attention. When it was over, she turned to him.

"Sorry—what did you say?"

"I said there won't be much more of this."

A dagger went to her heart, which seemed to stop beating for minutes. When she could speak, the words came out terribly middle-class-matron.

"I don't quite understand. Much more of what?"

"This. You and me together in the mornings."

"You don't mean your parents are coming home early?"

"No. I've—got a flat. Nearer college. So there's not so much traveling in the mornings and evenings."

"You're just *moving out?*"

"Pretty much so. I can't live with my parents forever."

Caroline's voice grew louder and higher.

"You're not living with your parents. It's six months before they come home. You're moving out *on me.* Do you have the impression that I'm the sort of person you can just move in with when it suits you and then flit away from when it doesn't suit you any longer?"

"Well—yes, actually. I'm a free agent."

"You *bas*tard! You *bas*tard!"

She would have liked to take him by the shoulders and

shake him till the teeth rattled in his head. Instead, she sat there on the bed, coldly furious. It was 7:15. The kettle whistled and poured boiling water onto the teabags in the teapot.

"Have some tea or coffee," said Ben on the screen to his politician guest, with a smile that came out as a death's-head grin. "It's about early-morning teatime."

"It's someone else, isn't it?" said Caroline, her voice kept steady with difficulty. "A new girl friend."

"All right, it's a new girl friend," agreed Michael.

"Someone younger."

"Of course someone younger," said Michael, taking up his book again and sinking into monetarist theory.

Silently Caroline screamed: Of course someone younger! What the hell's that supposed to mean? They don't come any older than you? Of course I was just passing the time with a crone like you until someone my own age came along?

"You're moving in with a girl," she said, the desolation throbbing in her voice.

"Yeah," said Michael from within his Hayek.

"Tea all right?" Ben asked his guest.

Caroline sat there, watching the flickering images on the screen, while the tea in the pot turned from hot to warm. The future spread before her like a desert—a future as wife and mother. What kind of life was that, for God's sake? For some odd reason, a future as *lover* had seemed, when she had thought about it at all, fulfilling, traditional, and dignified. Now any picture she might have of the years to come was turned into a hideous, mocking, negative image, just as the body beside her in the bed had turned from a glamorous sex object into a boorish, ungrateful teenager.

They were having trouble in the *Wake Up, Britain* studio, where the two link-up people had got mixed up as to who was introducing what. Caroline focused on the screen—she always enjoyed it when Ben muffed something.

"Sorry," said Ben, smiling his kindly uncle smile. "I thought it was Maria, but in fact it's me. Let's see—I know it's David, our resident medico, but actually I don't know what your subject is today, David."

"Poison," said David.

But the camera had not switched to him, and the instant he dropped the word into the ambient atmosphere Caroline —and one million other viewers—saw Ben's jaw drop and an expression of panic flash like lightning through his eyes.

"I've had a lot of letters from parents of small children," said David, in his calm, everything-will-be-all-right voice, "about what to do if the kids get hold of poison. Old medicines, household detergents, gardening stuff—they can all be dangerous, and some can be deadly." Caroline saw Ben, the camera still agonizingly on him, swallow hard and put his hand up to his throat. Then, mercifully, the director changed the shot at last to the doctor, leaning forward and doing his thing. "So here are a few basic rules about what to do in that sort of emergency—"

Caroline's was not a quick mind, but suddenly a succession of images came together: Ben's kiss that morning, his smile as he offered his guest early-morning tea, a bottle of paraquat standing next to the box of teabags in the kitchen, Ben's dropping jaw at the sudden mention of poison.

"Michael," she said.

"What?" he asked, hardly bothering to take his head out of his book.

She looked at the self-absorbed, casually cruel body and her blood boiled.

"Oh, nothing," she said. "Let's have tea. It'll be practically cold by now."

She poured two cups, and handed him his. He put aside his book, which he had hardly been reading, his mind congratulating himself on having got out of this lightly. He took the cup and sat on the bed watching the screen, where the sports man was now introducing highlights of last night's athletics meeting from Oslo.

"Boy!" said Michael appreciatively, sipping his tea. "That was a great run!"

He took a gulp, then two or three more to finish the cup, then handed it back to Caroline.

Caroline did not take up her tea, but sat there looking at the graceless youth. Round her lips there played a smile of triumphal revenge—a smile the camera whirring away in the secrecy of the study cupboard perfectly caught for Ben, for the criminal courts, and for posterity.

COUNT YOUR BLESSINGS

by SIMON BRETT

"Your wife tells me you're going to take up shooting," said Alex Paton, during a lull in the dinner-party conversation.

Kevin Hooson-Smith flashed a look of annoyance at his wife, Avril, but smiled casually and responded, "Well, thought it might be rather fun. You know, at some point. When I've got time for a proper weekend hobby. Old Andersen keeps us at it so hard at the moment I think that may be a few years hence."

He laughed heartily to dissipate the subject, but Alex Paton wasn't going to let it go. "But Avril said you'd actually bought a shotgun."

"Well . . ." Kevin shrugged uncomfortably. "Useful thing to have. You know, if the opportunity came up for a bit of shooting, one wouldn't want to say, No, sorry, no can do, no gun." He laughed again, hoping the others would join in. Surely he'd got the words right. If Alex Paton or Philip Wilkinson had said that, the others would certainly have laughed. But they didn't, so he had to continue, "You shoot at all, Alex?"

"Not much these days. Pop off the occasional rabbit if I go down to the country to see Mother. Father left me his pair of

Purdeys, which aren't bad. What make was the gun you got, Kevin?"

"Oh, I forget the name. Foreign."

"Dear, dear. Some evil Continental popgun." They all laughed.

"Absolutely," said Kevin. At least he'd got that right. "More wine, Alex?"

"Thank you."

"It's a '71 Pommard."

"I noticed."

Kevin busied himself with dispensing wine to his guests, but Alex was still not deflected from the subject. "Avril said she thought you were going off shooting this weekend."

"Oh, I don't know. Maybe. Will you have a little more, Elizabeth? Fine. No, I saw something about one of these weekend teaching courses, you know, in shooting . . . We all have to learn sometime, don't we?" Kevin laughed again.

"Oh, yes," Alex agreed. "If we don't already know."

Philip Wilkinson came kindly into the pause. "You know, anyone who's keen on shooting ought to chat up that new girl who's just started cooking the directors' lunches. Davina Whatsername—"

"Entick," Kevin supplied.

"Yes. Her old man's Sir Richard Entick."

Alex Paton was impressed. "Really? I hadn't made that connection. Well, he's got some of the best shooting in the country. Yes, keep on chatting her up, Kevin."

Kevin laughed again, but again alone. They were silent, though there was quite a lot of noise from the cutlery. Avril hoped the steak wasn't too tough. She had done it exactly as the Cordon Bleu monthly had said. Well, except that had said *best* grilling steak, but the best was so expensive. The stuff she had got had been expensive enough. She was sure it was all right.

Maybe they weren't talking because they were too busy eating. Enjoying it. The other two wives hadn't said much all evening. Maybe the wives of stockbrokers from Andersen Small weren't expected to say anything. Well, she wasn't going to be totally silent and submissive. Particularly with an empty wine glass.

"Hey, Kev, you missed me on your rounds. Could I have a bit more wine?"

Kevin somewhat ungraciously pushed the wine bottle toward her.

"Kev," Alex Paton repeated. "That's rather an attractive coining."

Kevin was immediately on the defensive. Though he smiled, Avril recognized the tension in his jaw muscles. "Actually, the name Kevin is quite old. Came across something about it the other day. Means 'handsome birth.' There was a St. Kevin way back in the Sixth Century. A hermit, I think. In Ireland."

"Ah," murmured Alex Paton. "In Ireland."

They all laughed at that, though neither Kevin nor Avril could have said exactly why. Emboldened by his success, Alex Paton went on, "And tell me, what about Hooson-Smith? Does that name go back to the Sixth Century?"

After the laugh that greeted that one they were all silent again. Kevin didn't start any new topic of conversation, so Avril decided it was her duty as hostess to speak. The sound of a car at the front of the house provided her cue.

"I bet that's our next-door neighbor moving his car. You know, he's really strange. Very petty. He gets terribly upset if he can't park his car exactly outside his front door. And I mean exactly. We have known him to get up at three in the morning and move it, if he hears someone moving theirs and leaving a space. I mean, isn't that ridiculous? It's no trouble just to walk a couple of yards, but he always wants to be exactly outside. I hope we never get as petty."

They were all looking at her. She didn't know why. Maybe she had spoken rather louder than usual. She felt relaxed by the wine. It had been a long day. All the usual vexations of the children and tidying the house and then, on top of that, cooking this dinner party. Kevin insisted that everything had to be just so for his colleagues from Andersen Small. She didn't really see why. It was not as if they had ever been invited to them. And the wives didn't seem real, just exquisitely painted clothes-horses, not real women whom you could have a good natter with.

Alex Paton broke the pause and responded to her speech. "Yes, well, fortunately that's a problem we don't have to cope with. We are blessed with a rather quaint, old-fashioned device called a garage."

After the laugh Philip Wilkinson started talking about the intention of Andersen Small to open an office in Manila, and the attention moved away from Avril.

Only Kevin was still looking at her. She seemed to see him through a swimmy haze. And there was no love in his expression.

"I don't like to leave the washing up till the morning, Kev."

"Well, do it now, if you feel that strongly about it." He was already out of his suit and unbuttoning the silk shirt that had been a special offer in the *Observer.* "All I know is, it's after one and I have a heavy day tomorrow. I have a long costing meeting with Andersen first thing."

"I've got a lot to do tomorrow too."

"Having coffee with some other under-employed woman, then tea with someone else."

"No, not that. I've hardly met anyone since we've been in Dulwich. Not like it was in Willesden."

"Granted the people here are rather different from those in Willesden. Better for the boys to grow up with." Kevin was now down to his underpants. He turned away from her to take them off, as if embarrassed.

"But the boys don't grow up with them. They spend all their time traveling back and forth to that bloody private school and don't seem to make any friends."

"Don't say 'bloody.' It makes you sound more Northern than ever."

"Well, I am bloody Northern, aren't I?"

"There's no need to rub everyone's face in it all the time, though, is there?"

"Anyway, I'm no more Northern than you are. I just

haven't tarted up my vowels and started talking in a phony accent that all my posh friends laugh at."

"They do not laugh at me!" Kevin was dangerously near the edge of violence.

Avril bit back her rejoinder. No, calm down. She hadn't wanted the evening to end like this. She lingered in front of the dressing table, unwilling to start removing her makeup. It had used to be a signal between them. Well, more than a signal. She would start to remove her makeup and he would say, "Come on, time enough for that. We've got more important things to do," and pull her down onto the bed. Now he rarely seemed to think they had more important things to do. Now, she felt, he wouldn't notice if she never even put on any makeup.

He was in his pajamas and under the duvet, his back unanswerably turned to her side of the bed. (Why a duvet? She hated it. She loved the secure strapped-in feeling of sheets and blankets, the tight little cocoon their bed had been back in the flat in Willesden.)

Then she remembered their new chore. "Have you potted James?"

"No."

"But I thought we'd agreed you'd do it."

"You may have agreed that. I haven't agreed to anything. Anyway, it's ridiculous, a child of six needing to be potted."

"If he isn't, he wets the bed."

"If he is, he still seems to wet it. It's ridiculous."

"It's only since he's been at that new school."

"I don't see what that has to do with it."

"It has everything to do with it. He hates it there. He hates how all the other boys make fun of him, hates how they imitate his accent."

"Perhaps that'll teach him to improve his accent."

"What, you want another phony voice in the family?"

"AVRIL! SHUT UP, SHUT UP, SHUT UP!" He was sitting up in bed, his face red with fury.

Avril again retreated and went and potted James. When she came back, Kevin was pretending to be asleep. The rigidity of his body showed he wasn't really. She knew his mind was working, rehearsing tiny humiliations, planning revenges, planning more success. He worked hard to make himself what he wanted to be.

She sat down at the dressing table and picked up a new jar of cream to remove her makeup. But she didn't open it. Somehow she felt something might still happen; he might get out of bed and put his arms round her. "Kevin . . ."

The totality of his silence again gave the lie to his appearance of sleep.

"Kev, did you mean that about not going away this weekend?"

"No, I'm going."

"On this shooting course?"

"Yes."

"But you told Alex you might not."

"Because it wasn't his business. I was bloody annoyed at you for starting talking about shooting anyway."

"But you only bought the gun this week. And they seemed to know about it. I thought at last there was a common subject we could all talk about."

"Well, you were wrong. In the future stick to talking about cooking or children or the next-door neighbor's car. And for Christ's sake let me go to sleep!"

"So you're definitely going this weekend?"

"Yes."

"Taking the car?"

"Yes. Why do you ask?"

"I was thinking, if you weren't here, I could take the kids up to see Mum."

"All the way to Rochdale?"

"It would be a break. She'd love to see them. And now you've taken over the fourth bedroom it's very difficult for her to come and stay down here."

"I need a study. But even more than that I need sleep."

"We could go up to Rochdale by train."

"What? Do you have any idea how much fares are these days?"

"I'd just like to see Mum. She's getting on and she was pretty knocked out by that bout of flu."

"If you can afford it out of the housekeeping, then go by all means."

"You know I can't. You'd have to pay."

"Well, I can't afford to."

"You can afford a brand-new shotgun and a shooting course and bottles of wine and—"

"Avril!" Kevin sat up again in bed. This time he was icy cool, even more potentially violent than he had been when he was shouting. "I make all the money that comes into this household, so will you please leave it to me to decide how it should be spent. From an early age I have tried to better myself and I intend to continue to do that. When I die, the boys will be left in a much better position than where I started. I know what I'm doing."

Avril sighed. "It depends on your definition of 'better.' From where I'm sitting, everything seems to be a lot worse than it ever was."

"I'm sorry, Avril. If you can't appreciate the improvements I've brought into our lives, then I'm afraid there is no point in continuing this rather fruitless discussion."

"Right." Avril opened the jar of cream. "Right, I am now going to remove my makeup."

"Fine." Kevin looked curiously at the jar. "What's that stuff? It's new."

"It's called rejuvenating cream."

"Left it a bit late, haven't you?" he said and turned back into the duvet.

By eight o'clock on Saturday night Avril was exhausted. The boys were so highly strung at the moment. They were so tensely on their best behavior at the new school that the release of the weekend made them manically high-spirited and quarrelsome. Kevin's absence didn't make things any easier. Though Avril often resented, or even laughed at, his performance as the stern Victorian *pater-familias,* it did curb the boys' worst excesses. Without him there, and having made no friends in the area, the boys put all their emotional pressure on their mother. She had to be playleader, entertainer, referee, and caterer.

By eight o'clock, when she had finally dragged them away from the television and got them into bed, largely by brute force, she was absolutely drained. She collapsed on the sofa in the sitting room and once again everything seemed to swim before her eyes.

A pall of depression draped itself over her. She tried to lift it by using her mother's eternal remedy, counting her blessings. She could hear her mother's voice, with its warm Lancastrian vowels, saying, "Now come on, our Avril, cheer up. Remember, there's always someone worse off than yourself. You just count your blessings, young lady."

She felt a terrible lonely nostalgia and an urge to ring her mother immediately. But no, Mum needed her help now; she mustn't ring and burden the old lady with her troubles. That was giving in.

No, come on, our Avril, count your blessings.

Right, for a start, there were a nice house, two lovely boys, a very successful husband making far more money than any of the other boys from Rochdale you might have married. Okay, marriage going through a sticky patch at the moment, but that was only to be expected from time to time. Kevin's was an exacting job, and it was only to be expected that some of the tension he felt should be released at home. It was her job as a wife to make that home an attractive place for him to return to and relax in.

And if he needed to get out sometimes on his own, she mustn't make a fuss. This shooting weekend would probably do him a lot of good. Do them both a lot of good, give them a break from the claustrophobia of marriage.

And he'd been so excited about the gun. He seemed to have spent all his spare time that week cleaning it and oiling it, fiddling with all the little pads and brushes that he had bought with it. And this weekend was his chance to show it off. It was no different from James's desire to take his new Action Man to school on his birthday.

And at least it wasn't a woman. Let him fiddle with guns to his heart's content so long as he wasn't fiddling with another woman. True, he hadn't been fiddling with her much recently, but that again was just a phase. It would get better.

She started to feel more confident. Good God, they hadn't kept the marriage going from Rochdale, through all his time at college, the squalid flat in Willesden, his awful job in I.C.I., bringing up small children, all that pressure and aggravation, for it to fall apart now.

No, it would be all right.

Good old Mum. It always worked. Count your blessings and you'll feel better. Come on, they breed them tough in Rochdale. Pick yourself up, get yourself a drink, and cook yourself some supper.

The sherry bottle was empty.

Oh, no. She couldn't really go out to the off-license and leave the boys alone in the house. They'd never wake, but—no, she couldn't. Anyway, come to think of it, she hadn't got any cash. The housekeeping allowance didn't seem to go far these days, and with that dinner party in the middle of the week there was nothing left.

Damn. She could really use a drink.

On the other hand . . . Upstairs in Kevin's study there was a whole huge rack full of wine. All those bottles that involved so much correspondence with what he called his "shipper" and so much consultation of books on wine appreciation and tables of good years and . . .

Yes, Kevin could certainly spare her a bottle of wine. A small recompense for her letting him go off for the weekend on his own. She wouldn't take one of his most precious ones, not one of the dinner-party specials, just something modest and warming.

His study was unlike the rest of the house. It was the spare bedroom, but he had moved the bed out and had the room decorated in dark green. There was an antique (well, reproduction) desk and leather chairs. It sought to capture the look of a gentleman's club.

The boys were never allowed inside. Avril was discouraged from entering except to clean. The difference in décor seemed symbolic of a greater difference, as if the room had declared U.D.I. from the rest of the house.

The wine rack covered one whole wall. The range was extensive. Kevin approached the purchase of wine as he did everything else, with punctilious attention to detail and a desire to do the correct thing.

Avril chose a bottle of 1977 Côtes du Rhône, which surely couldn't be too important. Anyway, he owed her at least that.

There was a corkscrew on his desk, so she opened it straightaway. The presence of the corkscrew suggested that Kevin himself drank an occasional bottle up there, which in turn suggested that somewhere he must have glasses.

She opened the closet by the window. She didn't notice whether there were any glasses. Something else took her attention.

Standing upright in the closet, with all its cleaning materials ranged neatly beside it, was Kevin's new shotgun.

Avril swayed for a moment. This dizziness was getting worse. She supported herself against the window frame and looked out into the road.

Parked exactly in front of their house was a silver-gray Volkswagen Golf.

It was Monday evening before she got a chance to confront him. He had arrived back late on Sunday, and Monday morning was the usual scrum of forcing breakfast into her three men and rushing the boys through heavy traffic to their distant private school.

All day she phrased and rephrased what she was going to say to him, and when the opportunity came she was determined not to shirk it. He had bought some sherry and poured her a drink, a perfunctory politeness which he performed automatically every evening before retiring upstairs with his briefcase to work until told that his supper was ready.

She took the glass, and before he could get out his "Just going up to do a bit of work," said, "I see you didn't take your shotgun away with you for your shooting weekend."

He looked first surprised, then very annoyed. "You've been up rooting round my study." When he was angry, his voice lapsed back into Lancastrian. The "u" in "study" sounded as in "stood."

"I went up there."

"Well, I wish you bloody wouldn't! I've got a lot of important papers up there and I don't like the thought of getting them all out of order."

But she wasn't going to be deflected so easily. "Stop changing the subject. I want to know why you didn't take your precious brand-new shotgun with you when you went off on this shooting weekend."

He smiled patronizingly. "Oh, really, Avril. You don't know the first thing about shooting. It isn't just something you can step straight into. You have to learn a lot of theoretical stuff first—you know, safety drill and so on. You don't start handling guns straightaway. I knew that, so I left the gun this time."

"This time? You mean there will be more weekends?"

"Oh, yes. As I say, it's not something you can pick up overnight."

She looked downcast.

He put his arms round her. "Why don't we go upstairs?"

She looked up into his eyes gratefully.

The phone rang.

"You get it. It's bound to be for you. Join me upstairs." And he went up.

After the phone call she found him in the study rather than the bedroom, but she was too upset to register his change of intention. "It was Mrs. Eady."

"Mrs. Eady?"

"Who lives next door to Mum. Kev, Mum's had a stroke."

"Oh, no. Is she—I mean, how is she?"

"Mrs. Eady says it wasn't a bad one, but I don't know what that means. I'll have to go up there."

"I suppose so."

"Straightaway. I'll have to. Can I take the car?"

"It's not going to be very convenient. I've got one or—"

"Kev . . ."

He crumbled in the face of this appeal. "Of course. Are you really going to go straight off?"

"I must. I can't just leave her."

"What about the boys?"

"You can manage for a couple of days."

"But getting them to school? If you've got the car—"

"Oh, God, yes. Look, there's Mrs. Bentley. Lives round in Parsons Road. Her son goes to the school. I'm sure she'd take them too."

"How well do you know her?"

"Hardly at all. But this is an emergency."

"Will you ring her?"

"No, you do it, Kev. I've got to dash." She started looking round the room for a holdall to take with her.

"I think it would be better if you rang, Avril. Avril? What are you looking at, Avril?"

It was nearly dark, but the study curtains were still open. The light from a streetlamp shone on the silver top of the Volkswagen Golf.

"That car. It's the third day it's been parked outside."

"So what? Lots of people park round here. It's near the station."

"But that car hasn't moved for three days."

"Perhaps someone's left it while they went on holiday."

"I don't think so."

"Well, what do you think?"

"I don't know, Kev." Abruptly she moved from the window. "I must go."

The cars on the M1 kept blurring, losing their shape and becoming little blobs of color. Avril clenched her jaw and tensed the muscles round her eyes, fighting to keep them open. In three nights she couldn't have had more than an hour's sleep. Driving through Monday night and then the worry about Mum.

The fact that the stroke had been so slight and Mum had seemed so little affected by it only made things worse. The incident became a divine admonition. It's nothing this time, but next time it could be serious, and there's you living over 200 miles away.

Not that Mum had said that. She wouldn't. She was temperamentally incapable of using any sort of emotional blackmail. But Avril's mind supplied the pressure.

No, Mum had been remarkably cheerful. She fully expected to die soon and regarded this mild stroke as an unexpected bonus, a remission. And she was delighted to see Avril, though very apologetic at having "dragged her all this way!"

Mum would be all right. Even if she were taken seriously ill, there would be no problem. She was surrounded by friends. Mrs. Eady kept an eye on her and there were lots more who were ready at a moment's notice to perform any small service that might be required. That was what really upset Avril, the knowledge that her mother didn't need her —that and the warmth she had encountered in her hometown. The world of ever-open back doors and ever-topped-up teapots contrasted painfully with the frosty genteel anonymity of Dulwich.

And yet they'd all seemed impressed by her life, not envious, but respectful, as if she and Kevin were somehow their ambassadors to a more sophisticated world.

She'd met Tony Platt in the supermarket. Tony Platt, who she'd gone out with for nearly a year and even considered marrying. And there he was, looking just the same except balding, and with three kids—three bouncing kids with cheerful, squabbling Lancastrian voices and not an inhibition among them.

Tony had been pleased to see her. Friendly and slow, as he'd always been. "Heard you were living down in the Smoke. Sorry we lost touch. You married Kevin Smith, didn't you?"

And he'd said she was looking grand, and she knew it wasn't true. She knew that strain reflected itself immediately in her face, pulling it down, etching deep lines in her skin. And makeup no longer seemed to smooth out the lines, but rather to highlight them. Still, if she could get some sleep, maybe she'd start to feel better. Yes, when she got home she'd get some sleep. Kevin had phoned each day and assured her that everything was all right.

The cars around her started to lose their outlines again. Must concentrate. Keep going. Only another 70 miles.

A car overtook her, fast, and then cut in in front of her. Too close. Far too close. She had to brake.

She focused on the car.

It was a silver-gray Volkswagen Golf.

I see, trying to get me now, she thought. Right, I'll show them.

She flattened her foot on the accelerator. They wouldn't get away with trying to frighten her.

Her car moved closer and closer to the large-windowed back of the Golf. It speeded up, but it couldn't get away from her. She was gaining.

Suddenly the Golf, pressed for space, swung out to overtake a truck in front. Avril snatched her steering wheel to the right too.

There was a furious hooting and a scream of brakes as the Range Rover overtaking her had to slam on everything to avoid a collision.

There was no collision. Avril swung back to the left and her car slowed down with a crunch on the hard shoulder. As she rubbed her swimming eyes, she could hear the voice of the Range Rover's driver ringing round her head. "You bloody fool! What the hell do you think you're doing?"

The car was still parked outside when she got back to the house—the silver-gray Volkswagen Golf.

Its license plate was different from the one on the motorway, but she wasn't necessarily fooled by that. Still she felt the hood to see if the engine was warm and listened for the tick of contracting metal. But there was nothing. It seemed the car had not been used recently.

Inside, the house was absolutely quiet. It was nearly half-past six. The boys should be back from school. She swayed with exhaustion as she stood in the hall.

No, must resist the temptation to go to bed. Must find where the boys are. Probably with Kevin. Perhaps he'd left work early to fetch them from school. Even Andersen Small must recognize emergencies.

Must be with Kevin. Nowhere else they could be. Unless

they were with that Mrs. Bentley. Anyway, better ring her to thank her for taking them to school.

"Oh, Mrs. Hooson-Smith, I must say I'm very relieved you've rung. I was beginning to wonder if I was going to have to look after your sons for the rest of my life."

"I'm so sorry. I thought you wouldn't mind just taking them to and from school. My mother's been ill and—"

"No, I didn't mind that at all, but I must confess having them to stay for the past three days has been a bit of a strain."

"I'm so sorry. I didn't know."

"Your husband had to go away on business."

"Oh, no."

"So on Tuesday afternoon I was faced with the alternatives of putting them up or turning them out onto the streets. I must say, I do regard it as something of an imposition. It's not as if they're even special friends of Nigel."

"I had no idea. I'm so grateful. I do hope they behaved themselves."

"To an extent. Of course, people have different standards. About a lot of things."

"Oh, dear. Did my husband warn you about James's bedwetting?"

"No, he didn't."

It was a quarter-past eight. The boys were finally in bed, though not asleep. Still arguing fiercely. They were upset and confused, and as usual they expressed their confusion by fighting.

Avril fell onto her bed without taking any of her clothes off. Just sleep, sleep.

The phone rang. She answered it blearily.

"It's Philip Wilkinson. Is Kevin there?"

"No, he's away on business. I don't know when he'll be back."

"He's not away on business. I saw him in the office this morning. Then he went off after lunch."

"Then I've no idea where he is. All I know is that he's been away on business for the last three days."

"He hasn't."

"What?"

"He's been in the office for the last few days. On and off. A bit distracted, but he's been there."

"Oh. Well, I'm sorry, we've got our wires crossed somehow. As I say, I have no idea where he is. I'm absolutely shagged out and I'm going to sleep."

She put the phone down and lay back on the bed. But, in spite of her exhaustion, sleep didn't come. Her mind had started working . . .

Kevin came back about half-past eleven. She heard the front door, then his footsteps up the stairs. But he didn't come straight into the bedroom as usual. She heard him going into the bathroom, where he seemed to be going through some fairly extensive washing and teeth cleaning. Eventually he came into the bedroom. "Oh, I thought you'd be asleep."

"As you see, I'm not."

"No. How's your Mum?"

"Better."

"Good."

He reached for his pajamas. "Oh, I'm tired out."

"Kevin, what do you mean by leaving the boys with Mrs. Bentley?"

"I had to do something. I was called away on business."

"You weren't."

"What do you mean?"

"That smoothie Philip Wilkinson rang to speak to you. In the course of conversation he revealed that you have not been away on business for the past three days."

"Ah." Kevin put his pajamas down. Slowly he started to put his clothes back on. As he did so, he spoke. Flatly, without emotion. "Right. In that case I'd better tell you. You'd have to know soon, anyway. The fact is, I have fallen in love with someone else."

"What, you mean another woman?"

"Yes. I have spent most of the past week with her."

"Most of the past week? The shooting weekend—"

"There was no shooting weekend."

"But how could you? What about me?"

"I don't think there's much left between us now, Avril."

"Who is she?"

"Her name's Davina Entick. She works at Andersen Small."

Avril started laughing. "Oh, God, Kevin, you're predictable. Clawing your grubby way up the social ladder. First you got the voice, then you got the job and the house. Then you looked around and you thought, What haven't I got? The right woman. I need a matching woman to make a set with my shotgun and my wine rack and all my other phony status symbols. So you start sniffing round some little feather-headed debutante.

"Well, let me tell you, Kevin Smith, it won't work. Okay, maybe you managed to get into bed with her. A man can usually manage that if he's sufficiently determined, and you've never lacked determination, Kevin Smith. But that's all you'll get out of her. You can't push your way into the upper classes. You've always been as common as dirt, Kevin Smith. And about as wholesome."

He knotted his silk tie. "I didn't expect you to understand. I'm sure you've forgotten what love feels like."

"If I have, it's only because I've been living with you for the past fourteen years."

"I'm going now."

"Oh, back to the little love nest in Mayfair?"

"Fulham, actually."

"Oh, Fulham—what a letdown. Couldn't you find a nice upper-class dolly-bird with the right address? Never mind, maybe you can trade them in at Harrod's. Fix yourself up with a nice shop-soiled Duke's daughter, how about that?"

Kevin still spoke quietly. "I'm leaving, Avril. I won't come back, except to pick up my things."

"Oh, yes, pick up your things." She rose from the bed and went across to the chest of drawers. "Why not take your things with you now? I'm sure Devonia or whatever her fancy name is won't want to soil her pretty little hands with washing sweaty shirts and horrid stained Y-fronts, will she?"

As she spoke, she opened the drawers and started throwing clothes at Kevin. "Here, have your things. Have your clean shirts and your socks and your Y-fronts and your vests and your handkerchiefs and your bloody Aran sweaters and—"

Quite suddenly she collapsed on the floor, crying.

Kevin, who had stood still while all his clothes were flung at him, looked down at her contemptuously. "And you wonder why I'm leaving you."

She heard the car start. But when she looked out of the window, it was out of sight. All she could see, through the distorting film of her eyes, parked exactly outside the house, was the silver-gray Volkswagen Golf.

"Mummy, why have you drawn the curtains?"

"It's nearly night-time, James."

"But it's not dark. It's summer."

"Look, if I want to draw the curtains in my own house, I will bloody well draw them."

"But you must have a reason."

Oh, yes, Avril had a reason. But not one she could tell. You can't tell your six-year-old son that you've drawn the front curtains because you can't bear another look at the car parked outside your house. You can't tell anyone that sort of thing. It doesn't make sense.

So, as usual, answer by going on to the attack. "Anyway, it's time you were in bed. Go on, upstairs."

"Am I going to have a bath?"

"No, you can have one tomorrow night."

"You said that last night."

"Look, I haven't got the energy to give you a bath tonight. Now *GO UPSTAIRS!*"

"Can't I wait till Christopher comes home?"

"No. You go to bed." Avril didn't want to think where her ten-year-old son was. Mrs. Bentley, who had very grudgingly picked up James from school, had brought back some message about Christopher's being off with some friends and making his own way home on the bus. Avril knew she should be worried about him, but her mind was so full of other anxieties that that problem would have to join the queue and be dealt with when its time came.

A new thought came into her head—a new thought, calming like a sedative injection. Yes, of course, that was the answer. She'd just have to go out and check. Then it would be easy. Just get James into bed and she could go. He'd be all right for a few minutes.

"Go on, James, upstairs, or I'll get really cross."

Her younger son looked stubborn and petulant, just like his father when he didn't get his own way. With an appalling shock Avril realized that she could never be free of Kevin. She could remove his belongings, fumigate the house of his influence, even move somewhere else, but the boys would always be with her. Two little facsimiles of their father, two little memento moris.

"I need some clean pajamas," objected James. "I haven't got any clean pajamas in my drawer, because you haven't done any washing."

Now she had no control over her anger. "And you know why you need clean pajamas every night, don't you? Because you wet your bloody bed like a six-month-old baby!"

She knew she shouldn't have said it. She knew all the child psychology books said that shouting at them only made the problem worse. And when she saw James's face disintegrate into tears, she knew how much she had hurt him. She was his defender. His father had told him off about it, but she was always the one who intervened, made light of it, said it'd soon be all right. And now she had turned against him.

At least it got him out of the room. He did go upstairs. Maybe, when all this was over, she'd have time to rebuild her relationship with her children. Now she was just too tired. It was Thursday. Kevin had left the previous Friday. A week ago. And still she had hardly slept at all. She lay back on the sofa. Strangely, she felt relaxed. Maybe now sleep would come.

But no, of course. Her good thought. Yes, her good peace-bringing thought. Yes, she must do that.

She stood up. The whole room seemed to sway insubstantially around her.

She went into the hall, then out the front door. She averted her eyes from the thing parked in front of the house and set off briskly up the road.

A five-minute walk brought her to her objective. It was where she had remembered it would be, in the middle of the council estate.

It was an old Citroën DS. The tires were flat and the back window smashed. Aerosols had passed comment on its bodywork.

But what she was looking for was affixed to the windshield. It was a notice from the Council, saying that the car was dangerous rubbish and would have to be moved. She noted down the details of the department responsible.

Back outside the house, she forced herself to look at the car. It hadn't moved. It was in exactly the same position. Resin from a tree above it had dropped onto the bodywork and dust had stuck to this, dulling the silver-gray sheen.

But it was still a new car. This year's model. Some residual logic in her mind told her that no Council was going to come and tow this away as dangerous rubbish. For a moment she wanted to cry. But then everything became clear.

She wondered why she hadn't seen it earlier. Yes, of course. The car had arrived on the supposed shooting weekend. The smart new car had arrived just at the time Kevin had gone off with his smart new girl friend. At last she understood why she felt threatened by it.

She was so absorbed that she didn't hear the police car draw up behind her.

It was only when the officer who got out of it spoke to her directly that she came back to life.

"Mrs. Hooson-Smith?"

"Yes."

"I've brought your son Christopher back. I'm afraid he was caught shoplifting from the supermarket."

Avril sat by the window in Kevin's study, looking down at the silver-gray Volkswagen Golf. Now that she knew whom it belonged to she could face it.

It was Saturday. People walked up and down the street

loaded with shopping or planks and paint pots for the weekend's Do-It-Yourself. She had sent the boys out. She didn't know where they had gone. Probably the park. The policeman had said she must keep an eye on them, particularly Christopher until his appearance in the Juvenile Court on Tuesday. But she couldn't yet. Not till all this was over.

It was sunny and very hot. But she didn't open the window. Her dressing gown was hot, but she couldn't be bothered to take it off, still less to get dressed. A sickly smell of urine wafted from James's room, but she was too distracted to go and change his wet sheets. Even to close the study door and shut out the smell.

She had to watch the car.

The phone rang.

It was a dislocating intrusion. Like someone forgetting their lines in the middle of a good play, a reminder of another reality.

She lifted the receiver gingerly. "Hello."

"It's Kevin."

He sounded businesslike. This was the way she had heard him speak into the phone on the rare occasions when she'd gone up to Andersen Small to meet him and had to wait in his office.

"Oh." She hadn't expected ever to hear from him again. He was a part of her life that she no longer thought about. It was strange to be reminded that he was still alive. He had no place in the weightless, transitional world she now inhabited.

"How are things, Avril?"

She didn't answer. She couldn't cope with the philosophical ramifications of the question.

"Listen, I've been thinking. I want to get things cut and dried."

Unaccountably she giggled. "You always did, Kevin."

"What I mean is, I want a divorce. I want to marry Davina."

"And does she want to marry you?"

"I haven't asked her yet, not in so many words. I wanted to get our end sorted out first, to feel free."

"Free," she echoed colorlessly.

He ignored the interruption. "Then I'll speak to Davina. It'll be all right. We have an understanding."

"I'm sure you have." Suddenly anger animated Avril's lethargy. "It'll be easy enough for her to have an understanding of you. All she has to understand is selfishness and petty-mindedness and social climbing. And I'm sure, from your point of view, she takes no understanding at all. You can't understand something when there's nothing there to understand."

"There's no need to be abusive. Particularly about someone you haven't met. Davina is in fact a highly intelligent girl."

Avril didn't think this assertion worthy of comment.

"Anyway, all I'm saying is that I will be starting proceedings for divorce, and it's going to be easier all round if you don't create any problems over it. I'll see that you and the boys are well looked after financially. By the way, how are the boys?"

"Fine," she replied. Why bother to tell him otherwise?

"Anyway, I'll be round at some point to pick up my things. I hope we'll be able to meet without too much awkwardness. We're both grownup people and I hope we'll be able to deal with this whole business in a civilized adult manner."

Avril put the phone down.

A civilized adult manner. She laughed.

Pick up my things. She laughed further.

If, of course, you have any things to pick up.

She took a bottle out of the wine rack and threw it against the opposite wall. It shattered satisfyingly.

She did the same with another bottle. And another and another, until the whole rack was empty.

It was enjoyable.

She looked round for further destruction.

She opened the closet by the window.

And there it was. Of course. The brand-new shotgun.

Kevin had a book about shotguns on his desk. Good old Kevin. Never go into anything without buying lots of books to show you how to do it. Do your homework, you don't want to look a fool.

The book made it easy to load the gun and showed how to release the safety catch. Avril slipped a cartridge into each barrel from Kevin's unopened box.

Then she opened the window a little and continued watching the silver-gray Volkswagen Golf parked outside . . .

It was early Sunday morning. Eight o'clock maybe. She had seen it get light a couple of hours earlier. All night she had watched the car outside. It would be terrible not to be there when they arrived.

She didn't know where the boys were. She vaguely recollected their coming back at lunchtime on Saturday. But they had found there was no lunch prepared and had gone out again. She thought they had said something about spending the night in the park, but she couldn't be sure. It had been difficult to take in what they said. Her dizziness and the mobility of everything that surrounded her seemed to have grown. It was as if her head had levitated and floated above her body in some transparent viscous pool.

But she knew she would be all right. Her body would hold up as long as was necessary.

The phone rang. This time its intrusion didn't seem so incongruous. It now took on the ambivalence of everything else she saw and heard. It might be real, it might not. It didn't matter much one way or the other. She answered it. As she did so, she thought to herself, "If it's real, then I'm answering it. If it's not, then I'm not." That was very funny, and she giggled into the receiver.

"Hello, is that Avril?"

"Yes. Almost definitely."

She giggled again.

"It's Mrs. Eady."

"Ah, Mrs. Eady."

"It's about your Mum, Avril. I'm afraid she's had another stroke. Doctor's with her now."

"Ah."

"And I'm afraid this one's more serious. Doctor says he doesn't think she'll last long."

"Ah."

"Look, Avril, can you come up? I mean, she's still alive now, but I don't know how long it'll be. They're going to take her into the hospital and—Avril, are you still there?"

"Oh, yes," said Avril wisely.

"Can you come up?"

"Come up?"

"To Rochdale."

"Oh, no, I'm very busy."

"But it's your Mum. I mean, she can still recognize me and—"

"No, I'm sorry. I can't do anything till they come."

She put the phone down . . .

It was nearly eleven o'clock when the girl arrived. She came up the road carrying two suitcases.

It was the suitcases that alerted Avril. Kevin had a nerve! To send the girl to pick up his things. A bloody nerve.

The girl walked up the road slowly, giving Avril plenty of time to look at her. No, she wasn't that pretty. Not even as young as she'd expected. Looked about her age. Very brown, though, very tanned.

Avril knew she would stop by the car and, sure enough, she did. The two cases were put down, and the girl fumbled in her handbag for car keys. I see, she'd load up with Kevin's things, then drive off in the car.

Avril could see everything very clearly now. The world around her had stabilized—in fact, she could see it in sharper detail than usual. She sighted along the barrels of the shotgun.

The girl had found her key and was bending to open the car door. Avril felt the trigger with her finger. Just one trigger. Kevin wouldn't approve of waste. Just one cartridge would do it.

She squeezed the trigger.

She was totally unprepared for the recoil, which knocked her off her chair. But when she picked herself up and looked out of the window she saw she had succeeded.

The girl seemed to be kneeling against the side of the car. Her back was a mass of red. The side windows were holed and frosted and there were small holes in the silver-gray bodywork of the Volkswagen Golf.

Kevin arrived in his car a moment later and parked behind the Golf. He was in a furious temper.

Davina had turned down his proposal. Not only that, she had laughed at him when he made it. She had let him know in no uncertain terms that at the moment she had no thoughts of marriage. She had added as a rider that, if she had been looking for a husband, she would have looked far above him.

So he was coming home with his tail between his legs. Avril, he knew, would welcome him. She had no alternative.

As he got out of the car, he couldn't help noticing the bloody mess beside the Golf. He stared at the body with his back to his house.

So it was the back of his head that received the main blast of the second barrel of his new shotgun. Some more holes appeared in the bodywork of the silver-gray Volkswagen Golf . . .

The Detective Inspector watched the police car drive off. "Well, she seemed to go docilely enough, Sergeant."

"Yes, sir. The only thing she seemed worried about was that the Golf would definitely get towed away. Said it was in her parking space. I assured her it would be, and she seemed quite happy."

"Strange. I mean, not her shooting the husband. Apparently he'd left her and gone off with some other woman, so there's a motive there. But the other woman she shot—completely at random."

"She's not hubby's girl friend?"

"Oh, Sergeant, wouldn't that be nice and neat?" The Detective Inspector smiled. "No, we've identified her from things in her handbag. Passport, airline ticket stubs—very well-documented. Just come back from a fortnight's package holiday in Sardinia."

"No connection with this family at all?"

The Detective Inspector shook his head. "Not yet. I personally don't think we'll ever find one. I think that poor woman's only offense was to use someone else's parking space."

AS GOOD AS A REST

by LAWRENCE BLOCK

Andrew says the whole point of a vacation is to change your perspective of the world. A change is as good as a rest, he says, and vacations are about change, not rest. If we just wanted a rest, he says, we could stop the mail and disconnect the phone and stay home: that would add up to more of a traditional rest than traipsing all over Europe. Sitting in front of the television set with your feet up, he says, is generally considered to be more restful than climbing the forty-two thousand steps to the top of Notre Dame.

Of course, there aren't forty-two thousand steps, but it did seem like it at the time. We were with the Dattners—by the time we got to Paris the four of us had already buddied up—and Harry kept wondering aloud why the genius who'd built the cathedral hadn't thought to put in an elevator. And Sue, who'd struck me earlier as unlikely to be afraid of anything, turned out to be petrified of heights. There are two staircases at Notre Dame, one going up and one coming down, and to get from one to the other you have to walk along this high ledge. It's really quite wide, even at its narrowest, and the view of the rooftops of Paris is magnificent, but all of this was wasted on Sue, who clung to the rear wall with her eyes clenched shut.

Andrew took her arm and walked her through it, while

Harry and I looked out at the City of Light. "It's high open spaces that does it to her," he told me. "Yesterday, the Eiffel Tower, no problem, because the space was enclosed. But when it's open she starts getting afraid that she'll get sucked over the side or that she'll get this sudden impulse to jump, and, well, you see what it does to her."

While neither Andrew nor I is troubled by heights, whether open or enclosed, the climb to the top of the cathedral wasn't the sort of thing we'd have done at home, especially since we'd already had a spectacular view of the city the day before from the Eiffel Tower. I'm not mad about walking stairs, but it didn't occur to me to pass up the climb. For that matter, I'm not that mad about walking generally—Andrew says I won't go anywhere without a guaranteed parking space—but it seems to me that I walked from one end of Europe to the other, and didn't mind a bit.

When we weren't walking through streets or up staircases, we were parading through museums. That's hardly a departure for me, but for Andrew it is uncharacteristic behavior in the extreme. Boston's Museum of Fine Arts is one of the best in the country, and it's not twenty minutes from our house. We have a membership, and I go all the time, but it's almost impossible to get Andrew to go.

But in Paris he went to the Louvre, and the Rodin Museum, and that little museum in the 16th arrondissement with the most wonderful collection of Monets. And in London he led the way to the National Gallery and the National Portrait Gallery and the Victoria and Albert—and in Amsterdam he spent three hours in the Rijksmuseum and hurried us to the Van Gogh Museum first thing the next morning. By the time we got to Madrid, I was museumed out. I knew it was a sin to miss the Prado but I just couldn't face it, and I wound up walking around the city with Harry while my husband dragged Sue through galleries of El Grecos and Goyas and Velasquezes.

"Now that you've discovered museums," I told Andrew, "you may take a different view of the Museum of Fine Arts. There's a show of American landscape painters that'll still be running when we get back—I think you'll like it."

He assured me he was looking forward to it. But you know he never went. Museums are strictly a vacation pleasure for him. He doesn't even want to hear about them when he's at home.

For my part, you'd think I'd have learned by now not to buy clothes when we travel. Of course, it's impossible not to —there are some genuine bargains and some things you couldn't find at home—but I almost always wind up buying something that remains unworn in my closet forever after. It seems so right in some foreign capital, but once I get it home I realize it's not me at all, and so it lives out its days on a hanger, a source in turn of fond memories and faint guilt. It's not that I lose judgment when I travel, or become wildly impulsive. It's more that I become a slightly different person in the course of the trip and the clothes I buy for that person aren't always right for the person I am in Boston.

Oh, why am I nattering on like this? You don't have to look in my closet to see how travel changes a person. For heaven's sake, just look at the Dattners.

If we hadn't all been on vacation together, we would never have come to know Harry and Sue, let alone spend so much time with them. We would never have encountered them in the first place—day-to-day living would not have brought them to Boston, or us to Enid, Oklahoma. But even if they'd lived down the street from us, we would never have become close friends at home. To put it as simply as possible, they were not our kind of people.

The package tour we'd booked wasn't one of those escorted ventures in which your every minute is accounted for. It included our charter flights over and back, all our hotel accommodations, and our transportation from one city to the next. We "did" six countries in twenty-two days, but what we did in each, and where and with whom, was strictly up to us. We could have kept to ourselves altogether, and have often done so when traveling, but by the time we checked into our hotel in London the first day we'd made arrangements to join the Dattners that night for dinner, and before we knocked off our after-dinner brandies that night it had been tacitly agreed that we would be a foursome throughout the trip—unless, of course, it turned out that we tired of each other.

"They're a pair," Andrew said that first night, unknotting his tie and giving it a shake before hanging it over the doorknob. "That y'all-come-back accent of hers sounds like syrup flowing over corn cakes."

"She's a little flashy, too," I said. "But that sport jacket of his—"

"I know," Andrew said. "Somewhere, even as we speak, a horse is shivering, his blanket having been transformed into a jacket for Harry."

"And yet there's something about them, isn't there?"

"They're nice people," Andrew said. "Not our kind at all, but what does that matter? We're on a trip. We're ripe for a change . . ."

In Paris, after a night watching a floorshow at what I'm sure was a rather disreputable little nightclub in Les Halles, I lay in bed while Andrew sat up smoking a last cigarette. "I'm glad we met the Dattners," he said. "This trip would be fun anyway, but they add to it. That joint tonight was a treat, and I'm sure we wouldn't have gone if it hadn't been for them. And do you know something? I don't think *they'd* have gone if it hadn't been for *us.*"

"Where would we be without them?" I rolled onto my side. "I know where Sue would be without your helping hand. Up on top of Notre Dame, frozen with fear. Do you suppose that's how the gargoyles got there? Are they nothing but tourists turned to stone?"

"Then you'll never be a gargoyle. You were a long way from petrification whirling around the dance floor tonight."

"Harry's a good dancer. I didn't think he would be, but he's very light on his feet."

"The gun doesn't weigh him down, eh?"

I sat up. "I *thought* he was wearing a gun," I said. "How on earth does he get it past the airport scanners?"

"Undoubtedly by packing it in his luggage and checking it through. He wouldn't need it on the plane—not unless he was planning to divert the flight to Havana."

"I don't think they go to Havana any more. Why would he

need it *off* the plane? I suppose tonight he'd feel safer armed. That place was a bit on the rough side."

"He was carrying it at the Tower of London, and in and out of a slew of museums. In fact, I think he carries it all the time except on planes. Most likely he feels naked without it."

"I wonder if he sleeps with it."

"I think he sleeps with her."

"Well, I know *that.*"

"To their mutual pleasure, I shouldn't wonder. Even as you and I."

"Ah," I said.

And, a bit later, he said, "You like them, don't you?"

"Well, of course I do. I don't want to pack them up and take them home to Boston with us, but—"

"You like *him.*"

"Harry? Oh, *I* see what you're getting at."

"Quite."

"And she's attractive, isn't she? You're attracted to her."

"At home I wouldn't look at her twice, but here—"

"Say no more. That's how I feel about him. That's exactly how I feel about him."

"Do you suppose we'll do anything about it?"

"I don't know. Do you suppose they're having this very conversation two floors below?"

"I wouldn't be surprised. If they *are* having this conversation, and if they had the same silent prelude to this conversation, they're probably feeling very good indeed."

"Mmmmm," I said dreamily. "Even as you and I."

I don't know if the Dattners had that conversation that particular evening, but they certainly had it somewhere along the way. The little tensions and energy currents between the four of us began to build until it seemed almost as though the air were crackling with electricity. More often than not we'd find ourselves pairing off on our walks, Andrew with Sue, Harry with me. I remember one moment when he took my hand crossing the street—I remember the instant but not the street, or even the city—and a little shiver went right through me.

By the time we were in Madrid, with Andrew and Sue trekking through the Prado while Harry and I ate garlicky shrimp and sipped a sweetish white wine in a little cafe on the Plaza Mayor, it was clear what was going to happen. We were almost ready to talk about it.

"I hope they're having a good time," I told Harry. "I just couldn't manage another museum."

"I'm glad we're out here instead," he said, with a wave at the plaza. "But I would have gone to the Prado if you went." And he reached out and covered my hand with his.

"Sue and Andy seem to be getting along pretty good," he said.

Andy! Had anyone else ever called my husband Andy?

"And you and me, we get along all right, don't we?"

"Yes," I said, giving his hand a little squeeze. "Yes, we do."

Andrew and I were up late that night, talking and talking. The next day we flew to Rome. We were all tired our first night there and ate at the restaurant in our hotel rather than venture forth. The food was good, but I wonder if any of us really tasted it?

Andrew insisted that we all drink *grappa* with our coffee. It turned out to be a rather nasty brandy, clear in color and quite powerful. The men had a second round of it. Sue and I had enough work finishing our first.

Harry held his glass aloft and proposed a toast. "To good friends," he said. "To close friendship with good people." And after everyone had taken a sip he said, "You know, in a couple of days we all go back to the lives we used to lead. Sue and I go back to Oklahoma, you two go back to Boston, Mass. Andy, you go back to your investments business and I'll be doin' what I do. And we got each other's addresses and phone, and we say we'll keep in touch, and maybe we will. But if we do or we don't, either way one thing's sure. The minute we get off that plane at J.F.K., that's when the carriage turns into a pumpkin and the horses go back to bein' mice. You know what I mean?"

Everyone did.

"Anyway," he said, "what me an' Sue were thinkin', we thought there's a whole lot of Rome, a mess of good restaurants, and things to see and places to go. We thought it's silly to have four people all do the same things and go the same places and miss out on all the rest. We thought, you know, after breakfast tomorrow, we'd split up and spend the day separate." He took a breath. "Like Sue and Andy'd team up for the day and, Elaine, you an' me'd be together."

"The way we did in Madrid," somebody said.

"Except I mean for the whole day," Harry said. A light film of perspiration gleamed on his forehead. I looked at his jacket and tried to decide if he was wearing his gun. I'd seen it on our afternoon in Madrid. His jacket had come open and I'd seen the gun, snug in his shoulder holster. "The whole day and then the evening, too. Dinner—and after."

There was a silence which I don't suppose could have lasted nearly as long as it seemed to. Then Andrew said he thought it was a good idea, and Sue agreed, and so did I.

Later, in our hotel room, Andrew assured me that we could back out. "I don't think they have any more experience with this than we do. You saw how nervous Harry was during his little speech. He'd probably be relieved to a certain degree if we did back out."

"Is that what you want to do?"

He thought for a moment. "For my part," he said, "I'd as soon go through with it."

"So would I. My only concern is if it made some difference between us afterward."

"I don't think it will. This is fantasy, you know. It's not the real world. We're not in Boston *or* Oklahoma. We're in Rome, and you know what they say. When in Rome, do as the Romans do."

"And is this what the Romans do?"

"It's probably what they do when they go to Stockholm," Andrew said.

In the morning, we joined the Dattners for breakfast. Afterward, without anything being said, we paired off as Harry had suggested the night before. He and I walked through a sun-drenched morning to the Spanish Steps, where I bought a bag of crumbs and fed the pigeons. After that—

Oh, what does it matter what came next, what particular tourist things we found to do that day? Suffice it to say that we went interesting places and saw rapturous sights, and everything we did and saw was heightened by anticipation of the evening ahead.

We ate lightly that night, and drank freely but not to excess. The trattoria where we dined wasn't far from our hotel and the night was clear and mild, so we walked back. Harry slipped an arm around my waist. I leaned a little against his shoulder. After we'd walked a way in silence, he said very softly, "Elaine, only if you want to."

"But I do," I heard myself say.

Then he took me in his arms and kissed me.

I ought to recall the night better than I do. We felt love and lust for each other, and sated both appetites. He was gentler than I might have guessed he'd be, and I more abandoned. I could probably remember precisely what happened if I put my mind to it, but I don't think I could make the memory seem real. Because it's as if it happened to someone else. It was vivid at the time, because at the time I truly was the person sharing her bed with Harry. But that person had no existence before or after that European vacation.

There was a moment when I looked up and saw one of Andrew's neckties hanging on the knob of the closet door. It struck me that I should have put the tie away, that it was out of place there. Then I told myself that the tie was where it ought to be, that it was Harry who didn't belong here. And finally I decided that both belonged, my husband's tie and my inappropriate Oklahoma lover. Now both belonged, but in the morning the necktie would remain and Harry would be gone.

As indeed he was. I awakened a little before dawn and was alone in the room. I went back to sleep, and when I next opened my eyes Andrew was in bed beside me. Had they met in the hallway, I wondered? Had they worked out the logistics of this passage in advance? I never asked. I still don't know.

Our last day in Rome, the Dattners went their way and we went ours. Andrew and I got to the Vatican, saw the Colisseum, and wandered here and there, stopping at sidewalk cafes for espresso. We hardly talked about the previous evening, beyond assuring each other that we had enjoyed it, that we were glad it had happened, and that our feelings for one another remained unchanged—deepened, if anything, by virtue of having shared this experience, if it could be said to have been shared.

We joined Harry and Sue for dinner. And in the morning we all rode out to the airport and boarded our flight to New York. I remember looking at the other passengers on the plane, few of whom I'd exchanged more than a couple of sentences with in the course of the past three weeks. There were almost certainly couples among them with whom we had more in common than we had with the Dattners. Had any of them had comparable flings in the course of the trip?

At J.F.K. we all collected our luggage and went through customs and passport control. Then we were off to catch our connecting flight to Boston while Harry and Sue had a four-hour wait for their T.W.A. flight to Tulsa. We said goodbye. The men shook hands while Sue and I embraced. Then Harry and I kissed, and Sue and Andrew kissed. That woman slept with my husband, I thought. And that man—I slept with him. I had the thought that, were I to continue thinking about it, I would start laughing.

Two hours later we were on the ground at Logan, and less than an hour after that we were in our own house.

That weekend Paul and Marilyn Welles came over for dinner and heard a play-by-play account of our three-week vacation—with the exception, of course, of that second-last night in Rome. Paul is a business associate of Andrew's and Marilyn is a woman not unlike me, and I wondered to myself what would happen if we four traded partners for an evening.

But it wouldn't happen and I certainly didn't want it to happen. I found Paul attractive and I know Andrew had always found Marilyn attractive. But such an incident among us wouldn't be appropriate, as it had somehow been appropriate with the Dattners.

I know Andrew was having much the same thoughts. We didn't discuss it afterward, but one knows . . .

I thought of all of this just last week. Andrew was in a bank in Skokie, Illinois, along with Paul Welles and two other men. One of the tellers managed to hit the silent alarm and the police arrived as they were on their way out. There was some shooting. Paul Welles was wounded superficially, as was one of the policemen. Another of the policemen was killed.

Andrew is quite certain he didn't hit anybody. He fired his gun a couple of times, but he's sure he didn't kill the police officer.

But when he got home we both kept thinking the same thing. It could have been Harry Dattner.

Not literally, because what would an Oklahoma state trooper be doing in Skokie, Illinois? But it might as easily have been the Skokie cop in Europe with us. And it might have been Andrew who shot him—or been shot *by* him, for that matter.

I don't know that I'm explaining this properly. It's all so incredible. That I should have slept with a policeman while my husband was with a policeman's wife. That we had ever become friendly with them in the first place. I have to remind myself, and keep reminding myself, that it all happened overseas. It happened in Europe, and it happened to four other people. We were not ourselves, and Sue and Harry were not themselves. It happened, you see, in another universe altogether, and so, really, it's as if it never happened at all.

THE THREE MUSKETEERS

by JEREMIAH HEALY

The first Monday of February started with a parking ticket for stopping in a snow-emergency zone and an irate phone call from a grandmother in Wiscasset, Maine, who couldn't understand why I hadn't found her runaway grandson, a kid about as traceable in Boston as the smoke from yesterday's cigarettes. I was just hanging up when Vincent Biaggi came into my office, closing JOHN FRANCIS CUDDY, CONFIDENTIAL INVESTIGATIONS so quietly I barely heard the click.

"Mr. Cuddy?"

"Yes," I said, rising and shaking hands with him. "You're prompt."

"I try to be."

Somewhere in his early thirties, Biaggi was just under six feet, with sharp features. He wore an expensive razored haircut and draped a black-cashmere overcoat on his arm. Muted glen-plaid Brooks Brothers suit, buttoned-down white shirt, regimental tie. A man who had confidence in his own competence. Once we sat down, however, he fidgeted in my office-surplus chair. Biaggi didn't seem used to fidgeting.

"How can I help you, Mr. Biaggi?"

"I'm not sure you can."

"Well, what's the problem?"

He stared at me.

"Domestic? Because I don't—"

"Domestic? Oh, you mean like divorce. No, no. I'm already divorced, and it's nothing like that."

"Business, then?"

"No. Well—"

I leaned back until my chair touched the windowsill. "Mr. Biaggi, we have to start somewhere."

"Yes, yes you're right. I'm acting in a way I'd never tolerate from one of my team. Indecisive. It's just—well, how much do you charge?"

I thought I saw it. Biaggi had a problem he'd already talked over with another investigator. Calling me earlier for an appointment was his way of window-shopping, to see if he'd been offered a fair price elsewhere.

I said, "Three hundred a day, even if it ends up being just a half day. All expenses, including but not limited to travel, lodging, and meals."

"You sound like an attorney, Mr. Cuddy."

"I had a year of law school. Long time ago."

"Yes, well—"

I decided to wait him out.

His mouth resolved into a determined line. "Mr. Cuddy, I'm sorry. I'm wasting your time here. I haven't made up my mind yet, and I'm experienced enough to have known that without coming here. It's just that I'm starting a new project at the office and this is the only time I could get away during the day."

"Tell you what, Mr. Biaggi." I yanked open the center drawer and spun one of my cards over to him. "You make up your mind, you give me a call and we can talk about it. Whatever it is."

He picked up the card, started to put it away, then pulled out a pen instead. "Can I have your home number?"

"You can reach me here."

"Please. I may have to call you tonight about going forward."

I counted to five silently, then gave him the number,

repeating the digits because he seemed nervous writing them down. He took out some sort of calendar, covered in burnished leather but fairly unwieldy, and slipped my card under a paper clip that kept the thing opened to the current week.

Biaggi stood, thanked me, and left.

Mentally, I kissed him off, then spent the rest of the day into the evening trying to find Woodrow from Wiscasset. I had prime rib at J. C. Hillary's on Boylston Street, a great saloon about three blocks from the condo I was renting from a doctor off in Chicago on a residency. When I got home about ten, my telephone tape showed one message in its green fluorescent window. Replaying it, I was surprised to hear:

"Mr. Cuddy. This is Vincent Biaggi at eight-oh-four on Monday night. I'm sorry I acted so stupidly today, but—I'm under some pressure. I need to speak with you, but I'm heading out and I can't call you later. Please call me after two P.M. tomorrow at my office."

He rattled off the number. I wrote it down, then rewound the tape to erase and reset. I read *The New York Times* from that morning about events that happened on Saturday and Sunday, then went to sleep.

Tuesday dawned bright, the first clear day since the January thaw. I laced up my running shoes, pulled on a cotton turtleneck and shorts, and shrugged into the Gore-tex two-piece I'd allowed myself for Christmas. I crossed Storrow on the Fairfield Street footbridge and did a leisurely six miles along the Charles River, the first three into a biting northwest wind. The macadam paths were packed solid with the snow and sleet of the previous week, which made jogging easier rather than harder. Once you got the hang of it.

I followed the run with a workout at the Nautilus facility down the street from the condo. It's a lot more pleasant to shop at the Prudential Star Market in the early morning, so after the workout I stopped to buy the week's staples. When I returned to the condo about 9:30, there was a brown Ford sedan double-parked in front of the building. It had the kind of antenna the driver doesn't need for easy listening.

A thirtyish, broad-shouldered woman got out from behind the wheel. "Cuddy, don't you ever answer the phone?"

"Cross, I look to you like I've been in to hear it?"

She gave me a sour smile. "You got something in the bag that'll spoil, take it upstairs. Otherwise, the lieutenant wants to see you. Don't take the time to change. I'll sign out another unit while they fumigate this one."

Lieutenant Robert Murphy is older, stockier, and gruffer than I am. Given the crap he had to swallow back when the department didn't consider blacks executive material, the gruffer part was to be expected.

"Garbage man found a citizen dead in an alley down by Quincy Market this morning. Medical Examiner says multiple stab wounds. The uniforms responding didn't find a wallet or watch, but the guy had this fancy calendar thing in his breast pocket, your name down for yesterday afternoon, and your card with home number in handwriting under a clip. Tell me about it."

I related everything I could remember about Biaggi coming to see me, focusing on his uncertainty.

"So he never told you what was bothering him?"

"No. M.E. peg a time of death?"

Murphy shook his head. "Biaggi was in the snow behind a dumpster, but he'd been out carousing with a couple of his college friends from seven till almost eleven, so we figure eleven to twelve, maybe one at the outside."

"These friends said Biaggi was with them from seven on?"

"Till eleven, when they split to head home. Why?"

"I got a message on my tape last night. Biaggi's voice, telling me it was eight-oh-four but I wouldn't be able to reach him because he was 'heading out.' "

Murphy turned that around a while. "Could be he meant heading out for another bar. The friends say they were pub-crawling, making dinner on the free counter stuff at the places they hit."

"Maybe he called from a good phone booth, but I didn't

hear any background music or bar noise on the tape. And from what he said to me, Biaggi seemed like a guy who kept track of things like the time. These friends from work?"

"One. A guy named Michael Doyle. The other guy, Sandor Fried, no."

"Biaggi said something about a team. What'd he do for a living?"

"He was a project leader for a consulting group called Harbor Consulting and Research. Down by Lewis Wharf."

"You been over there?"

"Yeah. They keep cops' hours."

Meaning I didn't. "Any help?"

"No. The dude's secretary went numb when we told her, then started crying like she meant to raise the mean high-water mark."

"Check on the ex-wife?"

"Tara Wheaton. One of Biaggi's friends gave me her address up in Marblehead. She didn't seem too broken up about it. Came to the door in a robe, claims she was on a flight from L.A. last night."

"Business or pleasure?"

"Business. Ms. Wheaton's a stewardess. We're confirming her story, but unless something comes up this here's going down as a mugging gone rough."

"Mind if I ask around a little?"

"For free?"

"Looks that way."

Sandor Fried's office told me he'd left for the day. Murphy had a home address for him in Wellesley. After I showered and changed, I drove out there.

Wellesley is the kind of chic suburb you'd build ten miles west of a city. Fried's house fit right in, a big colonial on two nicely landscaped acres.

The front door was answered by a gaunt woman wearing a black wig that should have had some grey in it if it was intended to appear natural. "What do you want?"

"Mrs. Fried?"

"Yes. What is it?"

"My name is John Cuddy." I showed her my identification. "I'm looking into the death of Vincent Biaggi, and Lieutenant Murphy directed me to your husband."

Her mouth moved the way a cow's does chewing cud. "Come in, then. Sandy's very upset already—don't make matters worse, all right?"

She pointed me to a sunken living room while she climbed a half staircase. The parlor floor was covered by clashing Kerman rugs. Disproportionate modern art loomed from the walls. Couches and chairs in blue leather were attended by tables of glass and brass. Not a place designed for kicking off your shoes.

The mantel had photos of two children, a boy and a girl, at various ages up to young teens. No shots of Fried or his wife.

From an upper level, I heard a man's voice say tiredly, "Sylvia, please," then Mrs. Fried's: "You got a choice, Sandy. Either I hear what he says from down there or I hear what he says from up here."

After some clumping on the stairs, a defeated man shambled into the room, followed closely by Mrs. Fried. Thinning black hair combed heroically from above one ear up and over the top of his head. Pinched eyes, a large open face, and a bearlike physique under sweatshirt and sweatpants.

"You're—?"

"John Cuddy, Mr. Fried. As I explained to your wife—"

"It's about Vinnie, right?"

"Right."

He became agitated. "I already told the police. We didn't see anything."

"By we, you mean Michael Doyle and you?"

"Right, right."

Mrs. Fried said, "You want my opinion, this tragedy doesn't happen if the three of you behaved like responsible adults instead of fraternity feebs."

"Sylvia, it was our one night out, okay?"

"Stupid."

"It was a tradition. We always—"

"Traditions can't be stupid?"

I said, "Mr. Fried, maybe if you just told me what happened last night."

"I'll try. Sit, sit, please."

Sandor Fried and I sat. Mrs. Fried stayed standing, arms folded across her chest, watching for openings.

"Vinnie, Mike, and I went to college together. We were real close, bio-sci and all, but afterward, with business pressures, we didn't see that much of each other."

"You said bio-sci?"

"Yeah. We majored in Biological Sciences. I went into pharmaceutical publishing. Mike tried med school, but he—that didn't work out. Vinnie got into consulting first, then Mike came into it later."

"Can you tell me about this tradition you had?"

"Sure. We decided to kind of revive something we did in college. Go to the bars and watch Monday Night Football."

Mrs. Fried said, "Except the three musketeers here didn't stop when football stopped. Oh, no, it's Monday, they've got to kill brain cells."

"Sylvia, do you mind?" Fried turned back to me. "We went out last night, must have been about seven when I got to HCR—Harbor Consulting, where I picked up Vinnie and Mike. We went to the Market, hit some bars, then said goodbye." Fried stopped. "God, that's a hard way to think about it. We said goodbye about eleven, maybe a little before."

"You were home eleven thirty-five, smelling like a distillery."

I said, "While you were at the bars, was anyone acting oddly?"

"Oddly?"

"Any other customer. Sizing you up or anything?"

"Oh. No, not that I noticed."

"Can you give me the sequence of bars?"

Closing his eyes, Fried seemed to concentrate. "Michael's Waterfront, because it's right by HCR there, then over to the market area itself. The Lord Bunbury, Donovan's, Lily's—no, no, we went down to the Ames Plow first, then Lily's."

"Anybody overdo it?"

"What, drinking? No, there's nothing like that with us."

"I'll bet," from Mrs. Fried.

"Did Biaggi say where he was going after leaving you?" I asked her husband.

"No. Not to me. He's free to—he was divorced, you know?"

"Fraternity feebs, all of you."

Deciding that Mr. Fried had taken enough from both Mrs. Fried and me, I thanked them and left.

Tara Wheaton lived in a cluster of duplex condominiums that overlooked a yacht club and the expanse of mansions on Marblehead Neck, across the winter-empty harbor. Her building was halfway up the slope from the water. There were no locks on the entryway doors, so I climbed the stairs to her unit and knocked.

The woman who opened the door was about five foot seven, with lustrous brown hair and hooded green eyes. She smiled and said, "You're John Cuddy?"

"Yes, but without more security downstairs you might not want to give a stranger the name of a visitor you're expecting."

The smile grew lazy. "I've gotten a lot better at making judgments since I got divorced. Come on in."

The first level contained a combination living room/dining room and a glass wall with sliding door to a balcony offering a teasing peek of the Neck over the condo roofs closer to the waterfront.

She said, "Like the view?"

"Impressive."

"I've always liked the ocean, but we bought this place just after we were married because there was no upkeep, and now you can't touch a single-family along the water." She gestured to the sectional furniture. "Have a seat."

We sat facing each other in the L-shaped arrangement. "I really appreciate your taking the time to see me under the circumstances, Ms. Wheaton."

"Tara."

"Tara."

She rose a little, tucking one leg under the other. "Look,

let's not play games for what you might think is my benefit. Vinnie and I were married, Vinnie and I got divorced. I'm sorry he's dead, but I'm not exactly crushed. Okay?"

"Okay."

"So why did you want to see me?"

"After the divorce, did you and Biaggi stay on good terms?"

"Good terms." She thought about it. "I guess so. I mean, we could talk on the phone without screaming at each other. That was part of the problem, actually."

"Talking on the phone?"

"No. No, I mean while we were married. Vinnie just wasn't the—most passionate guy around."

As I thought about a next question, Wheaton said, "Actually, I have to take that back. He was passionate enough about his job. And about studying back in school. It's just that work was all he was passionate about."

"You met each other in college?"

"Yeah. Sandy, Mike, and Vinnie were together from the beginning. They were seniors when I was a freshman. I met Mike first. He introduced me to Vinnie."

"Mike Doyle."

"Right."

"Did you date Doyle first?"

"Kind of. Well—" She played with the cuff of her slacks. "You have to remember, this was back in the mid-Seventies. I think Mike expected me to hop into bed with him. He was okay, but not special enough for me."

"You and Biaggi married in college?"

"Right after. Stupid thing to do, since I already signed up to see some of the world. But to be honest with you, it worked better that way."

"How do you mean?"

"Well, what Vinnie really wanted was kind of a guaranteed date more than a lifemate. He wanted somebody who was around on a regular basis, but not really a wife. A wife would cut a little too much into his work time. So, with me being gone a lot but here often enough, it was perfect."

"What soured it?"

"Oh, I got tired of flying, so I left the airline to become a house-spouse. Plus, I was pushing thirty, starting to think about having kids. Vinnie wasn't really into that, and with me being home a lot, I started to realize just how little we had. As a couple."

"So you got divorced?"

"Right. Real—amicable, as the lawyers said. I got this place, because to tell you the truth he wanted to be closer in to the job anyway. It's ironic, actually."

"Ironic?"

"Yeah. I mean, that Monday-night thing with Sandy and Mike is about the only thing he did for fun, I bet, and it got him killed."

"Anybody you know who might have benefited from that?"

"Benefited?"

"Yes."

"You mean, like if it wasn't some mugger?"

"That's what I mean."

She hugged herself and settled deeper into the cushions. "The police—they think it might be—"

"You never know. Anybody come to mind?"

"Lord, I don't think so. Vinnie was a hard worker, but all his family's gone and—I don't think he really knew anybody outside work and the guys."

"Sandy and Mike."

"Right."

"What do you know about them?"

"Well, Mike, like I said, was okay but nothing special. He knew it, too."

"How do you mean?"

"He's just the kind of guy—he's always going to be a B-plus, never an A, you know? He couldn't hack it in med school, got his job at HCR because Vinnie vouched for him, that kind of thing."

"Private life?"

"We all used to go out sometimes, kind of triple-date. Mike would never be with the same girl twice, and she'd always be kind of CBA."

"CBA?"

"Yeah. Cheap but alluring. Nothing upstairs. It was like he went through them to prove something."

"How about Sandy Fried?"

"Sandy? Just a teddy-bear. A great guy who made the mistake of marrying the first girl who was nice to him. Has kids he adores and a wife—you meet Sylvia?"

"Yes."

"Then enough said."

"How about you?"

"Me?"

"Yes. You benefit from Biaggi's death?"

The lazy smile. "You're direct about it, anyway."

I waited her out.

"No, I don't. Just the opposite, in fact. Vinnie agreed to give me alimony—'rehabilitative' alimony, I think they call it. Since I'd left the airline to make a home for him. I had six months of it left, but the deal with the lawyers was that if Vinnie died, the money stopped, and I can't claim anything from his estate or whatever. So I sure didn't want to see him die."

"I thought you said you were back with the airline?"

"I am. After Vinnie and I split, they took me back."

"But you still got the alimony."

"For a while. It's been a nice cushion, but I'm finding flying as a single woman isn't so bad, really, even with the AIDS scare and all."

"Well," I said, rising, "thanks for your time."

She leaned back in the sectional, uncrossing her arms and tossing her head toward the harbor behind her. "So you like the view, huh?"

"Nice."

"Even nicer from upstairs."

"I'll take your word for it."

The door to Michael Doyle's office was swung half open. I could see the heavy weathered beams and exposed red brick that had been touched up during the renovation of worthless wharf buildings to pricy office space. I knocked on the jamb.

"Mr. Cuddy! Mike Doyle. Come on in. Pleasure to meet you. Though I wish it were under better circumstances."

Doyle was medium height, with reddish-brown hair and agreeable features perpetually arranged in a "can-do" smile. He came across as the kind of guy you'd hope would join the family business. "What can I help you with here?" he said.

"I've already spoken with Sandor Fried. I wonder if you could tell me what you remember about last night."

"Sure." Doyle repeated everything about the evening that Fried told me, even the bars in the same order.

"Biaggi have any enemies?"

"Vinnie? Just the opposite. Not the most gregarious guy in the world, maybe, but always helping people out."

"When did he start here?"

"Oh, let's see. 'Eighty-four sometime."

"You started together?"

"Ah, no. Actually, Vinnie beat me by about a year."

"He help you get your job?"

The perpetual smile seemed to falter a bit. "Yes, he did. Like I said, always helping people out."

"What do you do here, exactly?"

"If you mean HCR itself, lots of things. If you mean me in particular, I consult with and advise bio-tech companies."

"Gene-splicing, that kind of thing?"

"Well, yes, sometimes. But more the marketing and development angles."

"And Biaggi?"

"The same, only different. I don't want to appear evasive, but we have a lot of sensitive matters under our wings, so to speak."

"Then Biaggi did bio-tech, too?"

The smile waggled again. "Yes. We were lab partners back in school, and we did pretty much the same sort of work here."

"But he got here first."

Doyle paused, then, very evenly, said, "Yes."

We were interrupted by an older Japanese woman with a

trace of an accent. "Michael, see if you can snap Linda out of her trance. She's got to retrieve Vincent's computer notes so you can get up to speed on this immediately. We're in Conference Room Two."

"Right away, Chieko."

After the woman had left us, I said, "Linda was Vincent's secretary?"

"Right."

"And 'this' is the new project Biaggi was shepherding?"

"Uh-huh. Look, I don't mean to be rude, but—"

"I understand. Can you point me out of here?"

"Sure."

Outside his office, he was gesturing down and to the right when a young woman with a plain face but striking figure burst upon us from a subsidiary hallway. The face remark may have been unkind, because her makeup was smeared by tears and kleenex.

She nearly collapsed against Doyle, sobbing. "Oh, Michael, what should I do? What should I do?"

"Hey, Linda, it's going to be a tough time for all of us." Doyle shot me a What-can-*I*-do look that contained something more than embarrassment and less than sympathy. I left him to snap her out of it.

I'd parked a block from HCR. From my car, I could see the main entrance of the wharf building clearly.

Linda came out at 3:30 and flagged down a taxi on Commercial Street. I followed to a small apartment house in the North End. She paid the cabbie and entered the lobby. If she wasn't so upset, she could have walked it in ten minutes.

I gave her a half hour to settle in, then went to the mailboxes. There were no Lindas, the only first initial "L" belonging to an L. Duran in Apartment H. I pushed the other buttons till someone unseen negligently buzzed me into the building.

Apartment H was third floor rear. No view, but private. I banged on the door. Linda Duran's voice came from the other side of a peephole. "Who are you?"

I held up my identification, wondering if the convex lens distorted it beyond reading. "My name's John Cuddy, Ms.

Duran. I'm investigating the death of Vincent Biaggi, and I think you want to talk with me. Now."

Doyle was livid, shocking even the HCR receptionist. "Where the hell do you get off pulling me out of a meeting! I saw you yesterday, without an appointment, and answered your questions."

"Mike, I thought it would be easier for you this way. I would have sent Linda, but I'm told she called in sick this morning."

"Would you please just tell me what you want?"

"Sure. It seems you've got another meeting to attend."

"What? What other meeting?"

"With Lieutenant Murphy and Sandy Fried. In Conference Room One. I'm sure you know the way."

Doyle entered in front of me. By the expression on Fried's face, I guessed Mike was shooting daggers at his college pal.

After we all were seated, Murphy said, "I'd like to get some things straightened out. Just so everybody knows the score, anyone here is free to leave any time they want." Nobody got up.

The lieutenant tilted his head toward me. "Cuddy here had a little talk with Linda Duran yesterday afternoon."

Fried looked at Doyle. Doyle glared at me.

I said, "Seems that Linda kind of clouds everybody's story."

When neither responded, I went on. "Seems Linda and Sandy have been seeing each other. Only Sandy's married, so it had to be on the sly. Monday nights were a good time."

Fried said, "No. Oh, God, no."

Doyle said, "Shut up, Sandy."

"Yeah, Sandy, listen to your friend, let Cuddy speak his peace."

"Thanks, Lieutenant. Seems Mike and Vinnie kept the tradition alive, though, partly to cover for old Sandy with Sylvia back in Wellesley. Great cover, too. Explains booze on the breath, the scent of perfume in the clothes, and all that kind of stuff. Problem, though, for Sandy: Vinnie gets killed, and by the time Sandy hears about it he's already told the wife it was just another boisterous night out with the boys."

Fried said, "Does Sylvia know?"

Murphy said, "Not yet. Now be quiet, listen to the man."

"So Sandy calls Mike, and Mike helpfully squares their stories so that Sandy's still covered. Sure, it'll throw the police off a little on possible time of death, especially since the killer took away not just the wallet but the watch, too, which might have broken and revealed the time of the attack. But, hell, it was just another mugging, no witnesses, so the cops were never going to catch the killer anyway. Right, Sandy?"

Doyle said, "Doesn't wash. I was with Vinnie till almost eleven."

"Sorry, Mike. Detective Cross and I spent most of last night running down the Monday-night bartenders. Four of them work Tuesdays, too, so it wasn't as tough as it sounds. We caught the last one at his house this morning. And guess what?"

Fried had stopped looking at anything but his hands twisting in his lap. Doyle still glared at me, the big vein pulsing at his temple.

I said, "Turns out you three were pretty well known, not by last name but as Monday-night regulars. The guy at the first bar remembers Mike and Vinnie coming in two nights ago, must have been just after eight because he started his shift then. My guess is Sandy was already at Linda's by seven, while Vinnie didn't leave HCR with Mike until almost eight. Vinnie wanted to speak with me about something. A suspicion, maybe?"

Nobody else jumped in.

"So, the guy at the second place also remembers just Mike and Vinnie. The woman at the third bar remembers Mike, but not Vinnie. The woman at the fourth place is sure Mike ordered two drinks and paid for them. The guy at the last stop remembers only Mike mentioning Vinnie was in the men's room. Now how about that?"

Doyle said, "Any of them say I had blood on me? Huh? No.

The guy who killed Vinnie'd be covered in his blood. So shove it."

I shook my head. "No, Mike. Shove it's what you did. In the alley. All that biological background, you knew that cold weather widens the brackets for time of death. You also knew where to stick the blade, what parts of the body were vital but wouldn't go off like geysers, especially given the layers of clothes Vinnie would be wearing this time of year."

Murphy said, "We checked with the Medical Examiner, Doyle. All the wounds are consistent with what Cuddy here is saying."

Fried jerked his head up. "What? What're you saying?"

Doyle said, "Shut up."

I engaged Fried. "I'm saying Vinnie preceded Mike to HCR and Mike resented that, despite or even because Vinnie helped Mike get his job here. I'm saying Vinnie was assigned some juicy new project and Mike especially resented that. And finally I'm saying that Mike stabbed Vinnie to death so he could succeed him as HCR's leading light in bio-tech consulting."

Fried showed the bewilderment of a refugee. "Mike? Mike, what's this guy trying to sell here?"

"Can it, Sandy. He can't prove a thing."

"Prove? Prove! What's with prove? You just say you didn't do it, right? Just say it, say it to me."

Doyle looked at Fried with something approaching revulsion. Fried said, "My God, Mike. Say it!"

Doyle dipped his head, chin resting on his chest. "I want a lawyer."

It took both Murphy and me to pull Fried off the third musketeer.

THE LAST TIME

by ANDREW KLAVAN

It was happening again. She was sure of it. Tim came back to the apartment late that Thursday. Not very late. Just late enough. "Sorry, darling, something came up," he mumbled. He never took his eyes off the floor. She knew on the instant.

He headed straight for the bathroom: another sign. He showered for nearly twenty minutes. Checking himself for stray hairs and lipstick stains, no doubt; sniffing at himself to make sure every trace of perfume was washed away.

Margaret sat in the living room, knitting. She stared over the tops of the clicking needles. Her lips were pressed together tightly. I will not permit it, she thought. He promised it was the last time.

She had no trouble finding out who it was. She knew it would be someone young, first of all. Someone blonde. Someone accessible, but not so close as to cause trouble when it was over. She knew they wouldn't meet after work too often. Tim wouldn't want Margaret to become suspicious. Not after the row she'd made. Not after he'd promised. No, for the most part, they would use the lunch hour. Tim was an account executive at an advertising firm and took long lunches. For the most part, it would be then.

Around noon on the Monday next, she planted herself on the corner of Madison Avenue and Forty-sixth Street, across from the stately old office tower which housed Tim's firm, and waited. She didn't disguise herself or hide behind a newspaper, or anything like that. She wasn't some sleazy private detective, after all. She simply stood and watched the entrance. She trusted the Manhattan lunch-hour crowds to hide her well enough.

Her husband came out at around twelve-thirty and headed north up Madison. Margaret followed. At Fifty-first Street, he turned east, leading her away from the avenue. She kept a safe distance, but there was really nothing to worry about—he was walking quickly, intently, without looking back. He made his way past the mobs of gold-coast lawyers on Park into the throngs of shoppers on Lexington and then to the rows of elegant brownstones between Second and First. One of the brownstones—a fine one, decorated with medallion reliefs, crowned with an exquisitely crafted cornice—was his destination.

Margaret hung back and watched him go in. She crossed the street and stared up at the building. The light in the third-floor window was the only one on. As she watched, Margaret caught the brief sweep of a fan of golden hair behind the pane: the eager lover rushing to the door.

She went into the vestibule and checked the name on the mailbox. Nora Wilkins. It seemed to her there'd been a Nora once before. There'll be no more of them, she thought as she walked away. I'm putting a stop to it here and now. This is the last time.

That night, when Nora Wilkins returned home from whatever ridiculous glamor job it was she held, Margaret was waiting for her. Margaret was a firm, no-nonsense sort—she'd made up her mind and she was going to act. But even she quailed a little at the sight of the girl. Nora was more than beautiful. She was nearly perfect—tall and thin, with gently rounded hips and high breasts that made her spring blouse shiver as she walked. Her face was delicate and sweet, her hair long and shiny and richly gold. Seeing her,

Margaret had to summon up an extra measure of courage before she stepped out of the first evening shadows to confront her.

"Miss Wilkins," she said. The girl stopped, puzzled. "My name is Margaret Cade. I'm—"

"I know who you are," Nora said. And archly: "Tim has told me about you."

Her composure took Margaret aback, but she pushed on. "Then you know why I'm here."

Nora eyed the small, prim older woman before her with unmistakable distaste. "Yes," she said with a sigh. "But let's not do this in the street, okay?"

Margaret nodded and followed her into the building.

Upstairs, Margaret waited silently while Nora opened her apartment door. They came into a brightly decorated living room. The angular metal furniture, the posters on the wall—everything struck Margaret with its youthfulness. She stood in the center of the room, feeling dowdy and tired with her brown-grey hair tied up in back, her navy-blue jacket buttoned almost to the neck.

Nora plopped onto a sofa: peach pillows on a shiny metal frame. She stretched her shapely legs out before her. "I didn't think you'd try something like this," she said. "Why would you humiliate yourself?"

Margaret answered quietly, "You'd be surprised at the lengths one goes to. I hope you never have to learn."

Nora shrugged. "I guess it's different for someone your age."

"I suppose so." There was silence after that. In the face of such arrogance, such coldness, such—cruelty was the only word for it—Margaret could think of nothing to say. She felt her resolve melting within her.

"Lookit," said Nora. "Tim's a grown man. He knows what he wants, what he needs. If you can't handle that, leave him. There's no law saying you have to stay."

"Isn't there?" said Margaret.

"Well—" Nora gave that infuriating shrug again "—what can I tell you? We all make choices in this life, Mrs. Cade."

"Yes," Margaret said, trying to keep her voice from trembling with anger. "And I can see you've made yours. Excuse me for bothering you."

She turned, left the apartment, and hurried down the stairs. In another moment, she was walking toward Second Avenue, wobbling unsteadily on her low heels. One word echoed through her mind over and over: *Stupid, stupid, stupid.* Her eyes were glazed, her lips white with the force of her rage . . .

On Friday, she gathered what she needed.

There was a length of rope in the kitchen broom closet. There were reinforced garbage bags under the sink. The butcher knife was hanging above the stove, but it took her a while to find the hacksaw. Tim had been using it and it was in a drawer of his desk. Margaret put the things in a tote bag and zipped it shut. This is it. This is really it, she kept thinking.

She took out her knitting and sat with it in the easy chair by the phone.

It was quarter past six when the call came.

"I'll be—a little late this evening. Sorry, darling." Tim was mumbling again. His voice fairly dripped with guilt. "We have to redo an account. It came up suddenly. I—"

She forced herself to smile brightly. "That's all right," she cooed into the mouthpiece. "I have plenty to do."

This is it, she thought as she hung up the phone. This is the last time.

She waited until full dark, then took a cab to Grand Central terminal. There, she took the subway up to Lexington and Fifty-first. She walked from there, gripping the strap of her tote bag in her right hand.

This time, the lights in the third-floor window of the elegant brownstone were the only ones that were *not* on. Margaret walked into the vestibule and pressed the button next to Nora's name. There was a long pause before Tim's voice came over the speaker. "—Who is it?"

"It's your wife," Margaret said. The quiet firmness of her voice surprised her.

There was another long pause. Then the buzzer went off

and the latch of the front door snapped open. Margaret pushed inside.

She carried the tote bag upstairs. When she stood before Nora's door, she shifted her grip on the strap, making sure it was secure. She reached for the doorbell, but Tim cracked the door open before she could ring. The look of terror and confusion in his eyes almost made her feel sorry for him.

"Margaret," he said, "I—"

She pushed the door in, brushed past him into the darkened room. "Turn on the light," she commanded.

Tim did. Nora was on the floor, her beautiful body bruised and mottled now, her face bloated and disfigured. The stocking was tied around her neck so tightly it was nearly buried in her flesh.

As Margaret stood staring, Tim shuffled up behind her. "Please," he whispered meekly, "please. You have to help me. I don't know what to do."

Margaret set the tote bag down on the floor and began to roll up her sleeves.

"Oh, all right," she said angrily. "But this is *absolutely the last time.*"

A TASTE FOR FOXGLOVE

by SHARON PISACRETA

Only bamboo chairs, baking under a punishing sun, were in evidence on the hotel roof at noon. Except for an occasional tourist intent on acquiring a tan at any cost, no one was foolish enough to sit out here in the middle of the day. Most foreigners in Athens quickly learned that during August one took shelter at midday—lying in hotel rooms in their underwear or sipping ouzo at the Laikon Bar and talking with Costas, the bartender, waiting for dusk, for a bit of shade and maybe a breeze blowing in from the harbor before venturing out to Plaka or Constitution Square or Piraeus.

The man who now walked onto the roof did so with cool indifference, as only a Frenchman of a certain age could do. As expected, all the chairs were unoccupied. He settled into one, wincing as the hot cane seared his bare legs. For the past week in Athens, the hotel roof had been his refuge, his only solace in an inferno. Here he could be alone for a while, gazing at the Parthenon shimmering in the heat across the city, its parched ruins clearly visible from his vantage point, or he could read, as he intended to now, a paperback copy of *Plexus,* already open in his hands.

It seemed only an hour had gone by, but he had read too much for such a short time to have elapsed. At any rate, his afternoon of quiet was at an end. Without turning around, he knew that she was there, her lavish perfume invading the hot, still air around him. Fortunately, she always drenched herself in fragrance—it gave away her presence, she who moved soundlessly like a wary jungle cat, no jangling bracelets on her wrists, no clacking beads about her neck, and invariably barefoot (an irritating American habit he had not been able to break her of). Yes, she was certainly barefoot now—silent, so silent—but her scent gave her away.

At first, he didn't move. He would let her think she had the advantage, that she could stand back smugly and observe him, watching him squint in the sunlight while trying to read and rub his forehead free of sweat. But after a few minutes he grew tired of the game, tired and angry at having to wait anxiously in this heat, helpless and exposed to the merciless Greek sky and her. How long must the game go on? How long would the fear and doubt continue? And at the last, his courage failed, his back damp with the heat and his own despicable fear. The pages of his book blurred before him. Why must she linger? To savor the moment or to work up her nerve?

There was the sound of movement behind him, running feet hitting the burning cement, a swish of fabric, and the overwhelming fragrance. Just before her hands closed on his neck, he let out a short cry, instantly regretted. Her laughter rang out full and loud on the deserted roof and his humiliation was complete as her hands fell away, leaving him safe and alive—this time.

Back in their room, he refused to talk to her. Instead, he squashed himself into the tiny bathtub and frantically scraped away the sweat and the peeling flakes of sunburned skin that covered him. It was madness to have stayed in a hotel without air conditioning. How could he sleep in such heat, how could he relax and stretch out and uncoil?

The bathroom door opened and she looked in at him, amused as always by the sight. "Lucien, I'm going out to see if I can buy some fruit," she said, smiling. "I have this incredible craving for grapes. I feel positively Dionysian."

With that, she was gone, while Lucien slumped back in the tub. He would never have believed it, but he felt as spent as an exhausted animal. He was so sorry he had started this whole thing, sorry he had aroused a once sleepy and contented woman, sorry he had taken the first step, sorry, so sorry, that he had ever tried to kill his wife.

But so many things had changed in the past twenty-six years. He wasn't the aspiring medical student any more, and she was no longer the young American coed who had spent her summers painting in France. Then her dreaminess and passive sensuality had held a certain charm for him. The fact that her father was the fast-food king of a chain of American restaurants had held a certain charm as well. But Lucien was an easily bored man—he should have remembered that before he married her and began to flood France with Uncle Chester's Chicken restaurants.

For soon enough he was bored. Bored with medical school, bored with the chicken franchises, bored with domestic life in the suburbs of Paris, bored with their three quiet children, even bored by the succession of women he (or his new wealth) had attracted. But, above all, he was bored with her, with Anne, his American wife, so calm and lazy, so confident, so disdainful of the French and Frenchmen, so unsophisticated and easy to manipulate. Divorce was out of the question—there was simply too much money involved and, as one of the newly rich, one wished to climb up the social ladder as unobtrusively as possible.

Still, he might not have attempted such a thing had there not been that redheaded woman from Lyons he hadn't yet grown tired of, who had insisted—threatened actually—that he must end the marriage or he would see no more of her. Oh, the mesmerizing control that infernal woman had exerted over him for a time—Lucien blushed to recall it. It now seemed almost unbelievable to him that while on holiday in Sardinia, he had actually tried to kill his wife. It had been an absurd thing to do, but he had been so restless. And of course it had failed.

Lucien also had to admit in retrospect that choosing the dried leaves of the *Digitalis purpurea,* otherwise known as foxglove, had been a rather idiotic and fanciful way to go about it. Maybe it was his memories of medical school that had compelled him—he had always loved studying toxicology. At any rate, he had measured out the necessary grains and mixed it in her orange juice. Anne normally gulped down her morning juice so quickly that the glass would be immediately drained.

But he was just too fine, too good. When the nausea and vomiting started, the irregular pulse, the dizziness, the pain in the abdomen, Lucien, the ex-medical student, found he was unable to go through with it. Instead, he drove his stricken wife eighty kilometres to the nearest private clinic and sat trembling in the corridor while they pumped her stomach.

And when he was finally allowed to see her, and he beheld her so pale and ill, so defenseless in the white bed, he did the maddest thing yet in a holiday already filled with folly. He told her the truth, shamefully whispering his confession while she listened without expression.

"Why didn't you just ask for a divorce?" she asked calmly, as though he were a stupid child. "I would gladly have given you one."

Lucien didn't know how to answer her. How could he tell her about the woman from Lyons and his fear of scandal and his reluctance to part with any of the Uncle Chester's Chicken money? How could he allow himself to appear even more contemptible than he already had? Besides, he was a little offended at the readiness with which Anne seemed to embrace the idea of leaving him. He had never imagined that she might be as weary of him as he was of her. If the circumstances were different, he might even have worked up a little anger. But the time was not right.

"Well, do you want a divorce?" There was no carelessness to her voice at that moment, only a firm timbre that signaled a decision had been made.

Choking back tears and shaking his head violently, he started to break down as only a severely controlled person could.

"Well, I think it would be a great mistake," she murmured, staring out the window for a moment, as though she were examining something in her mind. Lucien kept imagining the sound of a Sardinian police siren coming for him. "It wouldn't be fair, would it? After all, you've had your chance. Now it's my turn."

"What?" Lucien whispered, not sure he had heard correctly.

"It's my turn now," Anne replied, actually smiling. "You tried to murder me and you failed. Don't you think I deserve a chance to even the score?"

"What are you saying?"

Too weak to pull herself up, Anne simply lay back against the pillows, looking strangely at him for several moments. "Do you think you're the only one in this marriage who's bored?" she asked venomously. "Twenty-four years living in France—that's enough to drive anyone over the edge. But twenty-four years married to a man who smells of sour pork, who spits phlegm on city sidewalks, who can only sleep on his left side in complete darkness, who chooses the coarsest and most money-hungry women to be his mistresses, who refuses to speak English properly—" For someone who had just been poisoned, there was a lot of life left in her, Lucien thought with amazement as she paused for breath. "If it hadn't been for the children, who unaccountably love you, I would have swum across the Atlantic to get away from you!"

"Anne!"

"And you have the nerve to try and kill me?" she accused, her voice thick with anger. "My God, only a Frenchman could be so arrogant, so in love with himself! Well, this marriage doesn't end until *I* have *my* chance."

"I really don't understand what you're saying."

"I'll go along with whatever lie you've told these doctors," she went on. "I'll tell them about mixing up my medication or whatever *merde* you've handed them. What *did* you tell them, by the way?"

"That you like to make new herbal teas and you accidentally picked the wrong herb—"

Anne looked at him with such scorn that his voice trailed off.

"I'll go along with that story since I'm sure they aren't going to take your word for it. And I won't tell the police the truth, either. Unless you refuse to do as I ask."

It occurred to him that perhaps he should have put more foxglove in her juice.

"I may take precautions, though," she continued, pleased by the nervous expression on his face. "Maybe I'll leave a sealed letter for Father, explaining what you've tried to do today, with instructions 'to be opened in case of my death.' Or I may keep it our secret. But you'll never know if you play the game. In fact, there isn't much left for you *to* do once you agree to it. Your role in the game is simply to wait."

"Wait?"

"Wait and do nothing," she stated. "Wait the month, the year, or years before *I* try to kill *you.*" As weak as she was, Lucien heard the grim excitement in her voice. "I may fool you, tease you even. I may let you think I'm about to murder you, but you'll be wrong. When my real attempt comes, it will be terrible and shocking, like foxglove in a glass of orange juice. And if my serious attempt fails, then the ball will be back in your court, the next move will be yours. It will be your choice as to what should happen next. Divorce? Truce? Or another round by the same rules. You can even try to murder me again."

It was only then that Lucien finally began to cry. What a relief! There would be no scandal, no prison, no humiliating exposure. Only a few amateurish attempts to kill him by a woman who was too inattentive for a hand of canasta, a woman who made up her own rules for chess because she kept forgetting how it was played, a woman who had lost more than one game of croquet because she was too lazy to even cheat. A woman who, like most women, would lose this game before it ever began.

But he was wrong.

In two years, he had grown old. Even though he was not yet fifty, he walked with a painful shuffle. Listless, indifferent. The constant anxiety and unpredictability were eating away at him, sapping what little energy he had left. The family business suffered, he had no mistress, and he was violently bitter over the most unexpected turn of events: he had fallen in love—again—with Anne.

For while these two years had shattered him, Anne had flourished. She was more beautiful than he had ever remembered her—radiant, full of appetite and curiosity. She had even started painting again. Her brush with death had stirred her awake, setting her on a new course, so that at forty-six, she was emerging strong, sure, and magnificent. Life was so rich for her, so exciting, robust, and sensual she put her husband and three pale children to shame.

And above all she loved the game. It sharpened her wits and gave her discipline. It was a delightful, dangerous time, and she was resourceful and clever at making Lucien think that this was it, *this* was the real attempt. She would watch him worry and try to hide his concern, watch him inevitably succumb to his fear, and then witness his quiet relief when he realized that, no, she didn't mean it this time, not just yet, it had been just another false alarm. It was as though she had developed a taste for foxglove, a craving for danger and the deadly charms of poison.

How many times had she hinted at cyanide in the roast, gas leaks in the kitchen, faulty brakes in the Renault? And how many times had he believed her just enough to wear down his arrogance, his once certain belief that she would never really do it, that she didn't really want to do it because she must be as drawn to him as he now was to her.

For he *was* drawn to her, he wanted her more than he had ever wanted any woman, even that barbarous woman from Lyons. He was even more in love with her than when he had first started his seduction so long ago of that very young and appetizing Anne with her lazy laughter and long dark hair. Oh, yes, this was a game she was playing all too well.

The trip to Greece had been his idea. Their last holiday had ended with foxglove and the clinic. Lucien wanted to be alone with her. He wanted to regain his lost advantage. He wanted the game over with and beautiful, exciting Anne at his side again, her surrender as complete as his.

But Athens was a mistake. He knew that even before the

little rooftop scene. It was too hot and white, too filled with cars and tourists, with intense, shouting people and the remains of ancient passions. Crowds and cities only seemed to stimulate Anne. If they stayed in the city, he sensed she would make another mock attempt on his life. He was beginning to believe that she took too much pleasure in teasing him to ever really kill him. It had been two years, after all. Two years! She hadn't murdered him yet and she had had no lack of opportunity.

Yes, it was the stalking and the planning that she probably thrived upon, savoring his quiet discomfort and slowly dying confidence. She liked the pursuit—hunting him down, watching him tremble—but she would not have the stomach for the kill. Not Anne.

But by the time she discovered that for herself, he might be dead from the sheer, unrelenting stress. No, something had to be done. She had loved him once. And she must still. After all, he had tried to do away with her and she hadn't turned him in or left him or finally taken her gruesome revenge. Lying there in the tub, Lucien thought, two years, *mon dieu!* He would not allow them to leave Greece until this thing was settled once and for all. After all, the pangs of guilt only stretched so far. Enough was enough.

With what little energy he had left, Lucien decided that he must take charge again. He would court her as he had long ago in Paris. Seduce her, plead with her like a medieval troubadour, caress her under the Aegean night sky, whisper of his ardor, his hopeless passion, his overwhelming need to feel that she had forgiven him, that they could once again nestle in each other's arms without either one of them having to peer over a shoulder in wary expectation of a dagger or a hired assassin. He would exert himself as though his life depended upon it—since, in fact, it did.

When she returned with the grapes, he was dressed in white-cotton trousers and an open-necked shirt, his dark tan in sharp contrast against his clothing. He was ready to charm, to take control, his weariness and indifference noticeably absent. Anne seemed surprised at the change—but pleased as well, Lucien thought. He would never allow her to see him frightened again.

The holiday was almost over. He had to press his advantage now. "Get dressed, Anne," he said in melodious French. "It's getting late and we're going dancing."

Somehow it didn't surprise him when she obeyed him without even a sarcastic smile.

It had gone well. Anne had always loved to dance. Slender and graceful, she moved with her eyes closed, oblivious to anything around her, concentrating only on the music. Tonight she had danced barefoot at a club in Plaka and more than one man had followed her with his eyes. It was all Lucien could do to prevent himself from kneeling before her as the bouzoukis started another song and she tossed her hair back over her shoulder. She was softening, she was receptive. She had leaned against him all night, letting him do all the talking, dancing only when he wanted to dance, eating only the foods that he had chosen to order. Like the old days, only both of them were so much wiser.

And now they were back at the hotel, too keyed up to go in to bed. The air was heavy and the sidewalk hot beneath their sandals. Lucien suggested they take the elevator up to the roof, where they could talk looking out over the lights of Athens, where they could be alone, where he would make himself vulnerable for the last time.

Anne pressed the eleventh-floor button in the elevator.

"Let me stop first and wash my face," she said agreeably. "I've danced so much tonight, I'm drenched. I must look like an exhausted peasant."

"You're stunning," Lucien said quietly.

She smiled and stepped out at their floor. He didn't join her. "I'm going on up," he said. She nodded and the elevator doors closed between them.

It was dark and deserted on the roof. Without a moon to shed any light, Lucien stumbled onto a bamboo chair and bruised his shin. Yes, he thought, looking out over the city, let her follow me here to a dangerous place where I wait alone, where if she really wants to kill me it will have to be now—or, letter or no letter to Papa, Lucien would leave her and that would be an ending almost as final as death.

He gazed out at the darkened Acropolis, at the street far below, at the hotel balconies where an occasional couple stood very close before they wandered back into their rooms.

There was a swish of crepe. That lush strong scent. Almost instinctively he stiffened, and then he thought, No, not this time. He felt her standing behind him.

"Anne?"

"Yes," she said softly. He could hear uncertainty in her voice.

He stepped close to the railing and turned to face her. God, she was beautiful. Like a willing victim, a sacrifice to her righteous magnificence, Lucien let her see how helpless he was before her. He beckoned.

"If you want to do it, I will not struggle," he whispered softly.

"Yes," she whispered back. And then was silent.

"And do you know why, Anne?" he said as he turned his back on her, feeling the railing against his belly, seeing the long drop down, sensing that the time was right for such a risk. "Go on, my wild one, kill me if you want. Have it over and done with finally if it's what you truly want."

She said nothing.

Lucien went on, as if he were addressing the wind. "But I don't think it's what you really want, Anne. I think you want what I've wanted for so long now. I—"

He never finished the sentence, for he was pushed with ferocious force over the edge of the perilous railing. For a fleeting, horrifying second, he couldn't believe it had actually happened—my God, my God!

The fifteenth-floor balcony broke his fall. His hurtling body struck wicker chairs and concrete, luckily missed a glass table. He had fallen onto the terrace where continental breakfast was served two floors below. Only two floors—but the pain! He felt as though he were losing consciousness. And his body was twisted somehow. He couldn't be hurt as badly as it seemed. He couldn't be dying—not him, not now. He had to live to put an end to the game, to live happily with her again. If only he could manage to shout before he lost consciousness. He had to draw someone there, he had to be rescued—he mustn't die.

A door creaked open and light spilled in, then darkness as the door quickly shut again. "Oh, help, help me, please," he cried weakly. "I'm hurt. Please call an ambulance. Please."

As soon as he smelled that powerful fragrance, however, he stopped pleading. It was Anne, standing barefoot over him in her black-crepe dress, holding something large and heavy in her hands. She was so quiet. The game was really over. And he had only himself to blame. You Gallic imbecile, he thought in despair as darkness closed in on him. How could he have forgotten that women never play fair?

HIGH NOON AT MACH SEVEN

by CLARK HOWARD

Buddy Briscoe drove up to the main gate of Edmunds Air Force Base in a silver custom Corvette with enough options to pay for a second car. The two young Air Police enlisted men on duty at the gate gawked openly at it, one of them pursing his lips in a silent whistle. Thinking the driver of such fine wheels must be minimum a bird colonel, they both snapped to with robotlike salutes.

"Skip the military courtesy, boys," said Briscoe, "I'm a civilian. General Ludlow is expecting me." Briscoe handed one AP a telegram, which was quickly read and returned to him.

"Welcome to Edmunds, Mr. Briscoe. Please proceed straight ahead to the first cross-street, turn left, and you'll find base headquarters directly in front of you. The receptionist there will direct you to the base commander's office."

Briscoe eased the Corvette, glancing into his rearview mirror to see if the two young airmen were still admiring the car. They were. Just a flash of the good life, boys, he thought. Recalling the barren New Mexico desert over which he had just driven, he decided that they probably didn't see much of it at this godforsaken base.

Five minutes later, Briscoe was being ushered into the office of Lieutenant General Malcolm Ludlow, the ranking

Air Force officer at Edmunds. With Ludlow was his executive officer, Colonel Charles Wilder.

"We're *very* pleased to see you, Mr. Briscoe," the general said, almost in a tone of relief. "I want you to know that we sincerely appreciate your coming out to talk to us."

"You can thank North Aircraft, General," Briscoe replied neutrally. "They're paying for the trip and my time. You do understand that I haven't agreed to take the job yet?"

"Of course. Certainly. We're nevertheless grateful to you for giving us a chance to tell you about our problem. Did North Aircraft brief you at all?"

Briscoe shook his head. "All they said was that it was a testing problem. From the amount of money they offered me, I assume it's serious."

"It's serious." Ludlow turned to Wilder. "Colonel, why don't you fill in the details for Mr. Briscoe."

"Yes, sir." Colonel Wilder shifted in his chair to face Briscoe. "Our funding on North Air's X-44 and X-45 experimental jet fighters is what Congress refers to as 'contingency performance' funding. In order to receive the money to continue flight-testing these aircraft, we're required to achieve certain goals and objectives within a specific timeframe. The schedule is inflexible and non-extendable. If we fail to accomplish what we're supposed to in the time allotted, the remaining contingency funds pass on to the next approved project."

"To give you an example," General Ludlow said, "last year we had six-point-two million allotted to us for testing of the Bluejay experimental combat helicopter. We had six months to complete phase one of the testing. We were right on schedule until out of nowhere we had a freak snowstorm. It hadn't snowed on the low desert here in thirty-one years. The storm lasted eight days, put our entire program on hold. We tried to catch up, but ultimately went three days past the deadline. Three *days.* Four-point-one million dollars we would have received for phases two and three of the Bluejay Project went to the Navy to use on a new nuclear torpedo-guidance device. I wasn't here then, of course—my predecessor, General Bancroft, was base commander at that time.

He's now the air liaison officer at the U.S. Embassy in Ankara. Ankara, *Turkey.* Get the connection?"

"I think so," said Briscoe, smiling slightly. "What's your problem with the North aircraft?"

Ludlow nodded at Wilder and the colonel picked up the narrative. "A run of bad luck. We had two prototypes of the X-44 and two pilots, Colonel Dunbar and Major Reed, qualified to test them. Eight days ago Reed hit a weather-balloon guy wire and crashed on takeoff. Scratch one pilot and one prototype. Three days ago, our other pilot came down with a flu virus and is flat on his back. He's got a fever of a hundred and four degrees and is so weak he can barely sit up. Scratch another pilot. We're left with one prototype of the X-44, nobody on base qualified to fly it, and not enough time to get a new pilot checked out before the deadline on our contingency funds."

"And that, I presume, is where I come in," Briscoe said.

General Ludlow nodded. "If we don't complete testing of the X-44, we won't be allowed to even *start* on the X-45. And North Air has two test models already *built.*"

"What's left on the X-44 test schedule?" Briscoe asked.

"Five flights. Two altitude, two high-level trajectory, one speed."

"How much time left?"

"Six days."

Like the young AP at the front gate, Buddy Briscoe pursed his lips in a silent whistle. That would be pushing it. *Really* pushing it. Right to the edge.

"We know," General Ludlow said, reading Buddy's expression. "We realize what we're asking."

Briscoe drummed his fingertips soundlessly on the padded arm of the chair and studied Ludlow. There were five rows of military decoration ribbons above the general's left breast pocket, including the Distinguished Flying Cross, and here he sat praying that a *civilian* test pilot would save him from being assigned to some dead-end this late in his career. Briscoe noticed light perspiration on the general's nose. North Air was offering Buddy a bundle to get Ludlow off the hook so that tests on the next experimental model, the X-45, wouldn't be cancelled. But five tests in six days!

"There wouldn't have been any problem if Colonel Dunbar hadn't taken ill," the exec said. "He would have finished all the testing himself. I'm sure you've heard of Harvey Dunbar. He holds the altitude world record, the vertical dive world record—broke Mach six just last week. He's probably the best all-around test pilot in the world."

"Best *military* test pilot," Briscoe interjected. His tone remained casual, but his expression hardened a touch.

"That's what Colonel Wilder meant, of course," the general said quickly. "Everyone in aircraft testing knows that Buddy Briscoe is *the* best. Your reputation is unchallenged here, Mr. Briscoe."

"No question about that," Wilder amended. "I certainly didn't mean to imply otherwise."

Like hell you didn't, Buddy thought. They were giving him lip service now—saying he was the best, but not really meaning it. Both of these flyboys really believed that their Harvey Dunbar was the best pilot in the world. As far as they were concerned, civilian test pilots still wore leather caps and goggles. Briscoe and his peers called that kind of thinking The Right Stuff Syndrome.

"I'll have to study the X-44 test results up to now before I make a decision, General," he said.

"No problem. We have them all ready and we've got a room for you in our unmarried-officers quarters. Why don't you take the rest of the afternoon to look over the tests Dunbar has completed, evaluate what's left to do, and we can continue our discussion at dinner?"

"Fine," Briscoe said. He wanted to get away from these two men who had turned into desk pilots. Generals and colonels, he was convinced, were like corporation presidents and vice-presidents. They were your real good buddies when they needed you for something—the rest of the time they were convinced you were beneath them. Briscoe preferred dealing with aeronautical engineers and jet-aircraft mechanics. At least they were real people.

"See you this evening then," General Ludlow said, smiling and shaking hands.

"Fine," Briscoe said again.

The general's hand, he noticed, was cold and clammy.

They sent a car for him exactly at twilight to take him to the officers club. On the way, Briscoe admired the bursts of brilliant color set off by the sun as it left the cobalt New Mexico sky. Streaks of red and gold and yellow had drifted back from the quickly setting ball of fire like tinted vapor trails from a jet exhaust, piercing the fluffy white cumulus clouds left from the afternoon. Briscoe loved to fly in skies like that—he called them marshmallow-sundae skies. They were, to him, like the gigantic thunder waves daredevil surfers waited for, or the occasional straightaway Formula One drivers claimed lifted their racing tires a hundredth-millimeter off the track on a tissue-thin airstream. Special. Very special.

At the officers club, which Briscoe found to be surprisingly plush, General Ludlow and Colonel Wilder were waiting for him with another officer at the bar. The third officer, a mild-looking man of about fifty, wore a medical insignia instead of wings on his uniform lapel.

"Colonel Dan Bracken, our flight surgeon," Ludlow introduced. Briscoe shook hands with him. "What'll you have to drink?" the general inquired, waving over one of the enlisted men tending bar.

"Just some ginger ale," Briscoe said. He saw Ludlow and Wilder exchange glances. They knew he would not consume any alcohol if he planned to fly at dawn, and they were jumping to the obvious conclusion. "I haven't made up my mind yet," he told them. "The ginger ale is just in case. The numbers are off by one test—from the reports I saw, there are six left, not five."

"There's a report missing," Ludlow explained. "Colonel Dunbar flew a speed test on Friday—he's just been too ill to dictate the report. But he was doing it at home this afternoon—you can see it tonight. I have verbal assurance that the test was unremarkable."

The four men stood at the bar drinking and talking planes and flying and, on Bracken's part, physical conditioning for test pilots. "How's *your* high-altitude blood pressure, Mr. Briscoe?" he asked conversationally.

"One-eleven over eighty-two at a hundred thousand feet," Buddy replied confidently.

"Outstanding. Any inner-ear vibes?"

"Never."

"Throat spasms?"

"Never."

"Sinus strictures? Ocular expansion?"

Briscoe shook his head. "None of that, ever. I was born for the high sky, Doctor." His glance shifted to the two flight officers. "That's one of the reasons I'm the best test pilot in the world."

Dr. Bracken suppressed a smile during a moment of awkward silence, then Colonel Wilder said, "Isn't that Donna who just came in?"

They all looked at a slim redhead walking toward them in a gold summery wraparound dress. Briscoe had seen dresses like that before—they came off by removing one tiny knot on the left hip. The woman's hair was tightly curled close to her head like a beehive. Her upper lip curved down past the lower one just slightly at each corner. In front where her dress scooped low was a tanned sea of tiny freckles that disappeared into her cleavage.

"Hello, Donna," the three officers chorused when she got to them.

"Good evening, General, gentlemen," she answered in a soft southern voice. She handed an envelope to Ludlow. "I thought I'd run this over as soon as Harvey finished it. It's his handwritten report on Friday's flight."

"You should have let me send a driver for it, dear," Ludlow said. "You didn't have to trouble." He turned to Briscoe. "This is Donna Dunbar, Colonel Dunbar's wife. Donna, Buddy Briscoe."

She held out a hand that Briscoe found firm and cool when he took it. When he stepped closer, he could see an inch farther down the freckle mine.

"How's Harvey doing tonight, Donna?" asked Dr. Bracken.

"Much better, thanks. Fever's still around a hundred and one, but he managed to keep down some 7-Up a while ago."

"Good. Keep pouring clear liquids into him. I'll stop by in the morning after the test flight." The doctor looked at Briscoe. "If there *is* a test flight, that is."

Briscoe said nothing. The general offered Donna a drink but she declined. "Thanks anyway, but I'd better get back to my patient. Nice to meet you, Mr. Briscoe."

"Mrs. Dunbar," Buddy said, nodding.

After Donna Dunbar left, Ludlow handed Briscoe the envelope she had brought him. Briscoe removed the test-flight report and read it through.

"Unremarkable?" the general asked.

"Unremarkable," Briscoe confirmed. He became aware that all three officers were staring at him. Glancing across the room, he studied the door through which Donna Dunbar had walked out. In his mind he could still see her figure and that knot on her left hip. Flicking his eyes from the general to the exec to the flight surgeon, Briscoe finally looked over at the bartender. "Another ginger ale," he said.

The three officers smiled.

It was cold on the flight line at dawn: cold and clear, with the kind of cloudless, azure sky that pilots who pushed it to the edge liked to fly. In the ready room, Briscoe was suiting up in a set of his own silver pressure skins and a custom-made oxygen helmet he had brought with him in case he decided to take the job. Dr. Bracken was reading the cardiogram tape he had just run on Buddy. General Ludlow and Colonel Wilder waited patiently for the doctor's official approval.

"He's fine," Bracken said at last.

Briscoe grunted softly and continued dressing. Colonel Wilder pushed an intercom button. "Roll out the Forty-four," he ordered.

"Which test do you want to do today?" General Ludlow asked Buddy.

Briscoe shrugged. "A test is a test. It's your airplane, you decide."

"There's only one speed test left. Let's do that."

"You've got it."

Briscoe left the three officers at the edge of the flight apron when he walked out to the waiting aircraft. A lead mechanic wearing master sergeant's chevrons handed him a clipboard with a printed checklist attached, certification that the aircraft was ready to fly. Briscoe initialed it without reading it. He and the master sergeant locked eyes for a fraction of a second. The checklist was nothing but a piece of paper and they both knew it. Experimental planes either flew or didn't fly. The master sergeant gave Briscoe a thumbs-up sign and Briscoe winked. He climbed into the cockpit, adjusted his body against the two parachutes, and strapped himself in. Connecting his pressure and oxygen tubes, he pulled down his helmet visor and pushed a button that closed the canopy. He pushed another button and the cockpit and his suit began to pressurize.

"X-ray four-four requests clearance," he said, his voice transmitting through a mini-microphone inside his helmet.

"X-ray four-four, straight on," the tower replied. "The field is yours, sir." Nothing else on an airfield moved when an experimental aircraft took off.

Briscoe powered up and moved the aircraft down the runway. In seconds the plane was rolling at a hundred miles an hour. Before Briscoe lifted it off the ground, it was doing one-ninety. He took it up at thirty degrees, not banking, and used his first thruster. The craft shot forward like the bullet it was. Seconds later, the people on the ground heard a thunderclap as the plane passed Mach one.

In the cockpit with Buddy Briscoe, there was only a soft, perfect silence. Flying faster than the speed of sound, he left all noise behind.

Ninety minutes later, Briscoe was back on the ground.

"You registered Mach six-two," an elated General Ludlow said. "That's one-tenth faster than Colonel Dunbar could get it to fly."

"That's what it's all about, General," said Briscoe. "Flying faster than the pilot who flew before you. Or flying higher. Or diving straighter. Whatever. That's why they call it testing. Which one do you want done tomorrow?"

"Trajectory?" the general asked.

"You've got it." Briscoe got off the examining table when Dr. Bracken finished the post-flight study. "Incidentally, where's the nearest carwash? My Corvette's got a lot of desert dirt on it—I want to have it cleaned up."

"There's one in Alamagordo," Dan Bracken said.

Back in his room, Briscoe showered and put on fresh clothes, left the base, and drove thirty miles across the desert to Alamagordo. He found the carwash at the edge of a shopping mall. While the Corvette ran through, he watched its progress through the waiting-room viewing window.

"Nice wheels," he heard a soft southern voice say next to him. It was Donna Dunbar.

"Well, hello," Buddy said.

"Fast, I'll bet," Donna said, bobbing her chin at the Corvette.

"It gets me where I want to go. On the road, anyway." Buddy had to exert control to keep his eyes from glancing down above the scooped-neck blouse she wore. "How's your patient?"

"Better. You didn't exactly make his day by breaking his X-44 speed-test mark."

"News travels fast."

"On this base, just short of Mach one." They watched a long rigid hose shoot a stream of frothy foam all over the Corvette. Then their eyes met again and Donna said, "So how come a good-looking, successful fellow like you isn't married?"

"How do you know I'm not?"

"I found an article about you in one of the back issues of *Aviator* magazine. Harvey subscribes to it. Never throws an issue away."

"I'll bet he keeps them on a shelf in leatherette binders."

Donna suppressed a smile. "What makes you so smart?"

Buddy didn't bother to suppress his own smile. "Just a

hunch. Spit-and-polish types like to keep all their ducks in a row, that kind of dull stuff. And I'm not married because I don't want to be." Finally he had to look. "Where'd you get all the freckles?"

"In Georgia. I grew them. And the answer is yes, they are."

"Are what?"

"All over me."

"They'd be fools if they weren't," Briscoe said.

Their eyes were locked in a frank stare at each other that neither one of them wanted to be the one to break. Finally the carwash loudspeaker did it for them. "Number sixty-nine, please."

"That's me," said Donna, glancing at her claim check. "Take care."

As she started to leave, Buddy said, "Tell your husband to get ready for more bad news tomorrow. It's a trajectory test. I'm the best diver around."

"I'll bet," Donna said over her shoulder.

Buddy watched her walk out, get into a freshly washed station wagon, and drive off.

The next day, Briscoe took the X-44 to thirty thousand and brought it down to twenty in a fifty-degree dive. Then he climbed to forty and came down at sixty degrees to twenty-five thousand. From fifty thousand, he plunged to thirty at an angle of seventy-eight degrees. Then he shot up to sixty-five thousand feet and dove straight down at ninety degrees all the way to twenty-five thousand again, a forty-thousand-foot dive that made his eyeballs swell. When he pulled out of it, he could feel his kidneys shudder.

Back on the ground, he was told that the figures on all four trajectories had exceeded those registered by the previous test dives of Colonel Harvey Dunbar. "You're quite the pilot, aren't you?" said Dan Bracken as he gave Buddy his post-flight physical.

"Just the best, Doc, that's all," said Briscoe, "just the best." He paused a beat, then asked, "How's Dunbar's flu?"

"He's about got it whipped. Another two or three days of rest and I'll certify him back to duty."

After changing, Buddy got in his Corvette and drove back toward the unmarried-officers quarters. On the way, he saw Donna Dunbar's station wagon parked outside the base exchange. Pulling over, he went in and wandered around the huge, multi-merchandise store. He found Donna in the food section, pushing a grocery cart.

"Nice wheels," he said.

"Hello again," she said and smiled. "Break those records this morning?"

"Every one of them," Buddy confirmed.

"That'll put Harvey in a wonderful mood. I think I'll stay out the rest of the day."

"Sounds good to me. What shall we do?"

"You *are* fast, aren't you. Here, push my cart for me."

"Any time," Briscoe said, grinning.

He helped her finish the grocery shopping and carried the bags out to her station wagon. After he closed the tailgate, they stood in the morning low-desert heat without saying anything. In an arrangement of cacti growing between parking lanes, they saw a long black lizard darting after flies, its tongue shooting out at extraordinary speed to snag them. "That's a Mach two tongue," Buddy said.

"Everything is Mach something to you flyboys, isn't it," Donna asked rhetorically.

Buddy shrugged. "I guess so. When old Ernst Mach developed the ratio of the velocity of an object to the velocity of sound, he probably had no idea they'd name it after him. We probably ought to be thankful he had a *simple* German name, not something like Fritzengrubber. Can you imagine how that would sound: 'Pilot to tower, I just achieved Fritzengrubber three.' "

Donna laughed. "You're a case, Briscoe."

"Wait'll you get to know me better." His expression turned serious. "Did you mean it about staying out the rest of the day?"

"No, I'm sorry, I can't. Harvey still needs some taking care of." She saw disappointment filter into his eyes. "But he's going to his office for half a day tomorrow," she added. "In the afternoon. I thought I'd go for a swim at the officers-club pool. Around two."

Buddy smiled. "See you there."

On the third day of testing, Briscoe went for altitude. He took the X-44 from takeoff on a forty-five-degree climb to eighty thousand feet. On the second climb he went from fifty to eighty-five. For the next two hours, in increments of five thousand feet per attempt, he pushed the plane to ninety, ninety-five, one hundred thousand, one-five, and finally one-ten. When he was ready to return to the ground, he was exhausted. But on each climb he had exceeded the numbers achieved by Colonel Harvey Dunbar on previous attempts.

At the post-flight medical exam, Dan Bracken looked at Briscoe's blood under a microscope and said, "No alcohol for eight hours, Buddy. Your blood alkalinity is down. Drink a couple of Dr. Peppers or Cokes."

"All right to lie in the sun?"

"Sure. And better schedule trajectory tomorrow instead of altitude. I'd like you to stay under seventy-five thousand for at least twenty-four hours."

"Whatever you say, Doc."

Back in his quarters, Buddy drank two Dr. Peppers and despite their high caffeine content took a long nap. It was past one when he awoke. Feeling sluggish, he went out to the vending machines, got another bottle of Dr. Pepper, poured a bag of salted peanuts into it, shook it up, and drank it. Ten minutes later, feeling fine, he put on swim trunks and sandals, tossed a towel around his neck, and drove to the pool.

Donna was already there, in a yellow one-piece suit with the straps undone. Buddy walked over and stood looking down at her. "They sure are," he said.

Shading her eyes, she looked up and saw it was him. "Are what?"

"All over you." He nodded at a chaise next to her where she had put a book. "Saving this place for me?"

"Nobody but."

Sitting down, he admired her figure. "Woman with a body like yours ought to wear a bikini."

"I used to. But I have a Caesarean scar down my middle now that's not very pretty."

Buddy nodded. "How many children do you have?"

"None. That one was stillborn and I can't have any more."

"I'm sorry."

"Don't be. I didn't want kids anyway."

"I'm not sorry about the kids. I was talking about the bikini."

"Don't be sorry about that either, flyboy," she said, standing up. "This one shows enough. Swim?" She walked toward the pool.

They swam, sunned, ordered a snack, swam again, ate the snack when it came, then lay on their backs and talked without looking at each other.

"May I ask you a personal question?" she said at one point.

"Sure."

"How much do you get paid for what you do?"

"Depends," Buddy said.

"On what?"

"The plane, the tests, the risks involved."

"Give me an average."

"I'll give you an example. For these tests on the X-44, North Air is paying me twenty thousand per test."

"You'll make a hundred thousand dollars for five days of testing?" she asked incredulously.

"Yeah. But this is a high-risk, emergency job. Some tests are simple, low-risk runs that pay only seven-fifty or a thousand dollars. It varies. I make about six hundred thousand a year, gross."

Donna grunted. "Nothing gross about that. Do you know how much Harvey makes for doing the same thing? Sixty-two thousand a year."

"Yeah, but he gets to wear those snappy uniforms and have all the peasants salute him."

"Big deal."

"I *never* get saluted."

"Poor baby. Want me to salute you?"

Buddy looked over and smiled. "I'd rather salute you."

Donna returned his look knowingly. "Better get in the water, Briscoe, and cool off."

"I think you're right, Mrs. Dunbar." He got up, adjusted his swim trunks, and dove into the water. A couple of minutes later he returned and stretched out again. "All cooled off," he reported. "Temporarily anyway."

"That's a good boy."

"My turn for a question now."

"All right."

"How old are you?"

"Older than you," she replied.

"Not by much, I'll bet."

"I didn't say by much." After a moment, she said, "I'm thirty-nine. You're thirty-four. *Aviator* magazine again."

"Oh, yeah. Leatherette binders."

There was no stopping the afternoon from passing, and after a final swim Donna dried off to go home. "It's been real, Briscoe," she said.

Buddy took hold of her arm. "Let's cut out the games, Donna." All levity was gone from his tone.

"Take your hand off me, for God's sake," she said. "It's already going to be all over the base that we spent the afternoon together. Let's not make it any worse."

He took his hand away. "If you knew it was going to be a problem, why did you suggest it?"

"Because I wanted to be with you, dummy." Their eyes met and held. "I've wanted to be with you since we met the other night. Can't you *feel* it?"

"*I* can feel it," he said. "I just wasn't sure about you. Women *have* been known to tease, you know."

"Not me, Briscoe. I *never* tease. When I play, I mean it."

"When can we meet?" he asked, his voice becoming hoarse with anticipation.

She bit her lower lip, thinking. Then she said, "Two o'clock tomorrow afternoon in Alamagordo. The back row of the Desert Theater. You can't miss the place—it's right next to the motel."

Briscoe flew the second trajectory series the next morning. He stayed under seventy-five thousand feet, as Dr. Bracken had requested, but carried out six separate tests, four of which exceeded the results of his own records set two days earlier. He was on a roll, pushing the plane and himself to the very edge, exhilarated as always at doing something no man—no *pilot*—had ever done before him. He was master of the high sky and he reveled in it. He had already made up his mind to push it one more time—another few thousand feet, another few degrees—but Dan Bracken's voice came over the radio.

"Buddy, I think that's enough for today," the flight surgeon said. "I'm getting a blip or two on some of your body readouts. Let's wrap it up, what do you say? Over."

"I read you, Doc. Bringing her in." Buddy Briscoe was fearless, but he wasn't a fool. If his body was telling him something through Bracken's instruments, that was a wrap for Buddy. None of that "We live in fame and go down in flame" macho jazz for him. After all, he had a Corvette to support.

Back downstairs, while Bracken was examining him in the medical debriefing room, General Ludlow came in with an officer Buddy had never seen before. "Buddy Briscoe, Colonel Harvey Dunbar."

He was exactly what Briscoe had imagined he would be: tall, board-straight, chin up, sideburns ending exactly at the earlobes, thin lips, immaculate uniform. He was everything Buddy Briscoe was not. Only their eyes were the same—steely-grey and direct, deep and fearless. The eyes of men who knew what it was to push to the edge.

Buddy was still on the examining table and the two men couldn't shake hands, so they merely nodded. Dunbar's thin lips spread in a humorless smile without showing any teeth. "You flushed a few more of my records today, Mr. Briscoe. Congratulations."

"It's a good airplane," Buddy replied modestly.

"Speaking of which," General Ludlow said, "the two new X-45s arrive tomorrow from North Air. Colonel Dunbar will begin training a replacement for the late Major Reed at once, and testing on the new models can probably start right on schedule. Providing the final test of the Forty-four goes all right tomorrow."

"It will, General," Briscoe assured him.

"Going to flush the rest of my records?" Harvey Dunbar asked, displaying the same fixed smile.

"You never know," Buddy replied.

"Hell, personal records aren't important anyway," General Ludlow said. "It's the team effort that counts. The main thing is that we'll continue receiving our contingency funding."

Briscoe and Dunbar locked eyes for a moment. This was an administrator talking, a man who was no longer a pilot. To men who pushed it to the edge, personal records *were* important. When you were all alone so high in the sky that you could see the curvature of the earth, there *was* no team. There was just you and the airplane and the edge. *That* was personal.

"The general is right, of course," Dunbar said, giving lip service to his commanding officer. "It's been a real treat for our junior officers having someone on base who's been on the cover of *Aviator* magazine. Some of the younger pilots are a little jealous that their wives got to see you at the pool yesterday while they were up flying."

At the mention of the pool, Briscoe glanced at the officer but said nothing.

"They can all meet Mr. Briscoe tomorrow night at Dan's farewell party," said the general.

Briscoe turned to Dan Bracken. "Farewell party?"

"Yes, I'm bailing out," said the flight surgeon. "The Air Force put me through medical school and I've given it twenty years of service in return. Now I'm going to Maui, work three mornings a week in a clinic to supplement my retirement pay, and sip exotic drinks from a coconut shell."

"You'll be back," Ludlow scoffed. "I give you six months. One day my phone will ring and you'll *beg* me to let you re-up. You're a thirty-year man, Dan."

"Nope, twenty's plenty. Wait and see." Dan Bracken

looked at Buddy. "I hope you'll come to the party, Buddy." Pausing just a beat, he added, "Everybody will be there."

"Sure," Briscoe said, thinking of Donna Dunbar, "I'll come."

In the air-conditioned dimness of the Desert Motel that afternoon, Buddy lay on his stomach between lovemaking sessions while Donna dragged her fingernails lightly up and down his spine.

"Why don't you get goosebumps when I do this?" she asked. "Other men do."

"I'm not like other men," he said into the pillow.

"I'll second that," Donna purred. She put her lips close to his ear. "Have you rested enough?"

"What are you trying to do, kill me?" he asked in mock indignation.

"I thought you test pilots liked to push it to the edge."

Buddy rolled over and pulled her down against his chest. "I think you're a nymphomaniac, Mrs. Dunbar."

"So? Nymphomaniacs need love, too."

"Speaking of love, I met your husband this morning."

"Yes, he told me at lunch. What did you think of him?"

"Mr. Rule Book. I kept looking for a bulge in one of his pockets, to see where he carried his manual of Air Force regulations."

Donna smiled. "Want to know what he thought of you?"

"Not particularly," Buddy said aloofly. Donna kept smiling. Finally Buddy couldn't stand it. "All right, tell me."

"He called you a juvenile delinquent of the sky. Said you made up rules as you went along. Said you probably carried a lucky charm of some kind, like a rabbit's foot maybe." She shifted her weight and rolled one leg across his body. "Personally, I think you're both right on target."

In his final test of the X-44, the fifth test in five days, Briscoe made altitude climbs that no pilot had ever made before. He pushed the experimental plane to one hundred thirty-six thousand feet straight up, and then only leveled off because he was afraid his pressure suit would burst. All the time, Dan Bracken was speaking urgently to him from the ground.

"Buddy, level off. Do you read? Your systolic and diastolic lines are in the red zone. Level off at once. Do you read?"

Buddy pushed it a thousand more feet toward the edge.

"Briscoe, goddamn it, do you want your heart to burst! Level off! Now!"

There was a moment of chilling silence, then Buddy said, "Aloha, Doc. Leveling off."

When he got back to the ground, Bracken called him several choice names and said, "What the hell were you trying to do, spoil my party tonight?"

"Just wanted to give the natives something to talk about, Doc. Did you see those altitude figures? I went right to the edge."

"The edge of insanity. If you were in the Air Force, I'd have you grounded."

"Got you there, Doc. Listen, after you get checked out of this flying school, why don't you stop off in San Francisco and spend a few weeks with me? I've got a great highrise apartment next to Fisherman's Wharf and a book of telephone numbers you wouldn't believe. Women of every race, creed, color, and sexual proclivity."

Bracken looked at him in surprise. "Where did you ever learn a word like 'proclivity'?"

"Hey, I had a year of high school before I started flying." Buddy smiled engagingly. "I also lived for a while with a gal who had a Ph.D. We taught each other things. Now how about that visit? I'll let you have the bedroom with the view of Alcatraz."

"Oh, well. That settles it. Who could pass that up?"

"All right!" Buddy winked. "You may never get to Maui, Doc."

He threw his silver pressure suit over one shoulder and strolled into the pilots' locker room, whistling.

As he walked into the officers club that evening, under a large banner that read SO LONG, DOC, IT'S BEEN GOOD TO KNOW YOU!, he saw Donna at one of the refreshment tables with a plate in her hand. Going over, he said, "Good evening, Mrs. Dunbar."

"Good evening, Mr. Briscoe." She did not smile. Glancing around, she lowered her voice. "Harvey knows about us."

"What?"

"He told me at lunch today. Apparently he heard about our afternoon at the pool. He followed me to town yesterday. He saw me park in the theater lot and later walk next door to the motel. He saw me leave, too, then waited and saw you leave."

Briscoe looked around the crowded room until he saw Dunbar standing with a group of other officers. Picking up a canape, he took a bite, then asked, "What's he going to do about it?"

"I'm not sure. He said he had some thinking to do."

"Probably going to look it up in the regulations."

"Listen, he's looking this way. I'd better go—"

"Too late," Buddy said. "He's coming over."

Harvey Dunbar walked up to them, smile fixed. "Well, well. Mr. Buddy Briscoe. The world's fastest man, in the air *and* on the ground." Turning his smile to Donna, he added, "Not the fastest in bed, I hope, for your sake, dear."

Donna set down her plate and walked away. Dunbar faced Briscoe again, his smile fading.

"You're a real wing-walker, aren't you, Briscoe? A regular Hotshot Charlie."

"If I am, I guess that makes you Steve Canyon," Buddy replied.

"You can have my wife if you want her, Briscoe, but you're not getting my flight records," Dunbar told him evenly. "I can fly loops around you."

"*Nobody* can fly loops around me, Dunbar. And I've already *got* your records."

Dan Bracken walked up to them. "You boys look serious. Let me guess: you're talking about flying, right?"

"Among other things," said Dunbar. A thought seemed to suddenly occur to him. "Dan, what do you figure is the max speed a pilot can travel?"

"Well, astronauts have reached speeds of—"

"He didn't ask about astronauts," Buddy cut in. "An astronaut is a *passenger.* He asked about *pilots.*"

"How fast do you think a man can fly and maintain control of his own craft?" Dunbar rephrased it.

Bracken shrugged. "We know the body can withstand Mach six-two—Buddy proved that several days ago."

"Could it take Mach seven?" Dunbar asked. His eyes met Briscoe's and held.

"Mach seven? I don't know," the flight surgeon said. "That's forty-six hundred miles an hour—"

"Forty-six-ninety," Buddy corrected.

Bracken began to explain. "Even in a pressure suit, inside a pressure cockpit, there's still force being exerted against the kidneys, bladder, brain, and heart. Particularly the heart, which is likely to be the organ that explodes first. Medically speaking—"

"Forget professional opinions," Dunbar said curtly. "Off the record, Dan. What do you think?"

"Off the record?"

"Strictly," Buddy assured him.

Bracken shrugged again. "I think it's possible. But it's just a theory," he added quickly.

"Thanks, Dan," said Dunbar.

"Yeah, thanks, Doc," said Buddy.

Dunbar and Buddy walked to the bar together.

"Perrier and lime," Dunbar ordered.

"Ginger ale," said Buddy.

In the ready room at dawn the next morning, Dunbar and Buddy suited up in silence. There were no pre-flight physicals, no briefing on tests to be flown, no flight plans filed. As senior flight officer at Edmunds, Colonel Dunbar had simply ordered the two new X-45 experimental aircraft fueled and readied for flight.

When they were suited up, Buddy in silver, Dunbar in blue, they walked out silently together and crossed the flight apron. The same master sergeant was there, this time with two clipboards. Dunbar carefully studied the checklist on his clipboard before initialing it. Buddy as usual initialed his with barely a glance. The master sergeant saluted Dunbar, gave Buddy a thumbs-up, and walked away.

Harvey Dunbar and Buddy Briscoe stood for a moment looking at each other through open visors. There was no longer any animosity in their eyes. It had been replaced by excitement—the sheer, raw thrill of what they knew was coming: pushing it to a new edge.

"Mach seven, Buddy?" asked Dunbar.

"Mach seven, Harv," answered Briscoe.

They grinned at each other and walked toward their respective planes.

Six minutes later, there was a double sonic boom as the two aircraft achieved Mach one.

Twelve minutes later, there were two fiery explosions at sixty thousand feet as both X-45s achieved Mach seven and disintegrated.

At twelve-thirty that night, Dan Bracken walked naked into the kitchen of his home on officers row and got a bottle of beer out of the refrigerator. Returning to his study, he sat on the floor, took a sip, and handed the bottle to Donna, who was stretched out on his couch, not naked but almost. After the officers' wives and other consoling visitors had left her own house, she had turned off all the lights and slipped over to Dan's. She took a swallow of the icy beer and passed the bottle back to him.

"We'll be set up pretty good, I think," Dan said. "With your officer's widow pension, my retirement pay, and the two hundred thousand hazardous-duty insurance the Air Force carried on Harvey, I might not even have to work three mornings a week at that clinic on Maui."

"Hmm," said Donna.

Dan yawned and stretched luxuriously. "Give us more time to sip exotic drinks from coconut shells."

"Hmm," she said again. She was looking at a bookcase across from the couch. Its shelves were partly filled with back issues of *Modern Medicine,* all kept neatly in leatherette binders.

Odd, Donna thought. She'd never noticed them before.

WIDOW?

by FLORENCE V. MAYBERRY

Chris and I met at Lake Tahoe. That was a long time ago when both Reno, where I lived, and Tahoe were simpler, less glittered with gambling and neons. Especially Tahoe. It was still woodsy and real, an outdoor place for swimming, horseback riding, Girl and Boy Scout camps—nightclubs only in the background. That day I was with a noisy young crowd from Nevada University, none of us particularly dating anybody, just a crowd of Christmas-holiday students.

I remember exactly what I wore. White ski pants, black fur-topped boots, a white angora sweater and cap. As I walked through the lobby to the fireplace after a morning of tramping in the snow, I looked in a mirror and was quite set up with myself. Tall, slender, pink cheeks, auburn hair waving into the white cap. I sat on the divan before the fire and began unlacing my boots, planning to toast my feet while waiting for our luncheon table to be called.

I hadn't noticed the man seated at the far end of an adjacent divan, but suddenly there was a swift movement and this stranger was kneeling before me, finishing the unlacing, pulling off the boot, smiling up at me; massaging my cold toes. "Do you mind?" he asked.

I was too startled to know whether I did or not. To my

nineteen years, this man was very mature. Thirty-five, perhaps even forty. Forty-two, it turned out. No college boy I dated had ever paid attention to whether I had cold feet or not—other things were on their minds. And for sure none of them would have knelt before a girl, unless in horseplay. I hastily glanced around to see if any of my group saw us, but they hadn't yet come inside. Blood rushed into my cheeks as the second boot was loosened and the big warm hands of the stranger rubbed my toes. "I—I think I do," I said. Then, impulsively, "But it feels good."

"It would to me in your place," he said, and kept rubbing.

When my feet were good and warm, he returned to the other divan, sat down, and leaned forward, hands clasped between his knees. "My name is Christopher Langsted. I live in Reno. New, though—I'm only there a few weeks."

"I live there, too. I go to the University."

"And home? Where is that?"

"Fresno, California." I didn't have to say any more, but I did. "My mother lives there. My father lives in Winnemucca. They're divorced, both married again. But Dad wanted me to go to college in his native state. Mine, too. I was born in Reno." Silence constrained us while we contemplated the crackling fire, and each other. Then, why not? "Where's your home?" I asked him.

"Canada. British Columbia. But I've wandered a bit, lived in a great many places. Now it's Reno. I like it—it has mountains *and* prairie."

I laughed. "Not prairie—desert. We don't have prairies in Nevada."

He laughed with me. "I'm an ignorant foreigner, you'll have to—"

But what I had to do was lost as my gang crowded into the lobby and called for me to join them. "I guess our table is ready," I said. "Thank you for getting my feet warm."

"That was my pleasure," he said. Then, as I turned away, he caught my arm and said, "Forgive me, please. But when you first arrived this morning I saw you in the lobby, and I thought how delightful, but how impossible, it would probably be to meet such a lovely girl. But when you came in again just now and sat so near me, it seemed providence. That's why I was so bold. It must have seemed very rude, but I would have hated myself if I lost that chance. Could I know your name?"

"Autumn," I told him. And blushed. "Honestly. I know it's a peculiar name. But I was born in autumn. With red hair. Like autumn leaves, my dad said. My mother preferred Dawn, because that's when I arrived—so that's my middle name."

"Your parents were very perceptive. It's a beautiful name."

That's how it started with Chris and me.

Just after the Christmas holiday a note addressed to "Miss Autumn Dawn" arrived at my dorm—a formal, polite note: "Dear Miss Autumn Dawn, I neglected to obtain your surname, but hope this will reach you. I took the precaution of attaching a separate note to the registrar stating that you are a tall, slender young woman with auburn hair. It would give me the greatest pleasure if you would have dinner with me this coming Friday night, or any night you choose. My telephone number is—."

I called him. Perhaps because he was so courteous, so intriguingly mature. Except for my father, he was the oldest man who had ever asked me out for dinner. And my dad didn't bother any more since he had remarried. But more likely it was because Chris was so good-looking—the tall, lean type I saw in British movies, the whole effect enhanced by his odd, clipped Canadian accent.

He looked so quietly sophisticated in his beautifully tailored suit as he waited for me in the dormitory lounge. The eyes of the girls sitting around widened and looked heavenward as they took sidewise glances at him, and I knew stacks of questions would greet me when I came home that night.

He helped me into the waiting taxi and we rode down South Virginia Road to one of Reno's best restaurants. I'd been there before with my father, and with one or two boy friends who had big allowances. But it was different with Chris. The way he ordered, talked, danced made me feel precious, elegant, romantic—rather like the girls in expensive perfume ads.

When he delivered me back to the dormitory, he didn't kiss me goodnight. He took my hand, told me how charming I was, and asked if my study program would permit a similar evening soon.

I said it would and started up the steps. Then on impulse I ran back to him, pulled his face close, kissed his cheek, and hurried inside. When I was in the foyer, I looked back. He still stood on the walk, as though waiting for me to return. Even now, when I think of Chris, that's the way I remember him. Waiting for me.

It was on our next date that Chris told me he was in Reno for a divorce that he wasn't sure his wife would give him. But if all went well, would I marry him?

He kissed me that night. Because I said I would.

At the end of his six weeks' stay in Reno, Chris explained that his wife refused to sign the divorce papers and he would have to return to Canada to reason with her, but I was not to worry because he planned to make a generous financial settlement. "The subject hasn't come up before, because you didn't ask. But I'm quite well off. My parents are both dead and I'm their only child. I have timber holdings and mills I'll sell out while I'm in Canada—there will be plenty of money for her and for us." He added in an off-hand way, "Even though she is a very greedy lady."

This was his first direct comment on his wife and I was curious. "What was your trouble, Chris?"

"Let's not talk about that, Sweet."

"Why not? I should know. To avoid doing the same wrong things and losing you, too."

He shook his head, an indulgent smile loosening his set expression. "Not you, Autumn. You're too open, too honest. And too loving."

But once started, I was determined to learn more about their trouble. "Chris, I'm not just prying. My own past is involved. My parents divorced just as I reached my teens—and I hated it. I still do. They both love me, I'm sure they do, but when they each remarried I was an outsider. I don't blame them, that's just how things happen. It's a relief to know you don't have children to be hurt as I was. Can't you understand how deeply I fear doing something that could lead to divorce? Please don't leave me in the dark."

So he told me. The problem was adultery. She didn't want a divorce because marriage is a good cover for short-term affairs. And she also liked money. Money and marriage formed her insurance policy, with marriage the more stable part of that policy. As she grew older, the affairs were harder to come by. She was less attractive and lonely old age loomed ahead. "She still has some beauty," he said, "But it's become hard-edged, somehow not real—not because of age, but because of the way she thinks and lives. I'll be honest, Autumn. Once I loved her a great deal. She was fascinating, lovely—a recent widow, eight years older than I, but very attractive to me. She resembled you, Autumn. Blue eyes, lovely skin, delicate features. Her hair was the same auburn shade. Later, as it began to grey and thin, she wore wigs, but they were always auburn. The color suited her as it does you. Now, please, Sweet, no more. The past is over for me. Let it be for you, too."

He left that week for British Columbia to finalize his divorce papers and was gone almost three months. When he returned, he was thinner, his face strained, silver beginning to show at his temples. He held me close, dropping his head against mine almost as though too tired to hold it up. "It's finally settled, Autumn. Finished at last. As soon as the divorce is granted, we can be married."

He requested a closed hearing for the divorce to avoid publicity and insisted that I not be there. This was a relief. I didn't want to be there. Then, in Carson City, we were married the day after I received my degree from the university.

We chose Lake Tahoe for our honeymoon because we had met there and because Chris loved the mountains, trees, and lakes. It reminded him of the mountain property in British Columbia his father had given him while he was still in college. Chris had built a log cabin there for himself, even to the rock fireplace. The land was far from the highway, free of traffic, stores, and people—private and peaceful.

"Then why didn't you take me there instead of to Tahoe?" I asked him.

His face shadowed. "It's too soon. I don't want to think of any life before this one of ours."

I didn't press. I was too happy with what we had. Chris was tender and gentle—a younger father, an older and understanding lover, a gentleman who treated me like an honored guest in my own home.

We ended up with two houses, one rented at the Lake and one we bought, a charming old-fashioned house that overlooked the Truckee River in Reno.

In the fall, three years after we were married, Chris suddenly said, "Autumn, I think it's time we paid a visit to my—to our cabin in British Columbia. Do you think you can stand at least part of a Canadian winter? Snow gets heavy up there."

I was happy as a child. "It sounds wonderful! Oh, Chris, I've longed to see the cabin! Let's really stock up and be snowed in all winter! How soon can we leave?"

"As soon as you can get ready. You'll need all your snow things, and you'll need to shop. But don't bring blankets, there are plenty there. No electric blankets—there's no electricity at the cabin, just oil lamps. We can buy basic supplies at the country store about twenty miles away."

As we drove north, I grew more and more excited, entranced with the beauty of the northern country. Lakes edged with pine and fir trees spiked into the blue sky as though trying to catch the puffball clouds. Deer darted across the highway. There was a hardy simplicity in the people we met at gasoline and food stops. And the air was so clean and pure and exhilarating. I wanted us to live here always.

Deep in British Columbia, we turned off the highway onto a narrow road strewn with pine needles and started climbing up the mountain, our car seeming to twist upon itself as we followed the unrelenting sharp curves, up and up, the air thinning into winey sharpness. Miles down the highway, we had stopped at a small trading center to stock up on supplies, including kerosene for the lamps. "We'll have to hurry, even though these curves are tricky," Chris said. "The sun goes down early this far north." But even driving faster, my first sight of the log cabin was sheathed in twilight and by the time we carried everything indoors, the sky was dark except for the moon appearing and disappearing in the shifting clouds.

Chris lighted the lamps on the stone mantle above the fireplace and the broad pine kitchen table and hurried out again to search out fallen tree branches for our fire. He was elated, more boyish than I had ever seen him. I couldn't help it—I wondered if the elation came from remembering previous times here with his first wife. This had been hers, too—she must have been here with him. Perhaps even that last time three years ago when he had returned about the divorce.

I shook my head to banish the nagging thoughts. But I wondered if similar thoughts had troubled Chris while he was outside, because when he returned with an armload of wood he was no longer elated but quiet and pensive. Unspoken strain held both of us until the fire blazed in the fireplace, the little iron cookstove was hot, and coffee bubbled in a granite pot. Then the strain vanished. We began to laugh and chatter about everything in the cabin. I rubbed my hands admiringly over the varnished dark-yellow logs of the wall, carried a lamp into the compact bedroom, set it on a built-in chest, and lifted the thick Hudson Bay blankets stacked on the bunks. Chris shook out the narrow mattresses and reached his long arms across them to spread out the sheets we had brought with us. I dusted the furniture, hung our clothes in the cedar-lined closet, planned where I might hang pictures, curtains I might make.

We cooked supper and after the dishes were washed Chris drew me into his arms. "This is the way it always should have been," he whispered, his cheek against mine. His voice was taut, covering more than he said. He eased us into the big lounge chair before the fire. "I've been afraid to bring you here—afraid it wouldn't turn out right. But it is right. You've driven away the past, Autumn darling. She'll never come back."

I pushed off his lap. "You're still thinking about her! It's this cabin—you didn't do that in Reno! I won't stay here. You're not fair. You don't want to tell me about her, yet you keep thinking about her. Was it here in this cabin that you finally broke up? If it is, I hate it. I want to go home!"

His eyes went wide and sick. He stared at me a few moments, then arose, took his jacket from a wooden hook beside the outer door, and went into the dark night.

My tempers come fast and leave the same way. By the time he had left the deck that bordered the cabin and the crunch of his steps on the needle-covered ground became faint, I was sorry. I grabbed my sweater and ran after him, calling, "Chris, I didn't mean it! I'm sorry!"

I waited in the dark outside the cabin, lamplight from the small paned windows intensifying the black forms of the trees and the intimidating immensity of the mountain beyond them. Utter loneliness crowded in on me. "I'm frightened, Chris!" I screamed. "I'm *so* sorry! Please come back!"

When he appeared out of the sheltering trees, he hurried to me, held me close, kissed me, and said, "Sweet, I'm the one to be sorry. I shouldn't have mentioned—anything at all. We'll leave tomorrow, never return."

But in the morning the sun was bright, the sky so blue, the air so sweet and clear, I couldn't bear to leave and go back to the noise and brittleness of Reno. So Chris had memories. Who didn't? Together we would build our own memories in this lovely place.

It was like being newlyweds all over again, to nest in the snug cabin. I busied myself inside while Chris sought out fallen trees, sawed and split their trunks and branches, stacked firewood up the side of the cabin. "When snow comes, the wood beside the house will insulate it, help keep it warm. If I chop enough, we could last out the winter."

"What about food?"

"Oh, we probably *won't* stay. But if we should, there's always the store down the highway. If the car can't get out, I can snowshoe to the main road and catch a ride. The highway is kept clear."

Frost began to show around the window edges and one morning Chris said the clouds meant snow and he had better drive to the store for supplies. "Want to come along?" he asked.

I can't remember why I said no. Perhaps I feared we'd soon leave the cabin to avoid a snowbound winter and I wanted to hoard every minute of being in it. And Chris was so efficient, he didn't need my help with the shopping. Whatever the reason, I decided to stay and felt quite exhilarated by the prospect of a cozy day puttering about, perhaps exploring spots around the cabin I hadn't yet seen.

"I should be back by mid-afternoon or so. Are you sure you'll be all right? I haven't seen any wild animals around, but if a bear should show up run for the house and lock the door. It's too bad you don't know how to use the rifle."

"What rifle?"

"The one in the trunk of the car. In these mountains you never know when one might come in handy. Maybe I should give you a quick run-through, show you how to use it. If you did shoot something, we could hang it in the cache—you'd be a real pioneer lady."

I gave a feminine shudder and told him to keep his old rifle, I'd never shoot an animal.

The cache, actually, had been a problem for me when on the morning after our arrival Chris had pointed it out and explained its purpose: It was a small shedlike structure to one side of the cabin, built on top of four tall poles. Once Chris had spent an entire year here and had shot a deer for meat. He'd hung the carcass in the cache, where it stayed frozen through the winter, the tall poles keeping hungry animals from reaching it. My reaction was, the poor deer, the poor hungry animals—never mind the hungry man, there was a store down the road.

As he waved and drove away down the narrow, rutted road I thought how miraculously fortunate I was to have him appear out of nowhere and fall in love with me. Of *course* his first wife wouldn't have wanted to let him go—especially once her affairs were no longer so enticing and she was older. What kind of persuasion had he used to get her to finally release him? Money, he'd said—a great deal of money. But wouldn't she have had the money anyway even if she refused the divorce? Perhaps—could it be?—she had at last truly fallen in love with one of the men she was involved with.

What kind of woman was she, anyway? She resembled me, Chris had said. The eyes, the hair. She'd kept the hair color after she became grey by wearing a wig. Did I really look like her? Curiosity gnawed at me. If only I could find a photograph of her, left behind somewhere in the cabin. Things were always left behind after vacations. Impelled by the desire to know what she looked like, I started pulling out drawers, running my hand into crevices in the bedroom cupboards, even crawling under the bunks to feel the grooves in the log walls.

Finding nothing in the main cabin, I tackled the lean-to storeroom off the kitchen and dug through old packing boxes, castoff luggage, every nook and cranny of every shelf. Finally, a little ashamed of the clandestine search, I gave up.

The cabin was neat and sunlight had begun to brighten the lean-to window. The clouds were gone, the day had warmed. It would be lovely outdoors. Perhaps I could find dry grasses for bouquets.

As I left the cabin, my attention was caught by a tall ladder lying against one wall. I thought of the cache where Chris had kept the deer. It was a curiosity—I had never heard of one before this trip. Why not climb up and see what it was like inside? I dragged the ladder outside, steadied it against the floor of the small shed, climbed up, and peered through its narrow opening. Repulsed by a rank animal smell, I nevertheless continued looking into the shadowy interior.

In a far corner was a small mound—a small motionless animal, its shape and color barely discernible in the faint light. I shuddered, pitying the poor dead thing. It must have shinnied up a pole in search of food and then died, too timid to retreat, or frozen by winter.

Still staring at the creature, repelled but fascinated, I moved down a rung. Then the back of my neck tightened with irrational fear. The animal had hair nearly the color of my own. Dulled, yes, and dirty, but unmistakeably reddish. Could it be a fox? Part of a fox? But can a fox climb up a pole? No. A domestic cat, perhaps, strayed and hungry. I hastened back down the ladder, eager for the clean, cozy cabin and a cup of tea.

But as my feet touched the ground, another thought held me motionless. A long narrow green cloth had been beside the animal. Too wide for a pet's decorative neck ribbon. A scarf. Why would a green scarf be beside a dead cat? To wrap it for burial? Would a man be likely to do that? No, but a woman might. What woman? Chris's first wife, of course. But why put the pet in the cache instead of burying it?

I scurried up the ladder again and this time crawled across the straw-littered floor to the animal. I gingerly poked its fur with one finger. Dried dark-brown drippings streaked the dull red of its pelt. Blood, old blood. The poor thing had been badly injured. I picked it up by a hair tuft—and dropped it in horror. It was no animal! It was a tousled wig, matted with blood that once had poured through a gash in the wig's webbing. The green scarf half under the wig was also splotched with dried blood.

I dropped the hideous thing, backed onto the ladder and down to the ground. In mute hysteria, I ran into the forest and clung to a tall pine in a miserable effort to squeeze comfort from a natural, living thing.

Then I realized how foolish it was to be frightened by my own fertile imagination. There was sure to be a perfectly natural explanation for the red wig. Chris's wife could have left it behind, Chris never wanted to see it again, and tossed it into the rubbish. *And the wig climbed into the cache?* An animal attracted by the blood found it and carried it there. *But how did the blood get on the wig?* Perhaps two animals found it, fought, wounded each other, and bled. Their teeth had gashed the wig. *Then one animal carried the hairy, fleshless thing up one of the poles into the cache?*

My head whirled from the futile conjecture. I decided that when Chris returned, I would simply ask him about it.

It was nearly dark when Chris arrived, the car filled with groceries and packages. "Hi, Sweet! Miss me?" I ran to the car, eager for his tenderness and strength. "Oh, Chris, I did! I should have gone with you—it was horrible here alone, imagining scary things."

He swept me in his arms and held me, then asked me to help him carry the lighter stuff inside. In the house, he began rattling around with the stove. "Let's have some tea. You probably didn't eat all day. I didn't, either. But I picked up a lot of good things—we'll have a wonderful supper."

He was so normal, so comforting. I laughed, relieved, and sent him back to the car to pick up the rest of the things while I started supper.

After our meal, we settled before the fireplace and I brought up the episode of the cache.

"Today was a bad day, Chris. I was silly and broody. It's so good to have you home, to make me sensible. I do, sometimes, have too much imagination. But to be fair, Chris, part of what upset me today is your fault. You've been so secretive about your first wife. You've never even told me her first name. Not that it truly matters, but it leaves me feeling shut out and curious. Too curious, I suppose."

The firelight showed his face grow taut and I hurried on before he could stop me. "So today I looked for some trace of her. For a photograph or something that could give me a hint of what she was like. You said we looked alike. That her wigs were the same color as my hair."

His inward withdrawal became an inverse force, pushing me away from him. "Please don't stop listening, Chris—let me get this off my mind. Help me not to imagine something that isn't true—about what might have happened between you when you came back to Canada to talk about your divorce."

He stood abruptly. "Why do you continue prying? She's gone! She's out of our lives forever! We've been married three happy years. Why destroy that? Isn't it enough that I've adored you from the instant I first saw you? That life would mean nothing to me without you? Leave my past alone! It doesn't belong to you!"

"But *you* do," I said determinedly. "Everything about you, even your past. And this afternoon I found an auburn wig up in the cache. With dried blood on it." I stood and took his shoulder. "What happened, Chris? Did you argue? Did she fall against something, gash her head? Was the wig tossed in the rubbish and did an animal carry it away? A little animal that could climb the poles? How did it get there?"

He pushed me away. "Are you suggesting I killed her?"

I began to weep, stricken. "No, no! How could that be? She signed the divorce papers—you brought them back with you. That's how you got your divorce. But the wig—I couldn't help thinking something violent had to have happened. And it was so strange for the wig to be in—" I stopped, thinking: *a place where meat is kept, dead meat.*

His face congealed, like something dead itself. Without a word, he turned and walked outside. I started to follow, then stopped, believing he'd had too much of me for now, that he needed to regain his composure.

I sat, trembling, before the fire, getting up from time to time to add a log to keep it going. Almost an hour went by.

Frightened, I couldn't wait longer. I ran outside into the close-growing trees, calling his name. The spiney branches seemed to entrap my voice, muffle it. I turned back to the cabin, found a flashlight, and returned to the forest.

As a last resort, I got the car keys and drove slowly to the highway, stopping intermittently to shout his name. At the highway I stopped, uncertain. Should I turn toward the store, tell them my husband had run away from me, or try to find a phone box on the highway? Who would I telephone? My father? My mother? Say that my husband, whom they didn't know very well, had left me because he thought I'd accused him of murder? The police? No, that was worse. It would stir up a nasty inquiry, create a notoriety Chris would hate even more than that he'd dreaded about his divorce.

I decided to let him resolve the situation in his own way and not make it worse than I already had. I drove back to the cabin, hoping desperately to find him already there, worried about me, ready to talk.

But he wasn't there, and all that night he didn't return. In the morning, the wig and scarf were still in the cache and I vowed never again to mention them to anyone, even to Chris. The sky was overcast as I searched the woods again, and in the afternoon a light snow fell. I retreated to the cabin, careful to note any other human footprints than mine. There were none.

The snowfall ceased in the night and in the morning I could see indentations where I had walked, but still no other footprints. One more day, I promised myself. Then I'll leave for Reno.

Deep that night, I awakened. My eyes remained closed as I listened to the capricious creaking that houses make by themselves in the night. I could hear the faint scurry of a small animal outside on the window ledge. I heard, too, my rapid, shallow breathing—too rapid, too shallow.

I struggled to lift my eyelids and couldn't. I tried to raise my arms, to thrust aside the blankets which seemed intolerably heavy. Will as I might, my arms refused to move. My breath was getting short. Frightened, I struggled with the air itself, trying to force it into my constricted lungs. Was I paralyzed—was this a stroke brought on by anxiety? Surely not—I was too young, too healthy.

Smothering darkness crept up my body, up my neck, trying to capture my brain. This had to be a bad dream, not reality. But through quivering eyelids I could see moonlight shining through the window, the dark outlines of the chair with my clothes over its back where it stood near the window. My numbed lips mouthed at the air, trying to suck it into my starving lungs. I was awake, and I was dying.

Then great, gasping relief. Chris was there, standing beside the bunk. He bent close. I tried to force my paralyzed body into action, to cry out for help—beg him to lift me, put my feet on the floor, walk me back to life.

But he only stood there, not touching me. Chill emanated from him. He has wandered too long in the cold, I thought. "You found out," he said, his voice tired and flat. "And that killed me."

It's a nightmare—I'm asleep. Oh God, wake me, help me!

"I had to die after you found out," his empty voice said. "Only dying didn't solve anything. I thought I could just leave you, enter into emptiness. Nothingness. But that's not the way it is. I still exist—alone, in a void of loneliness. No one but me. That's the nothingness. I can't endure it, Autumn. I need you. You must come with me."

No! my mind shrieked. In an agony of panic, I tried to move.

"You must," his monotonous voice repeated. "I love you. I need you."

Did you murder her? I asked soundlessly.

"I suppose so. I didn't mean to, but we quarreled. She kept saying I would never be free. And I had to be free. To marry you. First I hid her in the cache. Then I took her far into the mountains. She will never be found—I know these mountains well. I told everyone she was upset about the divorce and had left Canada for good."

His presence became more ominous as he seemed to lean close to my face, willing the remnants of my breath to vanish. Even the darkness with its moonlit shadows began receding into nothingness. Terror crescendoed into heat, and the heat transformed into a flame of anger. Would he kill two wives? One through living strength, one through the magnetism of death? The anger burned through me and the tip of the little finger on my right hand quivered, the quiver strengthening through the entire hand.

"Lie still, Sweet," he whispered. "Don't resist. Come to me. A few moments and we will be together."

If you're dead, where is your body? my brain asked.

"You will never know—not in your world."

My right hand clenched and unclenched. Nerves stabbed up my arm, shooting electricity through my body, and I sat up as though catapulted. I moved to the edge of the bunk, swayed forward, and fell to the floor, drenched with icy sweat. "Chris!" I gasped, my hands groping in the darkness. No object obstructed them. I stood, fumbled for the matches, lighted the lamp.

"Chris!"

He wasn't there.

I threw on my robe and ran from the cabin, crying his name again and again. No answer. So it was a nightmare—it had to be a nightmare, ridiculous, abnormal, a miasma from my own subconscious.

But I had seen the window, the moonlight, the chair. The struggle for breath had been all too real. I had heard the skittering animal outside. I had been awake. Not lucid, perhaps, but awake.

I returned to the cabin and packed my belongings. When daylight came, I climbed one last time to the cache. Hating its touch, I carried the wig to the cookstove and burned it, forever destroying evidence of my terrible suspicion. When the flames died, I dampened the ashes, picked up my travel cases, and carried them to the car. Hesitantly, I opened the trunk. If a rifle had been there, as Chris had said, it was gone.

I loaded the suitcases inside, closed the trunk, and drove down the mountain road, onto the highway headed for the States and Reno. My head throbbed with nagging questions.

Can ghosts return? Can the dead threaten the living? Would Chris follow me to Reno?

As I said, that was a long time ago. I'm still in Reno. I was born here and it was the easiest place for me to get a job. Or to be in case Chris should come back—where he can find me, even if he is only a ghost.

That is, if there was a ghost. Neither Chris nor his wife were ever found. The police searched—I asked them to. They traveled all over the mountain range but no trace of bodies were discovered. So they settled on the theory that Chris and his wife are both in some foreign, lost place, she because she wants Chris and Chris to avoid a charge of bigamy.

Because Chris never got a divorce. There were no signed divorce papers. There was no closed-court hearing for me not to be present at. Oh, there was a wedding in Carson City, all right. I've got the license.

The question is, does it count?

If his wife was murdered, it does. I'm a widow.

If she wasn't, I'm not.

Since I'm the one involved, you might think I'd have reached a firm conclusion.

Sorry. I can't.

IN THE CLEAR

by PATRICIA McGERR

Frank Crawford was a careful man. Before taking any important action he figured the odds, balanced the gains against the costs, and made detailed plans. Although a moderate gambler, he did not bet more than he could afford to lose, seldom backed a longshot, and never drew to an inside straight. When his marriage at last became intolerable, he studied his alternatives with the same cautious deliberation that he gave a sales campaign for his appliance company.

After nearly 20 years of marriage the only feeling he had for Doris was a kind of mild contempt. The pleasing plumpness of girlhood had become middle-aged obesity. They had few common interests and her striving for intellectual improvement made her, in his eyes, an even greater bore. But she was an adequate housekeeper and put good meals on the table whenever he chose to come home to eat them.

For other satisfactions he looked elsewhere and had a longstanding arrangement with the manicurist in a shop near his office. Inge, though attractive and compliant, was not irreplaceable and he had no wish to make their relationship legal. Doris, on her side, was willing to ignore his infidelity as long as it did not disturb her comfortable existence. Thus there evolved a pattern that made it convenient for them to stay together while leading mainly separate lives.

Neither had any reason to seek a change until Julie Casement came to work for the agency that handled Frank's advertising.

Julie was small and slim with shaggily clipped black hair and large trusting brown eyes. Frank took her to dinner and when the evening ended he tried to analyze his odd sense of exaltation. The feelings she stirred in him were different from any he had ever known. Desire was softened by tenderness. He wanted to protect her from all the hurts of the world, even from himself. I'm in love, he decided with astonishment, in love for the first time in my life.

But she turned down his next invitation after one of her coworkers told her he was married. The regret in her tone encouraged him to argue, but it was no use.

"I suppose I sound dreadfully old-fashioned," she admitted, "but it's the way I was raised. I can't go out with you again."

"You must know there's more between us than a casual encounter," Frank persisted. "I care for you, Julie. Last night I thought you felt the same way."

"I do. But there's no point in talking about it. Please don't make it any more painful for me."

"I never want to cause you pain."

"Then say goodbye now. That's all there is to say."

He heard the click of her phone and put his own down more slowly. She was so dear, so good, so defenseless. She needed him to look after her. That evening at dinner he raised for the first time the question of divorce.

"You got some girl in trouble?" Doris asked harshly.

"Of course not."

"Then why the sudden rush to break up our marriage?"

"It's not sudden. Our marriage has been unsatisfactory for many years."

"You may not be satisfied," she countered, "but I am. I don't intend to change my whole way of life just because some bit of fluff has caught your eye."

Leaving the table, he drove across town to Inge's apartment. Responding curtly to her greeting, he strode to the kitchen and poured a generous measure of Scotch.

"What's bugging you?" she asked. "Your old lady giving you a hard time?"

"What's that to you?"

"My, we are in a foul mood. If you don't want to talk to me, why did you come?"

In answer he pulled her toward him and pressed his mouth on hers with a roughness that made her wince. Later, when he left her, his tension was somewhat eased but his spirits were still low. I've got two women, he thought morosely. Two bad bargains. Doris, fat and silly. Inge, hard and greedy. Then there's Julie. Gentle and sweet and unattainable.

Lying awake, he thought about divorce. Doris' opposition might wilt under pressure, but the price would be prohibitive. Living in a community property state, she'd take half of his savings, plus high alimony. He wanted Julie to have a life of luxury, not to scrimp on Doris' leavings. Nor should he make Julie, with her high standards, the cause of a messy divorce. But if Doris should die . . .

In the dark he let his mind play with the picture of himself as widower. Lonely, bereft, turning to Julie for comfort. Ah, yes, that would bring her to him. If only Doris were dead!

It was a concept to which his mind returned again and again in the days that followed: He began to look at his wife with eyes that saw her not as a woman but as a victim. His fantasies showed him a variety of methods—knife and gun, rope and poison. But he knew that when a woman is murdered, her husband is the Number One suspect. And if the investigation shows that the marriage was unhappy and the man had a younger mistress, the police will look no further. Yet if he ruled out both divorce and death, what was left? A long arid stretch of life without Julie.

What he needed was an undetectable poison or a weight that would drop on her head when he was far away. But those were, he knew, impossible dreams. If he killed Doris, he'd go to prison. If he divorced her, he'd be impoverished. He was in a trap with no exit. As a realist, he was learning to live with that fact until one afternoon he saw Julie. She was walking beside a well-dressed young man, her face raised to look up at him, absorbed in their conversation. The sight of her with someone else, the thought that he might lose her, was like a stab of physical pain. That was when he thought of Gregor.

Gregor operated a newsstand on a downtown street corner. In addition to papers and magazines, he sold candy, gum, cigarettes, and postcards. He also took bets on numbers and on a variety of sporting events. Through him, according to rumor, one could obtain loans at usurious interest. It was assumed, though no one said it out loud, that he had underworld connections.

Frank waited until evening, after the brisk rush-hour business, then approached to put $20 on a favorite in the next day's races. The transaction completed, he said with careful casualness, "By the way, a friend of mine has a problem. There's a guy who's—well, in his way, if you know what I mean. You know anybody who might—uh—have him taken care of?"

"Maybe." Without changing expression, Gregor scribbled numbers on a scrap of paper and handed it to Frank. "Ask for Dr. Brill."

"Doctor?"

"If he's looking for a permanent cure."

"Can you tell me what the—uh—doctor charges?"

"Two grand for a routine job with no complications."

"How does—"

"Look, you got the number. Tear it up, give it to your friend, do what you want. But don't tell me any more, don't ask me. You walk away and I forget we ever had this talk. Okay?"

"Right, Gregor."

He was trembling when he left him, the hand that held the phone number thrust deep in his pocket. I can't do it, he told himself. To put out a—what's the word?—a contract on Doris. To hire someone to kill her. It's a crazy notion. But he memorized the number before he burned the paper and he knew, deep within himself, that some day he'd make the call.

For the rest of the week he thought of little else. He must

not be rash or hasty. Before he took an irrevocable action, he must study all the angles, make careful preparations. First, there was the money. If Doris died violently, recent large cash withdrawals from his account would be a signal to investigators. Instead he began to squirrel small sums away in a metal box locked in the bottom drawer of his desk. A run of winning hands at his regular Friday-night poker session brought in over $300 which went into the box intact on Monday morning.

While the fund grew he also gave thought to eliminating, or at least obscuring, his motive. On Doris' birthday he invited another couple to dine with them at the city's best hotel. There he presented her with an expensive amber necklace and was, through the evening, ostentatiously kind and attentive.

"What are you up to?" she asked suspiciously when they were alone. "Buttering me up for something, I can see that."

"We're stuck with each other, old girl," he said with false jollity. "Why not make the best of it? It wasn't bad in the beginning, you know. If we both try a little, maybe we can get back to that."

"I guess it won't hurt to try," she conceded.

As his next move he brought home a packet of travel brochures with the suggestion that they celebrate their wedding anniversary on a Mediterranean cruise. He could count on her to display the folders to her bridge and luncheon partners who would become, if needed, witnesses to his concern for his wife's happiness. If needed. That remained the operative phrase. Several times he came close to calling the number given him by Gregor. Each time he drew back.

What finally decided him was a story in the Monday morning paper linking a series of robberies that had taken place throughout the city and its suburbs during the past few months. The method of operation was, according to police, similar enough to point to a single perpetrator, nicknamed the Bike Bandit because a motorcycle had, in several instances, been heard or seen near the scene of the crime. Seven residents had returned from an evening out to find their homes stripped of money, jewelry, and other small valuable objects. An eighth, surprising the thief in the act, had been struck with a heavy candlestick and left unconscious. She was recovering in a local hospital.

Frank, reading the story a second time, knew that if he was ever going to act, it had to be now. He left his office shortly before noon to make the call from an outdoor booth in an isolated area. When a voice said, "Answering Service," he asked for Dr. Brill.

"Leave your name and number and the doctor will call back."

"This is Mr. Smith," Frank said, and read off the number from the dial. He had about a ten-minute wait.

"Dr. Brill here." The new voice was clear and authoritative. "To whom am I speaking?"

"Mr. Smith. Gregor said you can help me with a—a permanent cure."

"You know the terms?"

"He told me two thousand."

"Right, if it's a standard operation."

"I thought it might be made to look like the Bike Bandit."

"That can be arranged. What's the patient's name and address?"

"Mrs. Frank Crawford, 4100 Rinegold Road."

"Have you set a date?"

"She'll attend a lecture from eight to nine thirty on Friday evening and get home about ten. If someone can be waiting in the house—"

"We'll handle the details. What about the husband? Will he be with her?"

"No, he has other plans for the evening."

"I assume you have the money ready."

"Yes."

"Then follow these instructions. Put the two grand in a plain brown envelope and leave it in locker number twenty-three at the airport before five p.m. on Wednesday. Got that?"

"Yes. Locker twenty-three on Wednesday. What about the key?"

"We don't need it. Just be sure the case is there on time."

"If you get full payment in advance, how do I know you'll carry out your end of the bargain?"

"How do you know a mechanic puts the parts he charges for in your car? You have to trust us, Mr. Smith. If you don't—well, it's your decision. If the money's in the box on Wednesday, the operation will take place Friday night. If not, the deal is off. No hard feelings either way."

Dr. Brill broke the connection but it was almost a minute before Frank hung up and walked out of the booth. I've done it, he thought. I've hired a killer. His mind veered away from the picture of Doris' dead body. He couldn't go through with it. He wasn't a murderer. He'd take the money from his desk, deposit it in the bank, and that would be the end of it. It would be as if the phone call had never been made.

But on Wednesday, Julie brought over an ad layout for his approval, and seeing her rekindled his desire. As soon as she left he sealed the money in an envelope and drove to the airport. On the way back he dropped the locker key into a roadside trashcan. His decision was irreversible.

On Thursday he stopped at the travel agency to make reservations on the cruise ship Doris had chosen. She was almost childishly pleased when he told her about it that evening. Everything was done. In one more day he'd be free. Then, on Friday morning, there was an unexpected snag. The man at whose house that night's poker session was scheduled came down with flu. Another player phoned to say the game was canceled.

"Oh, no!" Frank exclaimed. "We can't call it off now. We'll get a substitute."

"The problem is a place to play. Can you take us in?"

"No, that's not possible. How about Jim?"

"He's having his place painted. What's so bad about missing one week's game? You feeling lucky?"

"No, I just—" He paused, his mind working quickly. He'd overreacted. Mustn't leave the impression that the cancellation was important. "The thing is, my wife's going to an art lecture and if I tell her there's no game, she'll try to drag me along."

"I see your problem, pal." The other man chuckled. "My advice is, don't tell her. See you next week."

Frank sat looking at the silent phone. Damn. Damn. Damn! It was too perfect. I should have known something would go wrong. What do I do now? Call off the operation or postpone it? But the groundwork is all laid. It may be weeks before Doris and I have separate engagements for the same evening. And I'm sure Brill doesn't give refunds.

All right, calm down, think it through. All you've lost is an alibi. You've the rest of the day to set up another. Yet each idea was quickly discarded. Whatever he did must look natural. Any uncharacteristic activity would seem just what it was, an attempt to establish an alibi. He wasn't a moviegoer. He didn't bowl or shoot pool. He met his friends and customers for lunch not dinner. There was no one with whom he could, without strangeness, arrange to spend the evening. Except Inge.

His lips twisted wryly at the thought. She'd be a natural enough companion. And useless as an alibi. Who would believe a man's mistress if she said he was with her at the time his wife was murdered? And yet—He held onto her name a little longer. To call Inge when his poker game fell through was completely in character. If he took her to a public place and made sure they were visible and identifiable during the crucial time period, he'd be home free. With a lifting of spirits he reached for the phone.

Having made the date, he began to see ways it might serve as more than a simple alibi. Tonight he'd end the relationship, tell her he didn't intend to call her again. Then he could start fresh with Julie, with no old entanglements, no loose ends. More important, it would be one more piece in the mosaic he was building of an improved marriage.

Through the day he pondered his plans until every detail was perfect. He even rehearsed in the washroom the expression of stunned bereavement he would show the police. By the time he left his office he had begun to believe that the game cancellation was, in fact, a stroke of good luck.

He timed his arrival home for a few minutes before the friend with whom Doris was attending the lecture came by to pick her up. He walked with her to the car and helped her in.

"Have a good time," he told them both, "and soak up lots of culture. It will stand us in good stead in those foreign galleries. Did Doris tell you we're planning a cruise?"

"Yes, it sounds wonderful."

"See you later, hon." He patted her hand before closing the door, then watched with satisfaction as the car drove off. A touching farewell for Sue Farrell to describe when the police questioned her.

A short time later he was on his way to Inge's. Parking in an alley, he locked the car doors but left the lights on. Inge lived on the ground floor of an old remodeled house and he was about to knock on her kitchen door when he realized that if she noticed the car headlights on, he'd have to turn them off. Shaken a little by the near error, he walked around to the front.

Over drinks he told her that he'd reserved a table at a restaurant two blocks away.

"That Spanish place?" she protested. "I want to go some place fancy. You trying to cut expenses?"

"Somebody told me the guitarist is good. I'd like to hear him."

"Yeah? I didn't put on my Sunday best to eat rice and beans at a neighborhood joint."

"It's not that cheap." He cut short the argument. "Anyway, the reservation's made and I'm hungry. If you don't want to go—"

"Oh, all right." Sullenly she gave in. "Some great evening this is going to be."

Inge's shoes were not made for walking and her temper was not improved by Frank's insistence that the restaurant was too close to take his car. Her bad humor too, Frank congratulated himself, is in my favor. When the waiter tells the police we quarreled all through dinner, it will shore up my story of our split. He made no effort to be conciliatory but let her ramble on with her complaints. When the waiter put platters of paella in front of them he said loudly and harshly, "Shut up and eat. I'm sick of your bellyaching."

It was a silent meal. Inge sulked and Frank, secretly rejoicing, maintained an expression of grim displeasure. A mediocre flamenco dancer opened the 9:30 floor show. The guitarist wasn't much better, but Frank applauded with enthusiasm and sent the waiter to request "Adios, muchachas." The guitarist came to their table to lean soulfully over Inge as he sang. Frank thanked him with a five-dollar bill.

"What was that all about?" Inge challenged. "After being so mean all evening, do you think you can get round me with sentimental music?"

"No," he answered. "It's my way of saying goodbye. I won't be seeing you again." He signaled for the check.

"You what?" Smoldering resentment burst into flame. "You think you can brush me off like—like a squeezed lemon? You listen to me, Frank Crawford—"

"There's no need to shout."

"Oh, yes, there is." As expected, her voice rose higher. "You think you can pick me up and throw me away whenever you feel like it. Just let me tell you—"

"Hush, everybody's looking at us." He produced a credit card. The waiter took it and went away.

"I've got feelings too, you know." She pushed away the table and stood up. They were a center of attention for all the nearby diners.

"What do you want?" he asked with deliberate insult. "Severance pay?"

"You'll find out what I want," she said wildly. "You can't treat me like dirt and get away with it."

He signed the check, accepted his card and receipt, and stood. A glance at his watch showed it was 10:10. Right on schedule.

"Come on, let's get out of here." He took her arm. She jerked away and half ran to the door. Passing the maitre d' he mumbled in half apology, "The lady's a little upset."

Following her to the street, he let her stay a few paces ahead of him until she reached her apartment. She darted inside and slammed the door. And that suited him just fine.

Inge's part in the program was finished and she had, unwittingly, played it superbly.

He returned to the alley. His car was dark, the headlights no longer burning. He got behind the wheel, turned the key in the ignition, but the engine did not respond. As planned, the battery was dead. He walked through the alley to the next block where there was an all-night drugstore.

"Car trouble," he told the man on duty as he headed for the phone booth at the back.

"You'll have a hard time getting someone to fix it this time of night."

"I'm not going to try. It can stay where it is until morning. I just want to use your phone to call a cab."

In the booth he could not resist dialing his own number. It should be all over by now. He listened, hardly breathing, as the phone began to ring in his house. He counted up to ten. There was no answer. Satisfied, he called the cab company and gave the address of the drugstore. When he stepped out of the booth he was surprised to discover that he was drenched in perspiration. He mopped his face with his handkerchief as he moved to the counter and ordered coffee. When it came his hand was shaking so that half of it slopped over the counter as he tried to raise the cup to his lips.

The cab arrived quickly. Riding home he responded in monosyllables to the driver, discouraging conversation. He had to get his nerves under control, examine the plan for any last-minute flaws. He had left the restaurant at 10:15, entered the drugstore at 10:30. Even with wings he could not have got across town and back in that period.

The house, when the cab pulled up, was dark. The meter registered $2.45. Frank affected embarrassment.

"I'm afraid the smallest I have is a fifty," he said. "Can you change it?"

"You kidding, buddy? I don't carry that kind of cash on late night calls. Why didn't you break it in the drugstore?"

"I just wasn't thinking. If you'll come to the house with me, I'll get it from my wife."

"Okay, if that's how it's got to be." Grumbling, he accompanied Frank up the sidewalk. "Looks like your old lady's in bed. She won't like being routed out to pay your fare."

"She'll understand."

"Lucky you. Mine'd raise hell."

The driver waited on the porch while Frank unlocked the door and went inside. He took a quick breath, bracing himself, then flipped the switch that lighted the living room. Doris lay in the middle of the rug, arms outflung, eyes staring, mouth twisted in a grimace. Although the sight was expected, his sense of shock was genuine.

"My God! Doris—oh no!" He turned back to the cabman. "Something terrible has happened."

"What's going on, buddy?" The other man followed him in. "Oh, hey! Look at that! Is she dead?"

"I don't know." He dropped to his knees beside her, took her hand. It was cold, lifeless. "Call a doctor. Tell him to hurry."

"What you want is the police."

"Yes, I—you're right. Will you call them? The phone's in the hall."

"Sure thing." He went out.

Frank moved away from the body to a chair at the far end of the room and listened to the driver tell someone, "A lady's been killed." That's no lady, his mind appended with sick humor, that's my wife. All I have to do now is act dazed, broken, and tell the truth about how I spent the evening. When the driver came back he was slumped in the chair, his face buried in his hands.

"They'll be right over," the cabman reported. "He said for me to stay here and nobody should touch anything."

"Yes, fine. Thank you."

"Sorry about your wife, mister." He offered awkward sympathy. "Must be the guy they call the Bike Bandit. If the cops worked as hard chasing crooks as they do handing out tickets, he'd been in jail weeks ago."

His words rolled on but Frank stopped listening. He kept his face covered, his eyes closed, and his thoughts turned inward. At last the doorbell rang, the cabman went to answer it, and the room was suddenly full of men. One of them squatted beside the body. Another crossed the room to Frank who rose to meet him.

"Lieutenant Hamill, Homicide," he identified himself. "This your house?"

"Yes, I—I'm Frank Crawford. And that—" He forced himself to look again at Doris. "That's my wife."

"How about it, Doc?" Hamill asked the man on the floor. "She dead?"

"No doubt of that." He was matter-of-fact. "Offhand, I'd say a blow on the head with a heavy object."

"Okay, boys, you know what to do," Hamill told the others. "Is there some place we can talk, Mr. Crawford?"

"There's a den."

"What about me?" the driver protested. "I've got to get back on the street. I'm losing a night's work."

"Yeah? What's your part in this?"

"I brought the man home. I was with him when he found the body. I'm the one who called to report the crime."

"I haven't paid your fare," Frank remembered. "I was going to get it from—" He looked at the handbag that lay a few feet from Doris' hand and his voice died away.

"Send a bill," Hamill snapped. "Clancy, get the cabbie's story and let him go. All right, Mr. Crawford, take me to the den."

The smaller room showed signs of disarray. Desk drawers were partly open, a cabinet door swung loose. Nothing obvious, just enough to suggest that a search had been made.

"You keep any cash or valuables in here?" Hamill asked.

"No, I—oh!" A delayed memory struck him.

"Yeah? You notice something missing?"

"Not in here. But I just realized, when I found my wife, I—I took her hand—her left hand—and it was bare."

"Bare?"

"No rings. She always wore a big diamond. Almost a carat." Brill's man, he thought, had helped himself to a nice bonus. It was worth it, though, to add credibility.

"I see. Later I'd like you to go through the house and make an inventory of your losses. But first I want to get a sequence of events. When did you last see your wife?"

"About seven thirty this evening." He sat down, clasped his hands to stop their trembling. "A friend of hers picked her up to take her to a lecture."

"You know the friend's name and address?"

As he asked the question, the man he'd called Clancy entered unobtrusively and flipped open a small notebook.

"Mrs. George Farrell." Frank watched Clancy write it down. "She lives on Maple Drive. I'm not sure of the number."

"We can find her. After they left what did you do?"

"I had dinner with a friend."

"His name and address?"

"Actually, it was a woman."

"Oh?"

"Inge Ericson. 1421 Grant Street."

Again Clancy's pen moved. He and Hamill exchanged glances.

"I might as well tell you the truth, Lieutenant." Frank did not try to hide his embarrassment. "Inge and I were more than just friends. We've been having—well, I guess you'd call it an affair. But it's over. That's why I went to see her tonight—to break it off."

"Yeah?" the lieutenant's tone was neutral, showing neither belief nor doubt. "How come?"

"To be honest, my wife and I have been through some bad times. I wasn't the best of husbands—you'll hear that from a lot of people. But lately we've made an effort and it was starting to work. We planned to go on a cruise, a sort of second honeymoon. Doris was really looking forward to that. And now—now she'll never—" He broke off, covered his eyes with his hand, and held the pose for several seconds. Then he straightened and made a brave attempt to smile. "Sorry," he said. "Anyway, that's what I had to tell Inge."

"I see." Skepticism broke through. "What you're telling me, Mr. Crawford, is that at the time of your wife's murder you were in your girlfriend's apartment saying goodbye forever. I assume that Miss—Ericson, is it?—will tell the same story."

"We didn't stay in her apartment." Frank felt a secret

pleasure at the way the detective had swallowed his bait. "Inge's got a temper, and I figured she'd take the news better if there were other people around. So we went to a restaurant near where she lives. La Paloma." Got that, Clancy? he wanted to add.

"And then?"

"We had something to eat, watched the floor show, and I told her what I'd come to say."

"How'd she react?"

"She blew up a little and I took her home."

"How long did you stay in her apartment?"

"I didn't go in. She was still sore and there was nothing more to talk about, so I came home."

"Don't you have a car, Mr. Crawford?"

"Lord, yes, I almost forgot that part. I drove to Inge's but La Paloma is in walking distance. Then when I tried to start my car, I found I had a dead battery. It's still parked there."

"How'd you get the cab?"

"I phoned from a drugstore at the corner of 15th and Stevens. When we got here all I had was a bill too big for him to change. That's why he came into the house with me. I was going to get some money from Doris, but instead—" Again he gave way to emotion, hiding his face.

"That jibe with the hacker's story?" Hamill asked Clancy.

"Yeah. His sheet shows a pickup at ten thirty-five and we got the call at eleven twenty-seven."

"That fits. Get somebody to interview Mrs. Farrell, find out when she brought Mrs. Crawford home, what she saw and heard. Also check the restaurant, the drugstore, and the Ericson girl."

"Will do."

Clancy left. Hamill waited for Frank to recover. When he looked up, the detective's eyes were more sympathetic.

"I know this is a bad time for you, Mr. Crawford, but you've given us a straight story. I'm sure you understand that in a murder case, everything has to be doublechecked."

"You have your job to do." He matched the other's courtesy. "I'll do anything I can to help catch my wife's killer."

"We'll get him," Hamill promised. "The routine's going on while I talk to you."

As if in proof one of his subordinates came to the door. "The doc's finished," he reported. "Okay to take the body away?"

"Got enough pictures?"

"From every angle."

"Okay, let the morgue have her. What else do you know?"

"There are signs of forced entry by the back door. A couple of the neighbors say they heard a sound like a motorcycle being gunned around ten p.m."

Coincidence, Frank wondered, or part of the special Brill service?

The younger man left and Hamill turned back to Frank, his manner distinctly more friendly.

"We're getting a pattern," he said. "Maybe you've heard of a string of recent housebreakings?"

"The taxi driver said something about a—was it a Bike Bandit?"

"That's what the newspapers call him. He picks houses with no lights and no television playing and the occupants out for the evening. He steals small things, like money and jewelry, that he can carry on his motorcycle."

"Like my wife's ring."

"Exactly. Let's look around and see what else is missing."

With Hamill behind him Frank went upstairs and into Doris' bedroom. Like the den it gave the impression of a fast search. A jewel box lay open, its contents dumped in the middle of the bed.

"It's mostly costume jewelry," Frank said. "But she had a couple of good pieces—an amber necklace and a bracelet of heavy gold." He poked among the scattered articles. "They're not here."

"So he took the good stuff and left the junk. He knows values."

Continuing the inspection, Frank found that a pair of gold cufflinks had been taken from his bureau. That appeared to be the extent of the burglar's haul. They were in his bedroom when the phone rang. It was for Lieutenant Hamill.

He listened for a long time, responding with grunts and short exclamations that apparently expressed satisfaction with what he heard.

"That about covers it," he concluded, "except for Ericson. Get her story and we'll have the whole package. I'll be here for another hour or so." He put down the phone. "Your account is fully corroborated," he told Frank. "The restaurant owner, the waiter, even the guitar player—they all remember you. Your girl friend must have made quite a row."

"She was pretty mad," he agreed.

"The druggist remembers you too. And of course the cab company has a record of your call."

"Has someone talked to Mrs. Farrell?"

"Yes, she said the lecture ended about nine thirty and she drove your wife right home. The house was dark and everything looked normal."

"That's not much help."

"No, but at least the timing puts you in the clear. If you'll excuse me, I'll get on with my job. We have to go over the whole house for prints, et cetera. The fellow didn't leave any evidence in the other places, but sometimes they get careless and we get lucky. If you want to go to bed—"

"Thank you, no. I couldn't sleep. But I'll stay out of your way."

Frank remained upstairs while the lieutenant rejoined his associates. You're in the clear. In the clear. Hamill's words echoed soothingly in his brain. The tension that had carried him through the evening gave way to euphoria. His alibi was watertight and he was in the clear. Free of Doris. Free of suspicion. Two thousand dollars plus a diamond ring, an amber necklace, a gold bracelet, a pair of gold cuff links. He couldn't ask for a better bargain.

He was standing by the window gazing into the dark but contemplating a bright future when Hamill returned. Clancy was with him.

"You've found some evidence?" Frank asked them.

"Not here," Hamill answered. "But something else has come up. Tell me, Mr. Crawford, why did you go all the way to the drugstore to call a cab? Why didn't you use your girl-friend's phone?"

"We'd had a pretty heavy argument, you know about that. I didn't want to go back to her apartment."

"I'm sure you didn't. The druggist said you seemed very nervous, spilled coffee all over his counter."

"I suppose I was a little on edge. First the quarrel with Inge, then a dead battery."

"The cabdriver called you restless and fidgety."

"I may have been. What are you getting at, Lieutenant? What has all this to do with the murder of my wife?"

"With your wife? Not a thing. You know I sent a man to talk to Miss Ericson?"

"I heard you give the order."

"She didn't answer the doorbell and he couldn't get her on the phone. That worried him. Sometimes when a guy dumps a girl, she gets despondent, takes too many pills, or turns on the gas."

"Are you telling me that something's happened to Inge—"

"I think you know the answer to that as well as I do," Hamill snapped. "When they went in, they found her on the floor. The weapon, a heavy brass bookend, was lying by her side."

"Was she—is she—?"

"She's dead, Crawford."

"Oh, no! No, that can't be—"

"She yelled at you in the restaurant," Hamill said. "She made threats. A dozen or more people heard her. When you were back in her apartment, the fight got hotter. She wasn't willing to be dropped, maybe she had blackmail material. So you picked up the bookend, and crushed her skull. Is that how it happened?"

"No! No, you're wrong. I wasn't in her apartment. I only got as far as the door. She slammed it in my face." He paused, remembering how it had been. Himself on the out-side, Inge going alone into the dark house. "He must have already been there. The Bike Bandit. He went in while we were at the restaurant. She caught him robbing the place and he—he killed her."

"That's what we were meant to think," Hamill agreed. "Somebody did a good job of imitating the Biker's m.o. It might even have worked if the Bike Bandit hadn't gone out on his own tonight. But we know he was here in your house at ten o'clock. And a man can't be in two places at once, can he, Mr. Crawford?"

WEB OF CIRCUMSTANCE

by DONALD OLSON

Once they were married, a life apart from Edward seemed inconceivable to Cecile. She happily gave up her job to make a home for her husband in the pretty, gray-shingled bungalow on Wishing Tree Lane. To be a homemaker became her one and only ambition in life, and she dedicated herself to it with a spirit and efficiency that charmed the easygoing Edward. When he was shortly thereafter awarded a more lucrative sales territory in the furniture company that employed him, they were both delighted, even though it meant Edward would have to be away from home for two long weeks out of every month. But this would not last forever, and he promised that as soon as Cecile gave birth to their first child he would insist on being given a territory closer to home.

That Cecile was never to be able to bear children was the only disappointment in their marriage. Neither made any pretense of not caring, but they were so compatible, so much in love, and such reasonable, understanding, level-headed people they quickly adjusted to the reality of the situation, talked of eventually adopting a child or two, and happily settled into the pleasant routine of their lives. Edward's two-week absences only enhanced the joy of those periods when they were together; the years passed by swiftly and without a trace of discord. They considered themselves the luckiest of couples.

At 39, Cecile looked the same to Edward as on their wedding day, threads of gray hair and tiny fans of wrinkles at the corners of her blue eyes adding just the touch of attractive maturity to complement his thinning hair and blossoming stomach. Edward insisted that he did not go hungry while on the road for two weeks, but nonetheless he humored his wife by doing more than justice to the elaborate meals she cooked for him each and every day he was home.

At dinner his first day home in June, Edward asked, as usual, if anything had happened while he was away. Cecile told him about the new neighbors.

"Their names are Chester—Philip and Maribel. They're a little younger than us. Philip's an accountant—works at home. He's very good-looking. I see him lifting weights on their patio. I haven't met her, but he's very pleasant."

Edward showed surprise. Cecile was always so shy and retiring he couldn't imagine her becoming so quickly acquainted. Cecile explained that Philip Chester had come to the house one morning, steaming about the impossibility of having a phone installed right away, and asking if in the meantime he might impose on Cecile. The only other close neighbors were on an extended vacation trip.

Later, while Cecile was showing Edward what she'd been doing in the garden while he was away, Philip Chester appeared on the other side of the hedge separating the two backyards. Cecile introduced the two men. Edward saw that Philip Chester was quite as handsome as Cecile had described—tall, broad-shouldered, with thick blond hair and a charming smile.

"I'm ever so obliged to your wife for letting me use your phone. I tried to tell those idiots at the phone company I couldn't run my business without one."

Philip asked about Edward's work. Edward flung an arm around Cecile's waist and said how much he envied Philip for being able to work at home. The younger man responded with a mildly cynical smile. "Believe me, it has its drawbacks."

Afterward Cecile told Edward that Philip Chester had as much as admitted that his wife was addicted to the bottle. "I heard them arguing one night. She sounded like a royal nag. And Philip's so pleasant, didn't you think?"

"Oh, very."

When Edward next arrived home from his road trip and asked about the Chesters, Cecile replied that she still hadn't met Maribel and had done no more than exchange waves over the hedge with Philip, now that his own phone had been installed.

The day before Edward left was Cecile's birthday, and among his other gifts to her was a handsome diary with a tooled leather cover imprinted with her name.

"Edward, it's beautiful, but how on earth could I fill those big pages? Nothing ever happens to me except housework and gardening."

Edward gave her an affectionate squeeze. "That's the whole idea. I worry about you when I'm away, all alone here with so little to occupy your time. I want you to get out more, do things. Let these blank pages encourage you."

"Sweetheart, I've no desire to *do* things. I love our home and our garden. It's enough. I'm completely satisfied."

"Cecie, you're one in a million."

"So are you, Edward. What did we do to deserve such happiness?"

"That's easy. We found each other."

What Edward had said lingered in her mind, however, when she was once more alone. That she suffered spells of acute loneliness was true enough, but she'd always consoled herself with the knowledge that Edward would soon be home and two weeks of solitude was a small price to pay for the pleasure they would enjoy in each other's company. But then one sultry June afternoon, when she couldn't find a weed in the garden or a speck of dust in the house, Cecile settled herself on the porch glider and listlessly made a few jottings in the diary.

"Had breakfast. Drove to the market. Mended Edward's shirt. Finished my library book." These few lines occupied scarcely a quarter page. She smiled, sighed, and tossed the book down. Beyond the hedge she could see Philip Chester, dressed only in a pair of shorts that displayed his superb muscular development, playing with his poodle in the backyard. A moment later Maribel Chester, in a flowered housecoat, appeared on the patio. Cecile heard her scream at her husband: "You care more for that imbecilic *dog* than you ever did for me!" And then, to Cecile's astonished horror, the woman raised her arm and flung something at her husband. It flashed in the sun, sailed over the hedge, and landed in Cecile's bed of lupines.

Such a violation of the quiet summer afternoon was to Cecile like a glimpse into a private hell. She felt a sudden excess of joy at her own happily uneventful life, and a fresh awareness of her good fortune in having married Edward.

Philip Chester skirted the end of the hedge and carefully stepped among the flowers to retrieve what Cecile now saw to be a whiskey bottle. He looked up, saw her standing on the porch, and made a hapless, apologetic gesture in her direction. She felt very sorry for him.

Idly she again took up the diary and after a moment's thought proceeded to write a brief account of the incident. It would amuse Edward. Then, scarcely aware of what impulse prompted it, she added, "Philip came over and apologized for his wife's behavior. He was truly mortified. I invited him up on the porch for lemonade. He poured out to me all the miserable details of his life with that woman. But he didn't dare stay too long. She's insanely jealous."

Cecile reread the lines, was overcome with shame at her foolishness, and ripped the page from the book. From deep within her consciousness there filtered the memory of a schoolgirl crush on Mr. Erb, her sixth-grade math teacher, and those adolescent fantasies she'd confided to that long-forgotten earlier diary. But to be guilty of such whimsy at this time of life filled her with remorse. Whatever would Edward think? It was like a small act of betrayal, and only because to do so would attach too great a significance to the folly, she refrained from tossing the diary into the trash can.

Loneliness, however, no matter how ruthlessly denied, is a condition of the heart having nothing to do with reason, and when rain the following day prevented Cecile from spending any time in the garden, and when her bit of ironing and dusting left most of the day unoccupied, she lapsed into a mood of vague dissatisfaction. When the phone rang, she seized it eagerly, hoping it might be Edward, who would occasionally call if time permitted, or at least her friend Helen Bentley. Instead, it was a wrong number. She wandered out to the porch and stood gazing over the boxes of geraniums toward the Chester house, where she discerned no signs of life.

Mindlessly she walked back inside and found herself at her little writing desk, the diary open before her. She picked up the pen and started writing.

"Philip just called. Said his wife was away and could he come over. Said he desperately needed someone to talk to, and I was the most understanding person he'd ever met. I told him I didn't think it would be a good idea."

She felt a hot flush of guilt as she scanned what she'd written. Lunacy. Sheer lunacy. She started to shut the book, yet that blank expanse of page stared up at her challengingly. Once more the pen moved. "I was on the point of hanging up, however poor Philip sounded truly desperate. It would have been unkind to deny him a sympathetic ear. I agreed he might pop over for a few minutes. Oh, how distraught he looked. Said he couldn't possibly go on working in the house with Maribel raging at him constantly. I suggested he take an office downtown, but he said he couldn't afford it. He claimed to feel much better after talking to me. I was glad I'd been of help."

Thus began a habit that became as compulsive to Cecile as no doubt was Maribel Chester's drinking problem. The sense of shame gradually evaporated, for after all there was nothing to feel *guilty* about. A silly, harmless diversion, that's all it was, as innocent as a game of solitaire. She certainly harbored no secret passion for Philip Chester. Aggressively handsome men had never attracted her. She loved Edward and only Edward.

Nevertheless, the entries in the diary grew longer and longer, inevitably acquiring a moderately romantic cast.

"When Philip left today he surprised me with an unexpected kiss on the cheek. He could see I was offended. He apologized, but when I told him I couldn't possibly see him again he became boyishly contrite. Insisted he couldn't bear to be deprived of my 'shoulder to cry on,' as he put it. At last I relented, so long as he promised to behave himself."

Later in the week: "Philip ran into me at the market. Claimed it was accidental. Said his car was disabled and could he bum a ride home. But then he suggested we take a ride in the country, it was such a lovely day. We drove and talked for hours. He admitted the story about his car was a fib. When we parked and went for a walk in Allen Park he tried to kiss me. I'm determined never to see him again."

But of course she did, and in the weeks ahead, according to her diary, she saw Philip almost every day. Then when Edward came home she tried to atone for this imaginary betrayal by treating him with excessive affection, alarmed that he might detect something in her manner that might betray a guilty conscience. However, he merely remarked on how well she was looking, what a fresh color all the gardening seemed to be putting in her cheeks. Before he left, Cecile vowed to herself that she would burn the ridiculous diary as soon as he was gone.

Instead, it remained the high point of her day, and she would eke out the pleasure it excited in her by inscribing only a few lines at a time, in between her household activities, and saving a good quarter page for the evening.

One day there came a knock on the door and when she opened it to find herself staring into Philip Chester's wide blue eyes she blushed scarlet.

"Sorry to bother you, Mrs. Welland. Seems we've blown a fuse and are fresh out. Wonder if we could borrow one from you."

"A fuse? Oh—I—er—no, I'm sorry. We don't use them. Only circuit breakers." Which was untrue, but she was too flustered to allow him into the house. He looked at her strangely.

"Anything wrong, Mrs. Welland?"

"What? No, no. I was about to take something out of the

oven. Please excuse me." And she all but slammed the door in his face.

Later, in her diary: "Philip came to the door with some excuse about a fuse. I didn't dare let him in. This thing has gone far enough."

Yet soon she was agreeing in her imagination to accompany Philip on longer and longer excursions to neighboring communities, to picnics, museum visits, and on woodland walks. Eventually her sympathy for the beleaguered husband overcame her scruples.

"Philip came over, a trifle tight. Said that Maribel is beginning to suspect something, but he doesn't care. I'd never seen him so moody and downcast. I couldn't help myself. It simply happened. I was heartsick afterward, thinking of Edward. *It must not happen again.*"

Of course, it did.

Then something most disturbing happened just before Edward went back on the road following his two weeks at home late in July. One of the handles on his aging two-suiter had broken and he asked Cecile to leave it at the luggage store in town to be repaired. Meanwhile, he would drag out his other old suitcase and use that. Cecile thought no more about it until, just before leaving, he came lugging it downstairs.

"Oh, you found it," she said. "Was it in the attic?"

"No. In the closet."

Even then nothing registered, and it was only after he'd driven away that the thought struck her: the closet! Good heavens, that's where she kept the diary hidden. She rushed upstairs and pulled on the light. An oblong space in the film of dust showed where the old suitcase had been sitting, directly beneath the shelf where she kept the diary.

She had no way of knowing if the diary had been disturbed, and persuaded herself that it was most unlikely Edward might have noticed it there, and even if he had would probably not have touched it, although he might logically have wondered why she had secreted it there.

She awaited his return in a state of mild trepidation, and tried to believe it was no more than her imagination that accounted for what she believed to be a shade of reticence in his manner. He seemed, indeed, unusually quiet at dinner that evening.

"Is everything all right, darling?" she forced herself to ask. "Roast the way you like it?"

"Perfect. Why do you ask?"

"I don't know. You seem quiet."

"A grueling two weeks. Business isn't what it should be. Or maybe I'm losing my touch."

Relieved, she did her utmost to cheer him up. "Oh, Edward, isn't it time you stopped being on the road so much? It was different when you were younger. Couldn't you stay home more?"

"Would you really like that, Cecie?"

Did his tone betray a faint irony? No, it was only her imagination. It had to be.

"You *know* I would, Edward. Sometimes, when I'm alone all those days, I get frightened."

"Of what?"

"Oh, not of *things.* Burglars, anything like that. But of—loneliness. Sometimes it scares me."

He touched his napkin to his lips. "What are you trying to tell me, dearest?"

Surprising her quite as much as it did him, she burst into tears. Alarmed, he did his best to comfort her.

"Oh, Edward, if only you could stay *home.*"

"Now, now, Cecie. You've been such a fine brave girl all these years. So understanding. I'd no idea it affected you so much, being alone."

Gradually she composed herself, apologized for being so weak and foolish. Yet there remained a barely palpable strain in the atmosphere until Edward departed.

Three days later, while she was on the porch watering the geraniums, Cecile heard the sound of a siren on the next street, and a few minutes later was astonished to see a number of men, three in police uniforms, milling about the Chesters' backyard and patio. Curious, she walked across the lawn and peeped over the hedge. One of the plainclothesmen saw her and came forward.

"Is something wrong?" she inquired. "Has there been an accident?"

The man asked her name and said he'd be around to question her presently. When he came to her door she invited him into the living room. He identified himself as a Lieutenant Gregg of the detective force and quickly apprised her of what had happened: Philip Chester had allegedly returned home after an afternoon's fishing to find his wife dead.

Cecile's hand flew to her lips. "Dead? *Maribel?*"

"Strangled," he said impassively.

In a daze Cecile answered his questions. No, she didn't know the Chesters well at all, had never met Maribel, and spoken to Philip only on rare occasions. She explained about the telephone. And no, she'd heard nothing, no commotion of any sort, that afternoon. When pressed, she denied knowing anything about the Chesters' domestic relations. As she said this, Cecile tried unsuccessfully not to blush. Nor could she keep a slight stammer out of her voice. All she could think of were those fictional indiscretions she'd confided to her diary, and she felt sure the detective must be aware of her discomfiture.

When Edward came home and wanted all the details, Cecile referred him to the newspapers which she had saved. He read through them in absorbed silence as Cecile tried to concentrate on her knitting.

Later Edward went upstairs to his den to work on his bimonthly sales reports, and when he rejoined Cecile the details of the murder apparently remained on his mind.

"According to the papers, it happened sometime on the afternoon of the fourteenth," he remarked.

"Yes."

"Do you think he did it? One gets the idea he's the prime suspect."

"I can't believe that. You met him, Edward. He seemed such a pleasant man."

"Well, you'd know more about that than I would."

Her eyes jumped to meet his. He was regarding her with a placid, apparently unexceptional, curiosity.

"Me?"

"Well, you got to know him during all that phone business."

"Really, Edward, I hardly got to *know* him." She lowered her eyes and concentrated furiously on her knitting.

"Chester claims he was fishing all that afternoon. Only there's no one to back him up."

"If he's telling the truth, I'm sure someone will be able to verify it."

Edward sniffed. "Funny. He didn't strike me as the sportsman type."

"I don't know. He was always using those barbells on their patio."

"Vanity, not sport."

No doubt about it, Edward's tone was frankly damaging to Philip Chester's character. It wasn't like Edward. Cecile lost track of her stitches, flung the knitting aside, and went into the kitchen to prepare dinner.

That evening Edward took a walk and when he came home Cecile noticed at once how very pale he looked. "Edward? Are you all right?"

He took her hand and led her to the sofa. "Cecie, darling, I'm afraid I've done something quite inexcusable."

"Oh, Edward, not you."

"I never meant you to know. Cecie, you know how much I love you. Whatever happens, you must never forget that. I wouldn't for the life of me do anything to cause you the slightest unpleasantness."

Cecile was too disturbed to do more than stare blankly into his soft brown eyes. Edward's expression was thoughtful, almost philosophic.

"Remember, Cecie, when I had to fish my old suitcase out of the closet?"

Cecile caught her breath and held it. Edward's gaze grew even more compassionate. "I happened to see that diary I'd bought you sitting on the closet shelf. My dearest, I didn't mean to read it. I was amused that you hadn't used it. Then I saw that you had. Oh, my dear, I'd never have opened it if I'd thought there was anything you didn't want me to read."

"Edward, Edward. *Why* did you have to read it?"

"Believe me, I wish I hadn't."

She seized his hand. "Edward, it's not true. None of it is true. It was—it was, oh, silly, stupid make-believe. I swear."

"Cecie, don't. I understand. I really do. I know what loneliness can be like. I blame myself utterly. And you did your best to discourage him. That was perfectly clear. You can't help being the warm, understanding woman you are. It's why I love you."

Appalled, Cecile leaped to her feet. "Edward, stop! Oh, dear heart, as God is my witness, it is *not true.* Do you think I could ever be unfaithful to *you?* Never! Never! It was pure fantasy. I wouldn't take Philip Chester on a silver platter."

He tried to soothe her as he would a child. "Dearest Cecie, I tell you I understand. I forgive you. You were tempted beyond endurance. You don't have to pretend—"

"Pretending is what I *was* doing, Edward. I'm telling you the honest truth. It did not happen. Any of it. I swear."

Edward stirred uncomfortably. "Cecie, listen. I went to see Philip Chester tonight."

"You didn't."

"I had to, darling. He denied everything, of course. He laughed. He seemed only amused. And then I told him I had proof—your diary—"

"No!"

"I'd looked in your diary again yesterday. If you were with him as you said, all that day at Valley Ridge, he couldn't have murdered his wife."

Cecile had the sensation of reaching the brink of a dangerously high cliff and then falling numbly through space. Her voice lost its passion in the breathlessness of her fall. "He wasn't with me. He wasn't ever with me."

Edward sighed. She could see in his eyes the reflection of her own despair. With a muffled cry she turned from him and fled up the stairs to her bedroom.

Edward woke her late the following morning. "Come downstairs, Cecie. Lieutenant Gregg is waiting to see you."

The detective regarded her with apparent indifference to her ravaged appearance. "Philip Chester tells us you can prove he was nowhere near his house the afternoon his wife was killed. Something about a diary."

Cecile looked wanly from Edward to Gregg. "No. He denied there was anything between us. Ask my husband."

"Evidently, he's decided he'd rather have an alibi than go on shielding you."

Cecile stared at her husband. "Oh, Edward, what have you done?"

"Darling, it's your duty to show Lieutenant Gregg your diary. If you can give this man an alibi it would be morally wrong to withhold the information. He's promised to do all he can to keep you out of it, so long as you cooperate."

Gregg extended his hand. "The diary, Mrs. Welland?"

Cecile dragged herself upstairs to the closet and fetched the loathsome diary, hating the feel of it in her damp fingers. Gregg hastily skimmed through it, then looked up at her. "You understand this doesn't prove Chester's story. The two of you could have set it up in advance. We'll have to locate witnesses who can verify that the two of you were together in Valley Ridge."

Cecile shook her head. "You won't find any witnesses. There aren't any. I was never in Valley Ridge that day. Certainly not with Philip Chester. I've never been anywhere with Philip Chester."

When Gregg had departed, Cecile regarded Edward with a despairing look. "He didn't believe me. Any more than you did."

They heard nothing for two days. Edward tried to behave normally, to demonstrate by his attitude that he did truly understand and harbored no resentment against Cecile, but all he succeeded in creating was that atmosphere of excessive politeness that exists between strangers.

When Gregg next arrived, he made an extraordinary request. "We're still checking for witnesses. In the meantime, Mr. Welland, I'd be obliged if you'd allow me to take an impression of your fingerprints."

Edward stared. "Mine? Whatever for?"

"A friend of Maribel Chester's has come forward with information that the dead woman phoned her the morning she was strangled. She told this friend that she'd learned she was right about her husband having an affair with another woman. She said she was going to make Philip Chester sorry he'd ever been born."

Cecile clung now to Edward's hand. "You didn't go to her, did you, Edward?"

"No, of course not."

"As a matter of routine, Mr. Welland, we must check your prints against a couple of those still unidentified in the Chester house. And I trust you can account for your whereabouts the day she was murdered?"

"I can give you a list of all my accounts."

Cecile was by now in such a state of mental distraction that the entire web of circumstances acquired a comic dreadful unreality. "Lieutenant Gregg, you can't for a minute suspect *Edward.* What possible motive could he have for killing Maribel Chester? It's preposterous."

"I didn't say he was a suspect, Mrs. Welland. But as for that, it's not inconceivable that your husband might have gone to the Chester house, that Mrs. Chester might have threatened to expose you as her husband's lover, and that to prevent it . . . as I say, every possibility must be explored."

When they were alone, Cecile could no longer hold back the sobs she had fought to suppress while the detective was present. "Oh, Edward, what a dreadful mess I've got you into, all because of a silly, crazy whim. How can you ever forgive me? You should be furious. Any other man would despise me for what I've done."

"How could I despise you, Cecie? I love you. I've told you again and again that I understand the sort of loneliness that drove you to get mixed up with this man."

"But you *don't* understand. You refuse to believe the truth. If only you could believe that the diary was no more than a record of nonsensical daydreams."

On Thursday, Lieutenant Gregg paid them another call. His features were locked in an expression of official gravity.

"I'm sorry," he said. "But I have a warrant here for your arrest, Mr. Welland."

"No!" It burst like a scream from Cecile's lips. "No, that's impossible! There's been some horrible mistake. Edward could never kill anyone. Oh, if only you knew him as I do, Lieutenant. I've ruined his life, all because I wrote those insane lies in that diary. I was *lonely.* You've no idea what loneliness can do to a person."

Cecile turned to Edward and grasped his hand in both of hers. "Oh, Edward, Edward, I was so selfish. If only I'd thought of *your* loneliness. At least I was here in our own home. I wasn't forced to spend days and days with virtual strangers, sleeping and eating in dreary motels. And you never complained. Not once in all those years. Oh, tell him, Edward. Tell him you didn't harm that woman."

Edward's face was drained of color. "I didn't, Cecie. Of course I didn't. I swear it."

"Didn't you check his alibi, Lieutenant? Didn't you talk to all those people on the road?"

"We did."

"Then how can you charge him with murder?"

The detective's face lost a bit of its official impassivity. "I didn't say we were charging him with murder, Mrs. Welland. We finally broke down Chester's story. He *had* been having an affair with another woman. We've already questioned her. Chester's confessed to strangling his wife."

A cry of joy broke from Cecile's lips. "But in that case, why—"

"We checked out your husband's alibi more thoroughly than he may have expected." Gregg reached into his pocket and handed Cecile a photograph. "I'm sorry. I suppose we all have our ways of coping with loneliness."

Cecile stared at the picture, but Edward's was the only face that meant anything to her. She felt his arm gently encircle her waist. When he spoke, his voice expressed an anguished sorrow of regret at having to hurt her.

"Boy looks like me, doesn't he, Cecie? A fine lad. And you'd like Irene. She's a lot like you. Both so understanding."

Cecile raised her eyes imploringly to the detective's face. Gregg cleared his throat.

"The charge against your husband is not murder, Mrs. Welland. It's bigamy."

THE FEVER TREE

by RUTH RENDELL

Where malaria is, there grows the fever tree.

It has the feathery fern-like leaves, fresh green and tender, that are common to so many trees in tropical regions. Its shape is graceful with an air of youth, of immaturity, as if every fever tree is still waiting to grow up. But the most distinctive thing about it is the color of its bark, which is the yellow of an unripe lemon. The fever trees stand out from among the rest because of their slender yellow trunks.

Ford knew what the tree was called and he could recognize it but he didn't know what its botanical name was. Nor had he ever heard why it was called the fever tree, whether the tribesmen used its leaves or bark or fruits as a specific against malaria or if it simply took its name from its warning presence wherever the malaria-carrying mosquito was. The sight of it in Ntsukunyane seemed to promote a fever in his blood.

An African in khaki shorts and shirt lifted up the bar for them so that their car could pass through the opening in the wire fence. Inside it looked no different from outside, the same bush, still, silent, unstirred by wind, stretching away on either side. Ford, driving the two miles along the tarmac road to the reception hut, thought of how it would be if he turned his head and saw Marguerite in the passenger seat beside him. It was an illusion he dared not have and was allowed to keep for perhaps a minute. Tricia shattered it. She began to belabor him with schoolgirl questions, uttered in a bright and desperate voice.

Another African, in a fancier, more decorated uniform, took their booking voucher and checked it against a ledger. You had to pay weeks in advance for the privilege of staying here. Ford had booked the day after he had said goodbye to Marguerite and returned, forever, to Tricia.

"My wife wants to know the area of Ntsukunyane," he said.

"Four million acres."

Ford gave the appropriate whistle. "Do we have a chance of seeing leopard?"

The man shrugged, smiled. "Who knows? You may be lucky. You're here a whole week, so you should see lion, elephant, hippo, cheetah maybe. But the leopard is nocturnal and you must be back in camp by six p.m." He looked at his watch. "I advise you to get on now, sir, if you're to make Thaba before they close the gates."

Ford got back into the car. It was nearly four. The sun of Africa, a living presence, a personal god, burned through a net of haze. There was no wind. Tricia, in a pale yellow sun dress with frills, had hung her arm outside the open window and the fair downy skin was glowing red. He told her what the man had said and he told her about the notice pinned inside the hut: It is strictly forbidden to bring firearms into the game reserve, to feed the animals, to exceed the speed limit, to litter.

"And most of all you mustn't get out of the car," said Ford.

"What, not ever?" said Tricia, making her pale blue eyes round and naive and marble-like.

"That's what it says."

She pulled a face. "Silly old rules!"

"They have to have them," he said.

In here as in the outside world. It is strictly forbidden to fall in love, to leave your wife, to try and begin anew. He glanced at Tricia to see if the same thoughts were passing through her mind. Her face wore its arch expression, winsome.

"A prize," she said, "for the first one to see an animal."

"All right." He had agreed to this reconciliation, to bring her on this holiday, this second honeymoon, and now he must try. He must work at it. It wasn't just going to happen as love had sprung between him and Marguerite, unsought and untried for. "Who's going to award it?" he said.

"You are if it's me and I am if it's you. And if it's me I'd like a presy from the camp shop. A very nice pricey presy."

Ford was the winner. He saw a single zebra come out from among the thorn trees on the right-hand side, then a small herd.

"Do I get a present from the shop?" he asked.

He could sense rather than see her shake her head with calculated coyness. "A kiss," she said and pressed warm dry lips against his cheek.

It made him shiver a little. He slowed down for the zebra to cross the road. The thorn bushes had spines on them two inches long. By the roadside grew a species of wild zinnia with tiny flowers, coral red, and these made red drifts among the coarse pale grass. In the bush were red anthills with tall peaks like towers on a castle in a fairy story. It was thirty miles to Thaba.

He drove on just within the speed limit, ignoring Tricia as far as he could whenever she asked him to slow down. They weren't going to see one of the big predators, anyway, not this afternoon, he was certain of that, only impala and zebra and maybe a giraffe. On business trips in the past he'd taken time off to go to Serengeti and Kruger and he knew.

He got the binoculars out for Tricia and adjusted them and hooked them round her neck, for he hadn't forgotten the binoculars and cameras she had dropped and smashed in the past through failing to do that, and her tears afterward. The car wasn't air-conditioned and the heat lay heavy and still between them. Ahead of them, as they drove westward, the sun was sinking in a dull yellow glare. The sweat flowed out of Ford's armpits and between his shoulder blades, soaking his already wet shirt and laying a cold sticky film on his skin.

A stone pyramid with arrows on it, set in the middle of a junction of roads, pointed the way to Thaba, to the main camp at Waka-suthu and to Hippo Bridge over the Suthu River. On top of it a baboon sat with her gray fluffy infant on her knees. Tricia yearned to it, stretching out her arms. She had never had a child. The baboon began picking fleas out of its baby's scalp. Tricia gave a little nervous scream, half disgusted, half joyful. Ford drove down the road to Thaba and in through the entrance to the camp ten minutes before they closed the gates for the night.

The dark comes down fast in Africa. Dusk is of short duration and no sooner have you noticed it than it is gone and night has fallen. In the few moments of dusk pale things glimmer brightly and birds murmur. In the camp at Thaba were a restaurant and a shop, round huts with thatched roofs, and wooden chalets with porches. Ford and Tricia had been assigned a chalet on the northern perimeter, and from their porch, across an expanse of turf and beyond the high wire fence, you could see the Suthu River flowing smoothly and silently between banks of tall reeds.

Dusk had just come as they walked up the wooden steps, Ford carrying their cases. It was then that he saw the fever trees, two of them, their ferny leaves bleached to gray by the twilight but their trunks a sharper, stronger yellow than in the day.

"Just as well we took our anti-malaria pills," said Ford as he pushed open the door. When the light was switched on he could see two mosquitos on the opposite wall. "*Anopheles* is the malaria carrier, but unfortunately they don't announce whether they're *anopheles* or not."

Twin beds, a table, lamps, an air conditioner, a fridge, a door, standing open, to lavatory and shower. Tricia dropped her makeup case, without which she went nowhere, onto the bed by the window. The light wasn't very bright. None of the lights in the camp were because the electricity came from a generator. They were a small colony of humans in a world that belonged to the animals, a reversal of the usual order of things. From the window you could see other chalets, other dim lights, other parked cars. Tricia talked to the two mosquitos.

"Is your name Anna Phyllis? No, darling, you're quite safe. She says she's Mary Jane and her husband's John Henry."

Ford managed to smile. He had accepted and grown used to Tricia's facetiousness until he had encountered Marguerite's wit. He shoved his case, without unpacking it, into the cupboard and went to have a shower.

Tricia stood on the porch, listening to the cicadas, thousands of them. It had gone pitch-dark while she was hanging up her dresses and the sky was punctured all over with bright stars.

She had got Ford back from that woman and now she had to keep him. She had lost some weight and bought a lot of new clothes and had highlights put in her hair. Men had always made her feel frightened, starting with her father when she was a child. It was then, when a child, that she had purposely begun *playing* the child with its cajolements and its winning little ways. She had noticed that her father was kinder and more forbearing toward little girls than toward her mother. Ford had married a little girl, clinging and winsome, and had liked it well enough till he met a grown woman.

Tricia knew all that, but now she knew no better how to keep him than by the old methods, as weary and stale to her as she guessed they might be to him. Standing there on the porch, she half wished she were alone and didn't have to have a husband, didn't, for the sake of convention and pride, for support and society, have to hold on tight to him. She listened wistfully for a lion to roar out there in the bush beyond the fence, but there was no sound except the cicadas.

Ford came out in a toweling robe.

"What did you do with the mosquito stuff? The spray?"

Frightened at once, she said, "I don't know."

"What d'you mean, you don't know? You must know. I gave you the aerosol at the hotel and said to put it in that makeup case of yours."

She opened the case although she knew the mosquito stuff

wasn't there. Of course it wasn't there. She could see it on the bathroom shelf in the hotel, left behind because it was too bulky. She bit her lip, looked sideways at Ford.

"We can get some more at the shop."

"Tricia, the shop closes at seven and it's now ten past."

"We can get some in the morning."

"Mosquitos happen to be most active at night." He rummaged with his hands among the bottles and jars in the case. "Look at all this useless rubbish. 'Skin cleanser,' 'pearlized foundation,' 'moisturizer'—like some young model girl. I suppose it didn't occur to you to bring the anti-mosquito spray and leave the 'pearlized foundation' behind."

Her lip trembled. She could feel herself, almost involuntarily, rounding her eyes, forming her mouth into the shape of lisping. "We did 'member to take our pills."

"That won't stop the damn things biting." He went back into the shower and slammed the door.

Marguerite wouldn't have forgotten to bring that aerosol. Tricia knew he was thinking of Marguerite again, that his head was full of her, that she had entered his thoughts powerfully and insistently on the long drive to Thaba. She began to cry. The tears went on running out of her eyes and wouldn't stop, so she changed her dress while she cried and the tears came through the powder she put on her face.

They had dinner in the restaurant. Tricia, in pink flowered crepe, was the only dressed-up woman there, and while once she would have fancied that the other diners looked at her in admiration, now she thought it must be with derision. She ate her small piece of overcooked hake and her large piece of overcooked, bread-crumbed veal, and watched the red weals from mosquito bites coming up on Ford's arms.

There were no lights on in the camp but those which shone from the windows of the main building and from the chalets. Gradually the lights went out and it became very dark. In spite of his mosquito bites, Ford fell asleep at once but the noise of the air conditioning kept Tricia awake. At eleven she switched it off and opened the window. Then she did sleep but she awoke again at four, lay awake for half an hour, got up, put on her clothes, and went out.

It was still dark but the darkness was lifting as if the thickest veil of it had been withdrawn. A heavy dew lay on the grass. As she passed under the merula tree, laden with small green apricot-shaped fruits, a flock of bats flew out from its branches and circled her head. If Ford had been with her she would have screamed and clung to him but because she was alone she kept silent. The camp and the bush beyond the fence were full of sound. The sounds brought to Tricia's mind the paintings of Hieronymus Bosch, imps and demons and dreadful homunculi which, if they had uttered, might have made noises like these, gruntings and soft whistles and chirps and little thin squeals.

She walked about, waiting for the dawn, expecting it to come with drama. But it was only a gray pallor in the sky, a paleness between parting black clouds, and the feeling of let-down frightened her as if it were a symbol or an omen of something more significant in her life than the coming of morning.

Ford woke up, unable at first to open his eyes for the swelling from mosquito bites. There were mosquitos like threads of thistledown on the walls, all over the walls. He got up and staggered, half blind, out of the bedroom and let the water from the shower run on his eyes. Tricia came and stared at his face, giggling nervously and biting her lip.

The camp gates opened at five thirty and the cars began their exodus. Tricia had never passed a driving test and Ford couldn't see, so they went to the restaurant for breakfast instead. When the shop opened, Ford bought two kinds of mosquito repellent, and impatiently, because he could no longer bear her apologies and her pleading eyes, a necklace of ivory beads for Tricia and a skirt with giraffes printed on it. At nine o'clock, when the swelling round Ford's eyes had subsided a little, they set off in the car, taking the road for Hippo Bridge.

The day was humid and thickly hot. Ford had counted the number of mosquito bites he had had and the total was twenty-four. It was hard to believe that two little tablets of quinine would be proof against twenty-four bites, some of which must certainly have been inflicted by *anopheles.* Hadn't he seen the two fever trees when they arrived last night? Now he drove the car slowly and doggedly, hardly speaking, his swollen eyes concealed behind sunglasses.

By the Suthu River and then by a water hole he stopped and they watched. But they saw nothing come to the water's edge unless you counted the log which at last disappeared, thus proving itself to have been a crocodile. It was too late in the morning to see much apart from the marabout storks which stood one-legged, still and hunched, in a clearing or on the gaunt branch of a tree. Through binoculars Ford stared at the bush which stretched in unbroken, apparently untenanted, sameness to the blue ridge of mountains on the far horizon.

There could be no real fever from the mosquito bites. If malaria were to come it wouldn't be yet. But Ford, sitting in the car beside Tricia, nevertheless felt something like a delirium of fever. It came perhaps from the gross irritation of the whole surface of his body, from the tender burning of his skin and from his inability to move without setting up fresh torment. It affected his mind too, so that each time he looked at Tricia a kind of panic rose in him. Why had he done it? Why had he gone back to her? Was he mad? His eyes and his head throbbed as if his temperature were raised.

Tricia's pink jeans were too tight for her and the frills on her white voile blouse ridiculous. With the aid of the binoculars she had found a family of small gray monkeys in the branches of a peepul tree and she was cooing at them out of the window. Presently she opened the car door, held it just open, and turned to look at him the way a child looks at her father when he has forbidden something she nevertheless longs and means to do.

They hadn't had sight of a big cat or an elephant, they hadn't even seen a jackal. Ford lifted his shoulders.

"Okay. But if a ranger comes along and catches you we'll be in deep trouble."

She got out of the car, leaving the door open. The grass which began at the roadside and covered the bush as far as the eye could see was long and coarse. It came up above Tricia's knees. A lioness or a cheetah lying in it would have been entirely concealed. Ford picked up the binoculars and looked the other way to avoid watching Tricia who had once again forgotten to put the camera strap round her neck. She was making overtures to the monkeys who shrank away from her, embracing each other and burying heads in shoulders, like menaced refugees in a sentimental painting.

Ford moved the glasses slowly. About a hundred yards from where a small herd of buck grazed uneasily, he saw the two cat faces close together, the bodies nestled together, the spotted backs. Cheetah. It came into his mind how he had heard that they were the fastest animals on earth.

He ought to call to Tricia and get her back at once into the car. He didn't call. Through the glasses he watched the big cats that reclined there so gracefully, satiated, at rest, yet with open eyes. Marguerite would have liked them; she loved cats, she had a Burmese, as lithe and slim and poised as one of these wild creatures.

Tricia got back into the car, exclaiming about how sweet the monkeys were. He started the car and drove off without saying anything to her about the cheetahs.

Later, at about five in the afternoon, she wanted to get out of the car again and he didn't stop her. She walked up and down the road, talking to mongooses. In something over an hour it would be dark. Ford imagined starting up the car and driving back to the camp without her. Leopards were nocturnal hunters, waiting till dark.

The swelling around his eyes had almost subsided now but his neck and arms and hands ached from the stiffness of the bites. The mongooses fled into the grass as Tricia approached, whispering to them, hands outstretched. A car with four men in it was coming along from the Hippo Bridge direction. It slowed down and the driver put his head out. His face was brick-red, thick-featured, his hair corrugated blond, and his voice had the squashed vowel accent of the white man born in Africa.

"The lady shouldn't be out on the road like that."

"I know," Ford said. "I've told her."

"Excuse me, d'you know you're doing a very dangerous thing, leaving your car?"

The voice had a hectoring boom. Tricia blushed. She bridled, smiled, bit her lip, though she was in fact very afraid of this man who was looking at her as if he despised her, as if she disgusted him. When he got back to camp, would he betray her?

"Promise you won't tell on me?" she faltered, her head on one side.

The man gave an exclamation of anger and withdrew his head. The car moved forward. Tricia gave a skip and a jump into the passenger seat beside Ford. They had under an hour to get back to Thaba and Ford followed the car with the four men in it.

At dinner they sat at adjoining tables. Tricia wondered how many people they had told, for she fancied that some of the diners looked at her with curiosity or antagonism. The man with fair curly hair they called Eric boasted loudly of what he and his companions had seen that day, a whole pride of lions, two rhinoceros, hyena, and the rare sable antelope.

"You can't expect to see much down that Hippo Bridge road, you know," he said to Ford. "All the game's up at Sotingwe. You take the Sotingwe road first thing tomorrow and I'll guarantee you lions."

He didn't address Tricia, he didn't even look at her. Ten years before men in restaurants had turned their heads to look at her and though she had feared them, she had basked, trembling, in their gaze. Walking across the grass, back to their chalet, she held on to Ford's arm.

"For God's sake, mind my mosquito bites," said Ford.

He lay awake a long while in the single bed a foot away from Tricia's, thinking about the leopard out there beyond the fence that hunted by night. The leopard would move along the branch of a tree and drop upon its prey. Lionesses hunted in the early morning and brought the kill to their mate and the cubs. Ford had seen all that sort of thing on television. How cheetahs hunted he didn't know except that they were very swift. An angry elephant would lean on a car and crush it or smash a windshield with a blow from its foot.

It was too dark for him to see Tricia but he knew she was awake, lying still, sometimes holding her breath. He heard her breath released in an exhalation, a sigh, that was audible above the rattle of the air conditioner.

Years ago he had tried to teach her to drive. They said a husband should never try to teach his wife, he would have no patience with her and make no allowances. Tricia's progress had never been maintained, she had always been liable to do silly reckless things and then he had shouted at her. She took a driving test and failed and she said this was because the examiner had bullied her. Tricia seemed to think no one should ever raise his voice to her, and at one glance from her all men should fall slaves at her feet.

He would have liked her to be able to take a turn at driving. There was no doubt you missed a lot when you had to concentrate on the road. But it was no use suggesting it. Theirs was one of the first cars in the line to leave the gates at five thirty, to slip out beyond the fence into the gray dawn, the still bush. At the stone pyramid, on which a family of baboons sat clustered, Ford took the road for Sotingwe.

A couple of miles up they came upon the lions. Eric and his friends were already there, leaning out of the car windows with cameras. The lions, two full-grown lionesses, two lioness cubs and a lion cub with his mane beginning to sprout, were lying on the roadway. Ford stopped and parked the car on the opposite side to Eric.

"Didn't I say you'd be lucky up here?" Eric called to Tricia. "Not got any ideas about getting out and investigating, I hope."

Tricia didn't answer him or look at him. She looked at the lions. The sun was coming up, radiating the sky with a pinkish-orange glow, and a little breeze fluttered all the pale green, fern-like leaves. The larger of the adult lionesses, bored rather than alarmed by Eric's elaborate photographic equipment, got up slowly and strolled into the bush, in among the long dry grass and the red zinnias. The cubs followed her, the other lioness followed her. Through his binoculars Ford watched them stalk with proud lifted heads, walking, even the little ones, in a graceful, measured, controlled way. There were no impala anywhere, no giraffe, no wildebeest. The world here belonged to the lions.

All the game was gathered at Sotingwe, near the water hole. An elephant with ears like punkahs was powdering himself with red earth blown out through his trunk. Tricia got out of the car to photograph the elephant and Ford didn't try to stop her. He scratched his mosquito bites which had passed the burning and entered the itchy stage.

Once more Tricia had neglected to pass the camera strap around her neck. She made her way down to the water's edge and stood at a safe distance—was it a safe distance? Was any distance safe in here?—looking at a crocodile. Ford thought, without really explaining to himself or even fully understanding what he meant, that it was the wrong time of day, it was too early. They went back to Thaba for breakfast.

At breakfast and again at lunch Eric was full of what he had seen. He had taken the dirt road that ran down from Sotingwe to Suthu Bridge and there, up in a tree near the water, had been a leopard. Malcolm had spotted it first, stretched out asleep on a branch, a long way off but quite easy to see through field glasses.

"Massive great fella with your authentic square-type spots," said Eric, smoking a cigar.

Tricia, of course, wanted to go to Suthu Bridge, so Ford took the dirt road after they had had their siesta. Malcolm described exactly where he had seen the leopard which might, for all he knew, still be sleeping on its branch.

"About half a mile up from the bridge. You look over on your left and there's a sort of clearing with one of those trees with yellow trunks in it. This chap was on a branch on the right side of the clearing."

The dirt road was a track of crimson earth between green verges. Ford found the clearing with the single fever tree but the leopard had gone. He drove slowly down to the bridge that spanned the sluggish green river. When he switched off the engine it was silent and utterly still, the air hot and close, nothing moving but the mosquitos that danced in their haphazard yet regular measure above the surface of the water.

Tricia was getting out of the car as a matter of course now. This time she didn't even trouble to give him the coy glance that asked permission. She was wearing a red and white striped sundress with straps that were too narrow and a skirt that was too tight. She ran down to the water's edge, took off a sandal, and dipped in a daring foot. She laughed and twirled her foot, dabbling the dry round stones with water drops. Ford thought how he had loved this sort of thing when he had first met her, and now he was going to have to bear it for the rest of his life. He broke into a sweat as if his temperature had suddenly risen.

She was prancing about on the stones and in the water, holding up her skirt. There were no animals to be seen. All afternoon they had seen nothing but impala, and the sun was moving down now, beginning to color the hazy pastel sky. Tricia, on the opposite bank, broke another Ntsukunyane rule and picked daisies, tucking one behind each ear. With a flower between her teeth like a Spanish dancer, she swayed her hips and smiled.

Ford turned the ignition key and started the car. It would be dark in just over an hour and long before that they would have closed the gates at Thaba. He moved the car forward, reversed, making what Tricia, no doubt, would call a three-point turn. Facing toward Thaba now, he put the shift into drive, his foot on the accelerator, and took a deep breath as the sweat trickled between his shoulder blades. The heat made mirages on the road and out of them a car was coming. Ford stopped and switched off the engine. It wasn't Eric's car but one belonging to a couple of young Americans on holiday. The boy raised his hand in a salute at Ford.

Ford called out to Tricia, "Come on or we'll be late."

She got into the car, dropping her flowers onto the roadway. Ford had been going to leave her there, that was how much he wanted to be rid of her. Her body began to shake and she clasped her hands tightly together so that he shouldn't see. He had been going to drive away and leave her there to the darkness and the lions, the leopard that hunted by night. He had been driving away, only the Americans' car had come along.

She was silent, thinking about it. The American turned back soon after they did and followed them up the dirt road. Impala stood around the solitary fever tree, listening perhaps to inaudible sounds or scenting invisible danger. The sky was smoky yellow with sunset. Tricia thought about what Ford must have intended to do—drive back to camp just before they closed the gates, watch the darkness come down, knowing she was out there, say not a word of her absence to anyone—and who would miss her? Eric? Malcolm? Ford wouldn't have gone to the restaurant and in the morning when they opened the gates he would have driven away. No need even to check out at Ntsukunyane where you paid weeks in advance.

The perfect murder. Who would search for her, not knowing there was need for search? And if her bones were found? One set of bones, human, impala, waterbuck, looks very much like another when the jackals have been at it and the vultures. And when he reached home he would have said he had left her for Marguerite . . .

He was nicer to her that evening, gentler. Because he was afraid she had guessed or might guess the truth of what had happened at Sotingwe?

"We said we'd have champagne one night. How about now? No time like the present."

"If you like," Tricia said.

She felt sick all the time, she had no appetite. Ford toasted them in champagne.

"To us!"

He ordered the whole gamut of the menu, soup, fish, wiener schnitzel, creme brulee. She picked at her food, thinking how he had meant to kill her. She would never be safe now, for having failed once he would try again. Not the same method perhaps but some other. How was she to know he hadn't already tried? Perhaps, for instance, he had substituted aspirin for those quinine tablets, or when they were back at the hotel in Mombasa he might try to drown her. She would never be safe unless she left him.

Which was what he wanted, which would be the next best thing to her death. Lying awake in the night, she thought of what leaving him would mean—going back to live with her mother while he went to Marguerite. He wasn't asleep either. She could hear the sound of his irregular wakeful breathing. She heard the bed creak as he moved in it restlessly, the air conditioner grinding, the whine of a mosquito.

Now, if she hadn't already been killed, she might be wandering out there in the bush, in terror in the dark, afraid to take a step but afraid to remain still, fearful of every sound yet not knowing which sound most to fear. There was no moon. She had taken note of that before she came to bed and had seen in her diary that tomorrow the moon would be new. The sky had been overcast at nightfall and now it was pitch-dark. The leopard could see, perhaps by the light of the stars or with an inner instinctive eye more sure than simple vision, and would drop silently from its branch to sink its teeth into the lifted throat.

The mosquito that had whined stung Ford in several places on his face and neck and on his left foot. He had forgotten to use the repellent the night before. Early in the morning, at dawn, he got up and dressed and went for a walk round the camp. There was no one about but one of the African staff, hosing down a guest's car. Squeaks and shufflings came from the bush beyond the fence.

Had he really meant to rid himself of Tricia by throwing her, as one might say, to the lions? For a mad moment, he supposed, because fever had got into his blood, poison into his veins. She knew, he could tell that. In a way it might be all to the good, her knowing; it would show her how hopeless the marriage was that she was trying to preserve.

The swellings on his foot, though covered by his sock, were making the instep bulge through the sandal. His foot felt stiff and burning and he became aware that he was limping slightly. Supporting himself against the trunk of a fever tree, his skin against its cool, dampish, yellow bark, he took off his sandal and felt his swollen foot tenderly with his fingertips. Mosquitos never touched Tricia; they seemed to shirk contact with her pale dry flesh.

She was up when he hobbled in; she was sitting on her bed, painting her fingernails. How could he live with a woman who painted her fingernails in a game reserve?

They didn't go out till nine. On the road to Waka-suthu, Eric's car met them, coming back.

"There's nothing down there for miles, you're wasting your time."

"Okay," said Ford. "Thanks."

"Sotingwe's the place. Did you see the leopard yesterday?"

Ford shook his head.

"Oh, well, we can't all be lucky."

Elephants were playing in the river at Hippo Bridge, spraying each other with water and nudging heavy shoulders. Ford thought that was going to be the high spot of the morning until they came upon the kill. They didn't actually see it. The kill had taken place some hours before, but the lioness and her cubs were still picking at the carcase, at a blood-blackened rib cage.

They sat in the car and watched. After a while the lions left the carcase and walked away in file through the grass, but the little jackals were already gathered, a pack of them, posted behind trees. Ford came back that way again at four and by then the vultures had moved in, picking the bones.

It was a hot day of merciless sunshine, the sky blue and perfectly clear. Ford's foot was swollen to twice its normal size. He noticed that Tricia hadn't once left the car that day, nor had she spoken girlishly to him or giggled or given him a roguish kiss. She thought he had been trying to kill her, a preposterous notion really. The truth was he had only been giving her a fright, teaching her how stupid it was to flout the rules and leave the car.

Why should he kill her, anyway? He could leave her, he *would* leave her, and once they were back in Mombasa he would tell her so. The thought of it made him turn to her and smile. He had stopped by the clearing where the fever tree stood, yellow of bark, delicate and fern-like of leaf, in the sunshine like a young sapling in springtime.

"Why don't you get out any more?"

She faltered, "There's nothing to see."

"No?"

He had spotted the porcupine with his naked eye but he handed her the binoculars. She looked and she laughed with pleasure. That was the way she used to laugh when she was young, not from amusement but delight. He shut his eyes.

"Oh, the sweetie porky-pine!"

She reached on to the back seat for the camera. And then she hesitated. He could see the fear, the caution, in her eyes. Silently he took the key out of the ignition and held it out to her on the palm of his hand. She flushed. He stared at her, enjoying her discomfiture, indignant that she should suspect him of such baseness.

She hesitated but she took the key. She picked up the camera and opened the car door, holding the key on its fob in her left hand and the camera in her right. He noticed she hadn't passed the strap of the camera, his treasured Pentax, round her neck. For the thousandth time he could have told her but he lacked the heart to speak. His swollen foot throbbed and he thought of the long days at Ntsukunyane that remained to them. Marguerite seemed infinitely far away, farther even than at the other side of the world where she was.

He knew Tricia was going to drop the camera some fifteen seconds before she did so. It was because she had the key in her other hand. If the strap had been round her neck it wouldn't have mattered. He knew how it was when you held something in each hand and lost your grip or your footing. You had no sense then, in that instant, of which of the objects was valuable and mattered and which was not. Tricia held on to the key and dropped the camera. The better to photograph the porcupine, she had mounted on to the twisted roots of a tree, roots that looked as hard as a flight of stone steps.

She gave a little cry. At the sounds of the crash and the cry the porcupine erected its quills. Ford jumped out of the car, wincing when he put his foot to the ground, hobbling through the grass to Tricia who stood as if petrified with fear of him. The camera, the pieces of camera, had fallen among the gnarled, stone-like tree roots. He dropped onto his knees, shouting at her, cursing her.

Tricia began to run. She ran back to the car and pushed the key into the ignition. The car was pointing in the direction of Thaba and the clock on the dashboard shelf said five thirty-five. Ford came limping back, waving his arms at her, his hands full of broken pieces of camera. She looked away and put her foot down hard on the accelerator.

The sky was clear orange with sunset, black bars of the coming night lying on the horizon. She found she could drive when she had to, even though she couldn't pass a test. A mile along the road she met the American couple. The boy put his head out.

"Anything worth going down there for?"

"Not a thing," said Tricia. "You'd be wasting your time."

The boy turned his car round and followed her back. It was two minutes to six when they entered Thaba, the last cars to do so, and the gates were closed behind them.

THE FLAW

by JULIAN SYMONS

"Drink your coffee."

Celia sat feet up on the sofa, reading a fashion magazine, the coffee cup on the table beside her. "What's that?"

"I said drink your coffee. You know you like it to be piping hot."

She contemplated the coffee, stirred it with a spoon, then put the spoon back in the saucer. "I'm not sure it's hot enough now."

"I poured it only a couple of minutes ago."

"Yes, but still. I don't know that I feel like coffee tonight. But I do want a brandy." She swung her legs off the sofa and went across to the drinks tray. "A celebratory brandy. Can I pour one for you?"

"What are we celebrating?"

"Me, Giles, not you. I'm celebrating. But you want me to drink my coffee, don't you? All right." She went swiftly back, lifted the coffee cup, drank the contents in two gulps, and made a face. "Not very hot. Now may I have my brandy?"

"Of course. Let me pour it for you."

"Oh, no, I'll do it myself. After all, you poured the coffee." She smiled sweetly.

"What do you mean?"

"Just that we've both had coffee. And you poured it. But I gave it to you on the tray, remember?"

Sir Giles got up, put a hand to his throat. "What are you trying to say?"

"Only that if I turned the tray around you'll have got my cup and I shall have got yours. But it wouldn't matter. Or would it?"

He made for the door and turned the handle, but it did not open. "It's locked. What have you done with the key?"

"I can't imagine." As he lumbered towards her, swaying a little, she easily evaded him. "You think I'm a fool, Giles, don't you? I'm not, that's your mistake. So this is a celebration."

"Celia." His hand was at his throat again. He choked, collapsed onto the carpet, and lay still.

Celia looked at him thoughtfully, finished her brandy, prodded him with her foot, and said, "Now, what to do about the body?"

The curtain came down. The first act of *Villain* was over.

"I enjoyed it enormously," Duncan George said. "Is it all right if I smoke?"

"Of course." Oliver Glass was busy at the dressing-table, removing the makeup that had turned him into Sir Giles. In the glass he saw Dunc packing his pipe and lighting it. Good old Dunc, he thought, reliable dull old Dunc, his reactions are always predictable. "Pour yourself a drink."

"Not coffee, I hope." Oliver's laugh was perfunctory. "I thought the play was really clever. All those twists and turns in the plot. And you enjoy being the chief actor as well as the writer, don't you, it gives you an extra kick?"

"My dear fellow, you're a psychologist as well as a crime writer yourself, you should know. But, after all, who can interpret one's own writing better than oneself? The play—well, between these four walls it's a collection of tricks. The supreme trick is to make the audience accept it, to deceive them not once or twice but half a dozen times, to make them leave the theatre gasping at the cleverness of it all. And if that's to be done, Sir Giles has to be played on just the right note, so that we're never quite certain whether he's fooling everybody else or being fooled himself, never quite sure whether he's the villain or the hero. And who knows that better than the author? So if he happens to be an actor too, he must be perfect for the part."

"Excellent special pleading. I'll tell you one thing, though. When the curtain comes down at the end of the first act, nobody really believes you're dead. Oliver Glass is the star, and if you're dead they've been cheated. So they're just waiting for you to come out of that cupboard."

"But think of the tension that's building while they wait. Ready, Dunc."

He clapped the other on the shoulder, and they walked out into the London night. Oliver Glass was a slim, elegant man in his fifties, successful both as actor and dramatist, so successful that he could afford to laugh at the critic who said that he had perfected the art of overacting, and the other critic who remarked that after seeing an Oliver Glass play he was always reminded of the line that said life was mostly froth and bubble. Whether Oliver did laugh was another matter, for he disliked any adverse view of his abilities. He had a flat in the heart of the West End, a small house in Sussex, and a beautiful wife named Elizabeth who was fifteen years his junior.

Duncan George looked insignificant by his side. He was short and square, a practising psychiatrist who also wrote crime stories, and he had known Oliver for some years. He was typified for Oliver by the abbreviation of his first name, Dunc. He was exactly the kind of person Oliver could imagine dunking a doughnut into a cup of coffee or doing something equally vulgar. With all that, however, Duncan was a good fellow, and Oliver tolerated him as a companion.

They made their way through the West End to a street off Leicester Square where the Criminologists' Club met once a quarter to eat a late supper followed by a talk on a subject of criminal interest. The members were all writers about real or fictitious crime, and on this evening Oliver Glass was to speak to them on "The Romance of Crime," with Duncan George as his chairman. When he rose and looked around, with that gracious look in which there was just a touch of contempt, the buzz of conversation ceased.

"Gentlemen," he began, "criminologists—fellow crime writers—perhaps fellow criminals. I have come tonight to plead for romance in the world of crime, for the locked-room murder, the impossible theft, the crime committed by the invisible man. I have come to plead that you should bring wit and style and complexity to your writings about crime, that you should remember Stevenson's view that life is a bazaar of dangerous and smiling chances, and the remark of Thomas Griffiths Wainewright when he confessed to poisoning his pretty sister-in-law: 'It was a terrible thing to do, but she had thick ankles.' I beseech you not to forget those thick ankles as a motive, and to abandon the dreary books some of you write concerned with examining the psychology of two equally dull people to decide which destroyed the other, or looking at bits of intestines under a microscope to determine whether a tedious husband killed his boring wife. Your sights should be set instead on the Perfect Crime . . ."

Oliver Glass spoke, as always, without notes, fluently and with style, admiring the fluency and stylishness as the words issued from his mouth. Afterwards he was challenged by some members, Duncan George among them, about that conjectural Perfect Crime. Wasn't it out of date? Not at all, Oliver said, Sir Giles in *Villain* attempted it.

"Yes, but, as you remarked yourself, *Villain*'s a mass of clever tricks," Dunc said. "Sir Giles wants to kill Celia as a kind of trick, just to prove that he can get away with it. Or at least we think he does. Then you play all sorts of variations on the idea—is the poison really a sleeping draught? does she know about it?—that kind of thing. Splendid to watch, but nobody would actually try it. In every perfect murder, so called, there is actually a flaw." There was a chorus of agreement, by which Oliver found himself a little irritated.

"How do you know that? The Perfect Crime is one in which the criminal never puts himself within reach of the law. Perhaps, even, no crime is known to have taken place, although that is a little short of perfection. But how do we know, gentlemen, what variations on the Perfect Crime any of us may be planning, may even have carried out? 'The desires of the heart are as crooked as corkscrews,' as the poet says, and I'm sure Dunc can bear that out from his psychiatric experience."

"Any of us is capable of violence under certain circumstances, if that's what you mean. But to set out to commit a Perfect Crime without a motive is the mark of a psychopath."

"I didn't say without motive. A good motive for one man may be trivial to another."

"Tell us when you're going to commit the Perfect Crime, and we'll see if we can solve it," somebody said. There was a murmur of laughter.

Upon this note Oliver left, and strolled home to Everley Court, passing the drunks on the pavements, the blacks and yellows and all conditions of foreigners, who jostled each other or stood gaping outside the sex cinemas. He made a slight detour to pass by the theatre, and saw with a customary glow of pleasure the poster: *Oliver Glass in* Villain. *The Mystery Play by Oliver Glass.*

Was he really planning the Perfect Crime? There can be no doubt, he said to himself, that the idea is in your mind. And the elements are there—Elizabeth, and deliciously unpredictable Evelyn, and above all the indispensable Eustace. But is it more than a whim? Do I really dislike Elizabeth enough? The answer to that, of course, was that it was not a question of hatred but of playing a game, the game of Oliver Glass versus Society, even Oliver Glass versus the World.

And so home. And to Elizabeth.

A nod to Tyler, the night porter at the block of flats. Up in the lift to the third floor. Key in the door.

From the entrance hall the apartment stretched left and right. To the left Elizabeth's bedroom and bathroom. Almost directly in front of him the living room, further to the right dining room and kitchen, at the extreme right Oliver's bedroom and bathroom. He went into the living room, switched on the light. On the mantelpiece there was a note in

Elizabeth's scrawl: *O. Please come to see me if back before 2 A.M. E.*

For two years now they had communicated largely by means of such notes. It had begun—how had it begun?—because she was so infuriatingly talkative when he wanted to concentrate. "I am an artist," he had said. "The artist needs isolation if the fruits of genius are to ripen on the bough of inspiration." The time had been when Elizabeth listened open-eyed to such words, but those days had gone. For a long while now she had made comments suggesting that his qualities as actor and writer fell short of genius, or had pointed out that last night he had happily stayed late at a party. She did not understand the artistic temperament. Her nagging criticism had become, quite simply, a bore.

There was, he admitted as he turned the note in his fingers, something else. There were the girls needed by the artist as part of his inspiration, the human clay turned by him into something better. Elizabeth had never understood about them, and in particular had failed to understand when she had returned to find one of them with him on the living room carpet. She had spoken of divorce, but he knew the words to be idle. Elizabeth had extravagant tastes, and divorce would hardly allow her to indulge them. So the notes developed. They lived separate lives, with occasional evenings when she acted as hostess, or came in and chatted amiably enough to friends. For the most part the arrangement suited him rather well, although just at present his absorption with Evelyn was such . . .

He went in to see Elizabeth.

She was sitting on a small sofa, reading. Although he valued youth above all things, he conceded, as he looked appraisingly at her, that she was still attractive. Her figure was slim (no children, he could not have endured the messy, noisy things), legs elegant, dainty feet. She had kept her figure, as—he confirmed, looking at himself in the glass—he had kept his. How curious that he no longer found her desirable.

"Oliver." He turned. "Stop looking at yourself."

"Was I doing that?"

"You know you were. Stop acting."

"But I am an actor."

"Acting off stage, I mean. You don't know anybody exists outside yourself."

"There is a respectable philosophical theory maintaining that very proposition. I have invented you, you have invented me. A charming idea."

"A very silly idea. Oliver, why don't you divorce me?"

"Have you given me cause?"

"You know how easily it can be arranged."

He answered with a world-weary sigh. She exclaimed angrily and he gave her a look of pure dislike, so that she exclaimed again.

"You *do* dislike me, don't you? A touch of genuine feeling. So why not?" She went over to her dressing-table, sat down, took out a pot of cream.

He placed a hand on his heart. "I was—"

"I know. You were born a Catholic. But when did you last go to church?"

"Very well. Say simply that I don't care to divorce you. It would be too vulgar."

"You've got a new girl. I can always tell."

"Is there anything more tedious than feminine intuition?"

"Let me tell you something. This time I shall have you followed. And *I* shall divorce *you.* What do you think of that?"

"Very little." And indeed, who would pay her charge account at Harrods, provide the jewelry she loved? Above all, where would she get the money she gambled away at casinos and the races? She had made similar threats before, and he knew them to be empty ones.

"You want me as a kind of butterfly you've stuck with a pin, nothing more."

She was at work with the cream. She used one cream on her face, another on her neck, a third on her legs. Then she covered her face with a black mask, which was supposed to increase the effectiveness of the cream. She often kept this mask on all night.

There had been a time when he found it exciting to make

love to a woman whose face was not visible, but in her case that time had gone long ago. What was she saying now?

"Nothing gets through to you, does it? You have a sort of armour of conceit. But you have the right name, do you know that? Glass—if one could see through you there would be nothing, absolutely nothing there. Oliver Glass, *you don't exist.*"

Very well, he thought, very well, I am an invisible man. I accept the challenge. Elizabeth, you have signed your death warrant.

The idea, then, was settled. Plans had to be made. But they were still uncertain, moving around in what he knew to be his marvelously ingenious mind, when he went to visit Evelyn after lunch on the following day. Evelyn was in her early twenties, young enough—oh, yes, he acknowledged it—to be his daughter, young enough also to be pleased by the company of a famous actor. But beyond that, Evelyn fascinated him by her unpredictability. She was a photographer's model much in demand, and he did not doubt that she had other lovers. There were times when she said that she was too busy to see him, or simply that she wanted to be alone, and he accepted these refusals as part of the excitement of the chase. There was a perversity about Evelyn, an abandonment to the whim of the moment, that reached out to something in his own nature. He felt sometimes that there was no suggestion so outrageous that she would refuse to consider it. She had once opened the door of her flat naked and asked him to strip and accompany her down to the street.

Her flat was off Baker Street, and when he rang the bell there was no reply. At the third ring he felt annoyance. He had telephoned in advance, as always, and she had said she would be there. He pushed the door in a tentative way, and it swung open. In the hall he called her name. There was no reply.

The flat was not large. He went into the living room, which was untidy as usual, glanced into the small kitchen, then went into the bedroom with its unmade bed. What had happened to her, where was she? He entered the bathroom, and recoiled from what he saw.

Evelyn lay face down, half in and half out of the bath. One arm hung over the side of the bath, the other trailed in the water. Her head rested on the side of the bath as though her neck was broken.

He went across to her, touched the arm outside the bath. It was warm. He bent down to feel the pulse. As he did so the arm moved, the body turned, and Evelyn was laughing at him.

"You frightened me. You bitch." But he was excited, not angry.

"The author of *Villain* should be used to tricks." She got out, handed him a towel. "Dry me."

Their lovemaking afterwards had the frantic, paroxysmic quality that he had found in few women. It was as though he were bringing her back from the dead. A thought struck him. "Have you done that with anybody else?"

"Does it matter?"

"Perhaps not. I should still like to know."

"Nobody else."

"It was as though you were another person."

"Good. I'd like to be a different person every time."

He was following his own train of thought. "My wife puts on a black mask after creaming her face at night. That should be exciting, but it isn't."

Evelyn was insatiably curious about the details of sex, and he had told her a good deal about Elizabeth.

"I'm good for you," she said now. "You get a kick each time, don't you?"

"Yes. And you?"

She considered this. She had a similar figure to Elizabeth's but her features were very different, the nose snub instead of aquiline, the eyes blue and wide apart. "In a way. Being who you are gives me a kick."

"Is that all?"

"What do you mean?"

"Don't you like me?"

"It's wet to ask things like that. I never thought you were

wet." She looked at him directly with her large, slightly vacant blue eyes. "If you want to know, I get a kick out of you because you're acting all the time. It's the acting you like, not the act. And then I get a kick out of you being an old man."

He was so angry that he slapped her face. She said calmly, "Yes, I like that too."

By the time that night's performance was over his plan was made.

In the next two weeks Tyler, the night porter at Everley Court, was approached three times by a tall bulky man wearing horn-rimmed spectacles. The man asked for Mrs. Glass and seemed upset to learn on every occasion that she was out. Once he handed a note to Tyler and then took it back, saying it wouldn't do to leave a letter lying around. Twice he left messages to say that Charles had called and wanted to talk to Mrs. Glass. On his third visit the man smelled of drink and his manner was belligerent. "You tell her I must talk to her," he said in an accent that Tyler could not place, except that the man definitely came from somewhere up north.

"Yes, sir. And the name is—?"

"Charles. She'll know."

Tyler coughed. "Begging your pardon, sir, but wouldn't it be better to telephone?"

The man glared at him. "Do you think I haven't tried? You tell her to get in touch. If she doesn't I won't answer for the consequences."

"Charles?" Elizabeth said when Tyler rather hesitantly told her this. "I know two or three people named Charles, but this doesn't seem to fit any of them. What sort of age?"

"Perhaps about forty, Mrs. Glass. Smartly dressed. A gentleman. Comes from the north, maybe Scotland, if that's any help."

"No doubt it should be, but it isn't."

"He seemed—" Tyler hesitated. "Very concerned."

On the following day Oliver left a note for her. *E. Man*

rang while you were out, wouldn't leave message. O. She questioned him about the call.

"He wouldn't say what he wanted. Just rang off when I said you weren't here."

"It must be the same man." She explained about him. "Tyler said he had a northern accent, probably Scottish."

"What Scots do you know named Charles?"

"Charles Rothsey, but I haven't seen him for years. I wish he'd ring when I'm here."

A couple of evenings later the wish was granted, although she did not speak to the man. Oliver had asked her to give a little supper party after the show for three members of the cast, and because two of them were women Duncan was invited to even up the numbers. Elizabeth was serving the cold salmon when the telephone rang in the living room. Oliver went to answer it. He came back almost at once, looking thoughtful. When Elizabeth said it had been a quick call, he looked sharply at her. "It was your friend Charles. He rang off. Just announced himself, then rang off when he heard my voice."

"Who's Charles?" one of the women asked. "He sounds interesting."

"You'd better ask Elizabeth."

She told the story of the man who had called, and it caused general amusement. Only Oliver remained serious. When the guests were going he asked Duncan to stay behind.

"I just wanted your opinion, Dunc. This man has called three times and now he's telephoning. What sort of man would do this kind of thing, and what can we do about it?"

"What sort of man? Hard to say." Duncan took out his pipe, filled and lit it with maddening deliberation. "Could be a practical joker, harmless enough. Or it could be somebody—well, not so harmless. But I don't see that you can do much about it. Obscene and threatening phone calls are ten a penny, as the police will tell you. Of course, if he does show up again Elizabeth could see him, but I'd recommend having somebody else here."

This was, Oliver considered, adequate preparation of the ground. It had been established that Elizabeth was being pursued by a character named Charles. There was no doubt about Charles's existence. He obviously existed independently of Oliver Glass, since Tyler had seen him and Oliver himself had spoken to him on the telephone. If Elizabeth was killed, the mysterious Charles would be the first suspect.

Charles had been created as somebody separate from Oliver by that simplicity which is the essence of all fine art. Oliver, like Sir Giles in *Villain,* was a master of disguise. He had in particular the ability possessed by the great Vidocq, of varying his height by twelve inches or more. Charles had been devised from a variety of props, like cheek pads, body cushions, and false eyebrows, plus the indispensable platform heels. He would make one more appearance and then vanish from the scene. He would never have to meet anybody who knew Oliver well, something which he slightly regretted. And Charles on the telephone had been an actor whom Oliver had asked to ring during the evening. Oliver had merely said he couldn't talk now but would call him tomorrow and then put down the receiver.

In the next few days he noticed with amusement tinged with annoyance that Elizabeth had fulfilled her threat of putting a private inquiry agent on his track. He spotted the man hailing a taxi just after he had got one himself, and then getting out a few yards behind him when he stopped outside Evelyn's flat. Later he pointed out the man, standing in a doorway opposite to Evelyn. She giggled, and suggested that they should ask him up.

"I believe you would," he said admiringly. "Is there anything you wouldn't do?"

"If I felt like it, nothing." She was high on some drug or other. "What about you?"

"A lot of things."

"Careful old Oliver." What would she say if she knew what he was planning? He was tempted to say something, but resisted, although so far as he could tell nothing would shock her. She suddenly threw up the window, leaned out and gave a piercing whistle. When the man looked up, she beckoned. He turned his head and then began to walk away.

Oliver was angry, but what was the use of saying anything? It was her recklessness that fascinated him.

His annoyance was reflected in a note left for Elizabeth. *E. This kind of spying is degrading. O.* He found a reply that night when he came back from the theatre. *O. Your conduct is degrading. Your present fancy is public property. E.*

That Oliver Glass had charm was acknowledged even by those not susceptible to it. In the days after the call from Charles, he exerted this charm upon Elizabeth. She went out a good deal in the afternoons, where or with whom he really didn't care, and this gave him the chance to leave little notes. One of them ran: *E. You simply MUST be waiting here for me after the theatre. I have a small surprise for you. O.* And another: *E. Would supper at Wheeler's amuse you this evening? Remembrance of things past . . . O.* On the first occasion, he gave her a pretty ruby ring set with pearls, and the reference in the second note was to the fact that they had often eaten at Wheeler's in the early months after marriage. On these evenings he set out to dazzle and amuse her as he had done in the past, and she responded. Perhaps the response was unwilling, but that no doubt was because of Evelyn. He noticed, however, that the man following him was no longer to be seen, and at their Wheeler's supper mentioned this to her.

"I know who she is. I know you've always been like that. Perhaps I have to accept it." Her eyes flashed. "Although if I want to get divorce evidence it won't be difficult."

"An artist needs more than one woman," Oliver said. "But you must not think that I can do without you. I need you. You are a fixed point in a shifting world."

What nonsense I do talk, he said to himself indulgently. The truth was that contact with her nowadays was distasteful to him. By the side of Evelyn she was insipid. A great actor, however, can play any part, and this one would not be maintained for long.

Only one faintly disconcerting thing happened in this, as he thought of it, second-honeymoon period. He came back to the flat unexpectedly early one afternoon and heard

Elizabeth's voice on the telephone. She replaced the receiver as he entered the room. Her face was flushed. When he asked who she had been speaking to, she said, "Charles."

"Charles?" For a moment he couldn't think who she was talking about. Then he stared at her. Nobody knew better than he that she could not have been speaking to Charles, but of course he couldn't say that.

"What did he say?"

"Beastly things. I put down the receiver."

Why was she lying? How absurd, how deliciously absurd, if she had a lover. Or was it possible that somebody at the supper party was playing a practical joke? He brushed aside such conjectures because they didn't matter now. Nothing could interfere with the enactment of the supreme drama of his life.

Celia's intention in *Villain* was to explain Sir Giles's absence by saying that he had gone away on a trip, something he did from time to time. Hence the remark about disposition of the body at the end of Act One. Just after the beginning of the second act the body was revealed by Celia to her lover shoved into a cupboard, a shape hidden in a sack. A few minutes later, the cupboard was opened again and the shape was seen by the audience, although not by Celia, to move slightly. Then, after twenty-five minutes of the second act, there was a brief blackout on stage. When the lights went up, Sir Giles emerged from the cupboard, not dead but drugged.

To be enclosed within a sack for that length of time is no pleasure, and in any ordinary theatrical company the body in the sack would have been that of the understudy, with the leading man changing over only a couple of minutes before he was due to emerge from the cupboard. But Oliver believed in what he called the theatre of the actual. In another play he had insisted that the voice of an actress shut up for some time in a trunk must be real and not a recording, so that the actress herself had to be in the trunk. In *Villain* he maintained that the experience of being actually in the sack was emotionally valuable, so that he always stayed in it for the whole length of time it was in the cupboard.

The body in the sack was to provide Oliver with an unbreakable alibi. The interval after Act One lasted fifteen minutes, so that he had nearly forty minutes free. Everley Court was seven minutes' walk from the theatre, and he did not expect to need much more than twenty minutes all told. The body in the sack would be seen to twitch by hundreds of people, and who could be in it but Oliver?

In fact, Useful Eustace would be the sack's occupant. Eustace was a dummy used by stage magicians who wanted to achieve very much the effect at which Oliver aimed, of persuading an audience that there was a human being inside a container. He was made of plastic and inflated to the size of a small man. You then switched on a mechanism which made Eustace kick out arms and legs in a galvanic manner. A battery-operated timer in his back could be set to operate at intervals ranging from thirty seconds to five minutes. When deflated, Eustace folded up neatly into a size no larger than a plastic raincoat.

Eustace was the perfect accomplice, Useful Eustace indeed. Oliver had tried him out half a dozen times inside a sack of similar size and he looked most convincing.

On the afternoon of The Day he rested. Elizabeth was out, but said that she would be back before seven. His carefully worded note was left on her mantelpiece. *E. I want you at the flat ALL this evening. A truly sensational surprise for you. All the evening, mind, not just after the show. O.* Her curiosity would not, he felt sure, be able to resist such a note.

During Act One he admired, with the detachment of the artist, his own performance. He was cynical, ironic, dramatic —in a word, superb. When it was over he went unobtrusively to his dressing room. He had no fear of visitors, for he was known to detest any interruption during the interval.

And now came what in advance he felt to be the only ticklish part of the operation. The cupboard with the sack in it opened onto the back of the stage. The danger of carrying out an inflated Eustace from dressing room to stage was too great—he must be inflated on site, as it were, and it was possible, although unlikely, that a wandering stagehand might see him at work. The Perfect Crime does not depend upon chance or upon the taking of risks, and if the worst happened, if he was seen obviously inflating a dummy, the project must be abandoned for the present time. But fortune favours the creative artist, or did so on this occasion. Inflation of Eustace by pump took only a few moments as he knelt by the cupboard, and nobody came near. The timer had been set for movement every thirty seconds. He put Eustace into the sack, waited to see him twitch, closed the cupboard's false back, and strolled away.

He left the theatre by an unobtrusive exit used by those who wanted to avoid the autograph hunters outside the stage door, and walked along head down until he reached the nearest Underground station, one of the few in London equipped with lockers and lavatories. Unhurriedly, he took Charles's clothes and shoes from the locker, went into a lavatory, changed, put his acting clothes back in the locker. Spectacles and revolver were in his jacket pocket. He had bought the revolver years ago when he had been playing a part in which he was supposed to be an expert shot. By practice in a shooting range he had, in fact, become a quite reasonable one.

As he left the station he looked at his watch. Six minutes. Very good.

Charles put on a pair of grey gloves from another jacket pocket. Three minutes brought him to Everley Court. He walked straight across to the lift, something he could not do without being observed by Tyler. The man came over, and in Charles's husky voice, with its distinctive accent, he said: "Going up to Mrs. Glass. Expecting me."

"I'll ring, sir. It's Mr. Charles, isn't it?"

"No need. I said, she's expecting me."

Perfectly, admirably calm. But in the lift he felt, quite suddenly, that he would be unable to do it. To allow Elizabeth to divorce him and then to marry or live with Evelyn until they tired of each other—wouldn't that, after all, be the sensible, obvious thing? But to be *sensible,* to be *obvious*—were such things worthy of Oliver Glass? Wasn't the whole point that by this death, which in a practical sense was needless, he would show the character of a great artist and a great actor, a truly superior man?

The lift stopped. He got out. The door confronted him. Put key in lock, turn. Enter.

The flat was in darkness, no light in the hall. No sound. "Elizabeth," he called in a voice that did not seem his own. He had difficulty in not turning and leaving the flat.

He opened the door of the living room. This also was in darkness. Was Elizabeth not there after all, had she ignored his note or failed to return? He felt a wave of relief at the thought, but still there was the bedroom. He must look in the bedroom.

The door was open—a glimmer of light showed within. He did not remember taking the revolver from his pocket, but it was in his gloved hand.

He took two steps into the room. Her dimmed bedside light was switched on. She lay on the bed naked, the black mask over her face. He called out something and she sat up, stretched out arms to him. His reaction was one of disgust and horror. He was not conscious of squeezing the trigger, but the revolver in his hand spoke three times.

She did not call out but gave a kind of gasp. A patch of darkness showed between her breasts. She sank back on the bed.

With the action taken, certainty returned to him. Everything he did now was efficient, exact. He got into the lift, took it down to the basement, and walked out through the garage there, meeting nobody. Tyler would be able to say when Mr. Charles had arrived, but not when he left.

Back to the Underground lavatory, clothes changed, Charles's clothing and revolver returned to the locker for later disposal, locker key put in handkerchief pocket of jacket. Return to the theatre, head down to avoid recognition. A quick glance at his watch as he opened the back door and moved silently up the stairs. Nearly thirty minutes had passed.

He knelt at the back of the cupboard and listened to a few lines of dialogue. The moment at which the body was due to give its twitch had gone and Eustace proved his lasting twitching capacity by giving another shudder, of course not seen by the audience because the cupboard door was closed. Eustace had served his purpose. Oliver withdrew him from the sack and switched him off. With slight pressure to get out the air he was quickly reduced and folded into a bundle. Oliver slipped the bundle inside his trousers and secured it with a safety pin. The slight bulge might have been apparent on close examination, but who would carry out such an examination upon stage?

Beautiful, he thought, as he wriggled into the sack for the few minutes before he had to appear on stage. Oliver Glass, I congratulate you in the name of Thomas de Quincey and Thomas Griffiths Wainewright. You have committed the Perfect Crime.

The euphoria lasted through the curtain calls and his customary few casual words with the audience, in which he congratulated them on being able to appreciate an intelligent mystery. It lasted—oh, how he was savouring the only real achievement of his life—while he leisurely removed Sir Giles's makeup, said goodnight, and left the theatre still with Eustace pinned to him. He made one further visit to the Underground, as a result of which Eustace joined Charles's clothes in the locker. The key back in the handkerchief pocket.

As he was walking back to Everley Court, however, he realized with a shock that something had been forgotten. The note! The note which said positively that he would be at the flat during the interval, a note which if the police saw it would certainly lead to uncomfortable questions, perhaps even to a search, and discovery of the locker key. The note was somewhere in the flat, perhaps in Elizabeth's bag. It must be destroyed before he rang the police.

He nodded to Tyler, took the lift up. Key in door again. The door open. Then he stopped.

Light gleamed under the living room door.

Impossible, he thought, impossible. I know that I did not switch on the light when I opened that door. But then who could be inside the room? He took two steps forward, turned the handle, and when the door was open sprang back with a cry.

"Why, Oliver. What's the matter?" Elizabeth said. She sat on the sofa. Duncan stood beside her.

He pulled at his collar, feeling as though he was about to choke, then tried to ask a question but could not utter words.

"Come and see," Duncan said. He approached and took Oliver by the arm. Oliver shook his head, resisted, but in the end let himself be led to the bedroom. The body still lay there, the patch of red between the breasts.

"You even told her about Elizabeth's bedtime habits," Dunc said. "She must have thought you'd have some fun." He lifted the black mask. Evelyn looked up at him.

Back in the living room he poured himself brandy and said to Elizabeth, "You knew?"

"Of course. *Would supper at Wheeler's amuse you this evening?* Do you think I didn't know you were acting as you always are, making some crazy plan? Though I could never have believed it—it was Dunc who guessed how crazy it was."

He looked from one of them to the other. "You're lovers?" Duncan nodded. "My dreary wife and my dull old friend Dunc—a perfect pair."

Duncan took out his pipe, looked at it, put it back in his pocket. "Liz had kept me in touch with what was going on, naturally. It seemed that you must be going to do something or other tonight. So Liz spent the evening with me."

"Why was Evelyn here?" His mind moved frantically from one point to another to see where he had gone wrong.

"We knew about her from having you watched, and all that nonsense about Charles made me think that Elizabeth must be in some sort of danger. So it seemed a good idea to send your note to Evelyn so that she could be here to greet you. We put the flat key in the envelope."

"The initials were the same."

"Just so," Dunc said placidly.

"You planned for me to kill her."

"I wouldn't say that. Of course if you happened to mistake

her for Liz—but we couldn't guess that she'd put on Liz's mask. We just wanted to warn you that playing games is dangerous."

"You can't prove anything."

"Oh, I think so," Dunc said sagely. "I don't know how you managed to get away from the theatre—some sort of dummy in the sack I suppose—no doubt the police will soon find out. But the important thing is that note. It's in Evelyn's handbag. Shows you arranged to meet her here. Jealous of some younger lover, no doubt."

"But I *wasn't* jealous, I didn't arrange—" He stopped.

"Can't very well say it was for Liz, can you? Not when Evelyn turned up." The doorbell rang. "Oh, I forgot to say we called the police when we found the body. Our duty, you know." He looked at Oliver and said reflectively, "You remember I said there was always a flaw in the Perfect Crime? Perhaps I was wrong. I suppose you might say the Perfect Crime is one you benefit from but don't commit yourself, so that nobody can say you're responsible. Do you see what I mean?" Oliver saw what he meant. "And now it's time to let in the police."

A SOMEWHAT HAPPY ENDING

by ROBERT TWOHY

Brenda Frassup got home from the dentist and went upstairs to rinse out her mouth, but forgot about it the moment she stepped into the bathroom because the first thing she saw, on the tiles near the tub, was her new lightweight carving knife, blade all red.

Second thing to hit her was that the tub was full of red water, from which poked a couple of fat white knees.

"Roy?"

Lying low in the water she could vaguely make out the porky shape of her husband.

But Roy was in Cleveland, not due home until Friday. This was Wednesday.

But often he'd cut a business trip short. And always on return from Cleveland his first act was to take a bath.

Near the knife lay a heap of clothes—greenish shirt, shorts, blue slacks, purple socks—Roy never had any sense of what colors went with what.

Brenda looked at the still water and fiddled with her neat little chin, pondering. Who would have come sneaking in and stabbed him? Frank?

No, Frank had no call to get drastic—Roy was away on business trips most of the time. (He was an industrial-waste executive.) He hardly got in the way of Brenda and Frank's long-running affair.

Who then? *Someone* had finished him, that was for sure.

Well, whoever—it was the cops' problem. The bottom line was that with Roy dead the stylish house, the Mercedes, both bank accounts, all the stocks and bonds, and everything in the safe-deposit box now belonged to her. Plus, on his $500,000 insurance policy she had hit Big Casino. So her twelve-year-old marriage had wound up really well.

No doubt early in the afternoon Roy had called from the airport to tell her to pick him up. But she was at the dentist, so he'd come home by cab—and was all by himself for the killer.

A smile touched her pretty if somewhat sharp-featured face. Things work out, sometimes.

She went downstairs, got the number of the police from the operator, and when she dialed a man answered and asked what was the problem.

She told him.

He got Roy's name, and hers, and their classy address. "You sure he's dead?"

"Yes. There were no bubbles or anything."

"What kind of knife is it?"

"It's got a narrow blade, about eight inches long, comes to a point almost—so you can get between close bones without having to gouge, y'know? The handle's real nice, kind of artistic-looking. Swedish-made, I think."

The man said that some men would be over and not to touch anything. She promised she wouldn't.

She sat back on the couch and looked around the niftily furnished living room and felt not bad at all.

But Frank should get word of what had happened so he'd know that their affair better go on the shelf for a while.

She called his office (he worked at a pest-repellent plant) and in a cold voice like a bill-collector, the voice she always used when she called him at work, she asked if she could speak to Mr. O'Zonickle.

A wait, then: "He seems to be out. Can I take a message?"

Brenda said coldly that she'd call later.

Which meant that she'd have to try him at home, which meant that she'd probably get Lucy. But at least Lucy would pass him the word about Roy's murder and Frank would know he was being signaled to cool things for the nonce.

Lucy's dumb voice came on during the fourth ring. "Yuh? Who?"

"Brenda. Were you taking a nap?"

"Yuh. Whuh time zit?"

"After four."

"Whuff. Gotta start thinking of dinner. Frank said he might be home early. Whuz new, Brenda?"

Brenda and Lucy had been friends since each was a young married, before industrial waste caught on, carrying the Frassups up and away from the tacky old neighborhood where the O'Zonickles still lived. The women remained friends, more or less, and saw each other from time to time. Brenda was sure that Lucy, with her remarkably low IQ, had no idea of the ongoing thing with Frank. Nobody else knew about it either. It had been kept very low-profile.

Brenda said, "Roy's been murdered."

"Who?"

"Roy."

"Been what?"

"Murdered."

"You're kidding."

"No. He's in the tub under the water, which is all bloody—which my new lightweight carving knife, which is on the floor by the tub, is too. I was out and somebody sneaked in and got the knife from the kitchen drawer and went up and stabbed him."

A sudden coughing spasm hit Lucy. "You all right?" asked Brenda.

"Yuh. I'm s'prised is all. So Roy's dead in the water. That's terrible." Another spasm.

Brenda said somewhat sharply, "What's all the coughing?"

"Smoking too much prob'ly. Better stop talking. G'bye. I'm sorry to hear the news. Anything I or Frank can do, lemme know." She hung up.

Brenda sat fiddling with her chin. Odd—mixed in with the coughs had been sounds like giggling.

What was funny?

The phone rang. She picked it up, said "hello," and heard, "Brenda?"

It was like she'd read in a suspense story once—an icy hand seemed to grasp her heart. Another phrase, "it couldn't be," spun around in her head—it simply could not *be!*

"Brenda?"

It had to be someone mimicking Roy's voice. He lay upstairs in the red water.

"Brenda? D'you hear me? I'm calling from Cleveland. It's a jungle here. I'll be home tomorrow, flight blah-blah-blah, meet me at the airport, blah-blah-blah."

There could be no doubt. No mimic could get so exactly the particular soupy, sickening sinus whistle that came with his words.

She said, "Who's in the bathtub?"

"What?"

"If you're in Cleveland, who's in the bathtub?"

"What are you talking about?"

"Someone's in the bathtub."

"What bathtub?"

Frank's sense of what colors went with what was as gross as Roy's!

"Brenda, what the hell's going on?"

An afternoon not long ago she'd got up and half noticed purple socks in his heap of clothes by the bed.

She set the phone back on its cradle, went up and into the bathroom, looked at the socks, then at the two vacuous-looking knees. They told her nothing—knees had never meant anything to her.

She turned up her cuffs, knelt, reached, hooked hair, and hauled. The hair was sand-colored. She'd have liked a different color.

She hauled harder. The head popped up. Frank O'Zonickle's blue eyes gazed at her, sheepish, like he felt like two cents to be here in this condition.

She let go and the head slid back under.

The phone was ringing.

She went down and stood looking at it until it got quiet. Roy had finally given up trying to find out what was going on.

Brenda sat on the couch, dialed. Lucy's voice—"Yuh?"

"You knew all the time."

"Knew what?"

"That it was Frank."

"What was Frank?"

"In the tub."

"With Roy?"

"Roy's not in the tub. Just Frank."

"You said it was Roy."

"All I saw was the knees. Then Roy called from Cleveland and I pulled the head up and it's Frank. *Stop that lousy coughing!*"

"So Frank ducks off work and comes sneaking like Sylvester the Cat to your place, and starts making himself all pretty and sweet—and you come home and find a gone goose. I love it!"

Brenda thought dully, he never took a bath here before—why'd he do it today?

Lucy gradually cheered down. Her tone got sly. "Wait a minute, there's something fishy. Wait, I'm getting it. I've got it. Here's what happened—you came home and saw from the rear this fat glob sitting in the tub, and—yeah, that's it—it was all steamy prob'ly and you didn't see clear, you weren't expecting Frank, he'd sneaked over to give you an afternoon s'prise party, so you thought it was Roy back from Cleveland. From the rear naked they'd look alike, yards of pork, 'cept Roy's bald and Frank has hair—sorry, *had* hair—" She spasmed briefly, then resumed. "But he was prob'ly soaping his head so in the steam he looked bald. You flashed on the big inheritance you'd get, freaked out, ran down to the kitchen, grabbed your new carving knife, ran back, and—I've got it, don't I? Isn't that how it happened?"

She tacked on, purrily, "It'll be in'resting to see how you try to lie your way out of it."

Brenda took a deep breath to calm herself, but it didn't help. She screamed, "*You're* the liar! Pretending to believe it was Roy when you knew it was Frank all the time!"

"How could I?"

"Because you followed him—like you've probably done before!"

"I don't have a car—he takes the car!"

"By cab then! You saw him leave work and come here and go in the back door with the key I gave him. You followed him in—"

"How?"

"He always forgets—forgot—to lock the door after him.

"You heard the bath water, sneaked upstairs, peeked in, saw him in the tub, figgered it'd be real cute to finish him and hang it on me, ran down to the kitchen, got my new carving knife, ran back, and stabbed him!"

"So that's gonna be your lie, is it? Well, lemme tell you, they'll see right through you!"

Brenda listened, said, "Door chimes."

"I heard."

"The cops. I'll tell them who's the killer!"

"You won't have to. They'll know by your lying eyes."

That was the beginning of the O'Zonickle case. And pretty much the end of it. The carving knife showed no fingerprints. Each woman said the other had put the three terminal holes in Frank's back. And the D.A. couldn't nail down which one was the liar.

Brenda's lawyer conferred with him and told him that dumb she was, but not so dumb as to think that stabbing her husband in their own bathtub with their own artistic carving knife made in Taiwan was something she could expect to get away with. The D.A. pointed out that it was O'Zonickle, not her husband, who had been stabbed. The lawyer conceded that, but said that the same reasoning applied. If for any private reason she wanted to finish off Frank, she'd have picked a different place and a less personal weapon.

Then Lucy's lawyer came to confer. He told the D.A. that even if Lucy *had* followed Frank to Brenda's, which she hadn't, she couldn't possibly have expected that he'd plop his fat frame into the tub and be a sitting goose there—so why would she have gone in the house after him? How could she think she'd get advantage over him? He outweighed her by ninety pounds.

The D.A. forbore suggesting that maybe she'd followed him countless times, just waiting for the one time that things would break right, with Brenda off somewhere, her Mercedes not in the driveway, and that day had come last Wednesday. He forbore suggesting it because if it was true, it was just blind luck, on which with no evidence you can't make a case.

Anyway, Lucy's attorney went on, there was no motive to hang on her. Frank's affair with Brenda was no big deal to her—she'd known of it for months and all she thought of it was two morons had found each other.

The house was gone over for clues but there were none—and no signs of forced entry. But Brenda's story that Frank always forgot to lock the back door meant that her lawyer could claim that anyone could have slipped in and done the murder, for whatever reason—or maybe, times being as they are, for no reason at all.

Some days passed. Frank got buried. Nothing was charged to Brenda or Lucy. No other suspects turned up.

The D.A. was an orderly man—he liked things symmetrical, which the O'Zonickle case wasn't. It ran on three legs, which was why it stumbled around and got nowhere. He added a fourth leg—Roy.

Brenda, Frank, Lucy, Roy—four people about equally devoid of redeeming qualities, thought the D.A. Like attracts like. Brenda and Frank had found each other. Why not Lucy and Roy?

The concept pleased him. It gave the case balance.

But that was all it gave. Because a check of the local cab companies developed nothing. And clever questions asked around Roy's industrial-waste factory and around the two neighborhoods, the stylish one and the tacky one, turned up no one who knew of any affair between Roy and Lucy, or would say they did.

So the D.A. had no evidence of any kind. And no one was going to confess.

More days passed, and turned into weeks, then months. New murders took the spotlight. The O'Zonickle case was shoved into the enormous file marked UNSOLVED and became forgotten, even by the D.A.

But before forgetting it it would have been interesting if he'd learned that not many months after Frank passed away Roy divorced Brenda and, some time later, married Lucy.

Brenda got a settlement which, if it wasn't all she'd envisioned in those glorious minutes before Roy's call from Cleveland, wasn't altogether shabby either. And Roy got Lucy, who, for whatever weird reason, he apparently wanted. And she got *her* heart's desire of becoming a lady of position, living in the stylish house, and snubbing all her old friends. Her only regret was that she couldn't snub Brenda, who moved to southern California, where she's having a lively time no doubt.

So things worked out, if not perfectly, at least pleasantly for all but one of the people involved in the O'Zonickle case—which is about the most you can expect of any murder.

I think it's pleasing, in these cynical times, to come on a case with a somewhat happy ending.

RECIPE FOR A HAPPY MARRIAGE

by NEDRA TYRE

Today is just not my day.

And it's not even noon.

Maybe it will take a turn for the better.

Anyway, it's foolish to be upset.

That girl from the *Bulletin* who came to interview me a little while ago was nice enough. I just wasn't expecting her. And I surely wasn't expecting Eliza McIntyre to trip into my bedroom early this morning and set her roses down on my bedside table with such an air about her as if I'd broken my foot for the one and only purpose of having her arrive at seven thirty to bring me a bouquet. She's been coming often enough since I broke my foot, but never before eleven or twelve in the morning.

That young woman from the *Bulletin* sat right down, and before she even smoothed her skirt or crossed her legs she looked straight at me and asked if I had a recipe for a happy marriage. I think she should at least have started off by saying it was a nice day or asking how I felt, especially as it was perfectly obvious that I had a broken foot.

I told her that I certainly didn't have any recipe for a happy marriage, but I'd like to know why I was being asked, and she said it was almost St. Valentine's Day and she had been assigned to write a feature article on love, and since I must know more about love than anybody else in town she and her editor thought that my opinions should have a prominent place in the article.

Her explanation put me more out of sorts than her question. But whatever else I may or may not be I'm a good-natured woman. I suppose it was my broken foot that made me feel irritable.

At that very moment Eliza's giggle came way up the back stairwell from the kitchen, and it was followed by my husband's laughter, and I heard dishes rattle and pans clank, and all that added fire to my irritability.

The one thing I can't abide, never have been able to stand, is to have somebody in my kitchen. Stay out of my kitchen and my pantry, that's my motto. People always seem to think they're putting things back in the right place, but they never do. How well I remember Aunt Mary Ellen saying she just wanted to make us a cup of tea and to cut some slices of lemon to go with it. I could have made that tea as well as she did, but she wouldn't let me. I couldn't tell a bit of difference between her tea and mine, yet she put my favorite paring knife some place or other and it didn't turn up until eight months later, underneath a stack of cheese graters. That was a good twenty years ago and poor Aunt Mary Ellen has been in her grave for ten, and yet I still think about that paring knife and get uneasy when someone is in my kitchen.

Well, that young woman leaned forward and had an equally dumfounding question. She asked me just which husband I had now.

I don't look at things—at husbands—like that. So I didn't answer her. I was too aghast. And then again from the kitchen came the sound of Eliza's giggle and Lewis' whoop.

I've known Eliza Moore, now Eliza McIntyre, all my life. In school she was two grades ahead of me from the very beginning, but the way she tells it now she was three grades behind me; but those school records are somewhere, however yellowed and crumbled they may be, and there's no need for Eliza to try to pretend she's younger than I am when she's two years older. Not that it matters. I just don't want her in my kitchen.

That young woman was mistaking my silence. She leaned close as if I were either deaf or a very young child who hadn't paid attention. How many times have you been married? she asked in a very loud voice.

When she put it like that, how could I answer her? Husbands aren't like teacups. I can't count them off and gloat over them the way Cousin Lutie used to stand in front of her china cabinets, saying she had so many of this pattern and so many of that.

For goodness' sake, I had them one at a time, a husband at a time, and perfectly legally. They all just died on me. I couldn't stay the hand of fate. I was always a sod widow—there weren't any grass widows in our family. As Mama said, it runs in our family to be with our husbands till death us do part. The way that girl put her question, it sounded as if I had a whole bunch of husbands at one time like a line of chorus men in a musical show.

I didn't know how to answer her. I lay back on my pillows with not a word to say, as if the cat had run off with my tongue.

It's sheer accident that I ever married to begin with. I didn't want to. Not that I had anything against marriage or had anything else special to do. But Mama talked me into it. Baby, she said, other women look down on women who don't marry. Besides, you don't have any particular talent and Aunt Sallie Mae, for all her talk, may not leave you a penny. I don't think she ever forgave me for not naming you after her, and all her hinting about leaving you her money may just be her spiteful way of getting back at me.

Besides, Mama said, the way she's held on to her money, even if she did leave it to you, there would be so many strings attached you'd have to have a corps of Philadelphia lawyers to read the fine print before you could withdraw as much as a twenty-five-cent piece. If I were you, Baby, Mama said, I'd go and get married. If you don't marry you won't get invited any place except as a last resort, when they need somebody at the last minute to keep from having thirteen at table. And it's nice to have somebody to open the door for you and carry your packages. A husband can be handy.

So I married Ray.

Well, Ray and I hadn't been married six months when along came Mama with a handkerchief in her hand and dabbing at her eyes. Baby, she said, the wife is always the last one to know. I've just got to tell you what everyone is talking about. I know how good you are and how lacking in suspicion, but the whole town is buzzing. It's Ray and Marjorie Brown.

Ray was nice and I was fond of him. He called me Lucyhoney, exactly as if it were one word. Sometimes for short he called me Lucyhon. He didn't have much stamina or backbone—how could he when he was the only child and spoiled rotten by his mother and grandma and three maiden aunts?

Baby, Mama said, and her tears had dried and she was now using her handkerchief to fan herself with, don't you be gullible. I can't stand for you to be mistreated or betrayed. Should I go to the rector and tell him to talk to Ray and point out where his duty lies? Or should I ask your Uncle Jonathan to talk to Ray man-to-man?

I said, Mama, it's nobody's fault but my own. For heaven's sake let Ray do what he wants to do. He doesn't need anyone to tell him when he can come and go and what persons he can see. It's his house and he's paying the bills. Besides, his taking up with Marjorie Brown is no discredit to me—she's a lot prettier than I am. I think it's romantic and spunky of Ray. Why, Marjorie Brown is a married woman. Her husband might shoot Ray.

I don't know exactly what it was that cooled Ray down. He was back penitent and sheep-eyed, begging forgiveness. I'm proud of you, Ray, I said. Why, until you married me you were so timid you wouldn't have said boo to a goose and here you've been having an illicit affair. I think it's grand. Marjorie Brown's husband might have horsewhipped you.

Ray grinned and said, I really have picked me a wife.

And he never looked at another woman again as long as he lived. Which unfortunately wasn't very long.

I got to thinking about him feeling guilty and apologizing to me, when I was the one to blame—I hadn't done enough for him, and I wanted to do something real nice for him, so I thought of that cake recipe. Except we called it a receipt. It had been in the family for years—centuries you might say, solemnly handed down from mother to daughter, time out of mind.

And so when that girl asked me whether I had a recipe for a happy marriage I didn't give the receipt a thought. Besides, I'm sure she didn't mean an actual recipe, but some kind of formula like let the husband know he's boss, or some such foolishness.

Anyway, there I was feeling penitent about not giving Ray the attention he should have had so that he was bored enough by me to go out and risk his life at the hands of Marjorie Brown's jealous husband.

So I thought, well, it's the hardest receipt I've ever studied and has more ingredients than I've ever heard of, but it's the least I can do for Ray. So I went here and there to the grocery stores, to drug stores, to apothecaries, to people who said, good Lord, no, we don't carry that but if you've got to have it try so-and-so, who turned out to be somebody way out in the country that looked at me as if I asked for the element that would turn base metal into gold and finally came back with a little packet and a foolish question as to what on earth I needed that for.

Then I came on back home and began grinding and pounding and mixing and baking and sitting in the kitchen waiting for the mixture to rise. When it was done it was the prettiest thing I had ever baked.

I served it for dessert that night.

Ray began to eat the cake and to savor it and to say extravagant things to me, and when he finished the first slice he said, Lucyhon, may I have another piece, a big one, please.

Why, Ray, it's all yours to eat as you like, I said.

After a while he pushed the plate away and looked at me with a wonderful expression of gratitude on his face and he said, oh, Lucyhoney, I could die happy. And as far as I know he did.

When I tapped on his door the next morning to give him his first cup of coffee and open the shutters and turn on his bath water he was dead, and there was the sweetest smile on his face.

But that young woman was still looking at me while I had been reminiscing, and she was fluttering her notes and wetting her lips with her tongue like a speaker with lots of things to say. And she sort of bawled out at me as if I were an entire audience whose attention had strayed: Do you think that the way to a man's heart is through his stomach?

Excuse me, young lady, I wanted to say, but I never heard of Cleopatra saying to Mark Antony or any of the others she favored, here, won't you taste some of my potato salad, and I may be wrong because my reading of history is skimpy, but it sounds a little unlikely that Madame de Pompadour ever whispered into the ear of Louis the Fifteenth, I've baked the nicest casserole for you.

My not answering put the girl off, and I felt that I ought to apologize, yet I couldn't bring myself around to it.

She glanced at her notes to the next question, and was almost beet-red from embarrassment when she asked: Did the financial situation of your husbands ever have anything to do with your marrying them?

I didn't even open my mouth. I was as silent as the tomb. Her questions kept getting more and more irrelevant. And I was getting more stupefied as her eyes kept running up and down her list of questions.

She tried another one: What do you think is the best way to get a husband?

Now that's a question I have never asked myself and about which I have nothing to offer anybody in a St. Valentine's Day article or elsewhere. I have never gone out to *get* a husband. I haven't ever, as that old-fashioned expression has it, set my cap for anybody.

Take Lewis who is this minute in the kitchen giggling with Eliza McIntyre. I certainly did not set out to get him. It was some months after Alton—no, Edward—had died, and people were trying to cheer me up, not that I needed any cheering up. I mean, after all the losses I've sustained I've become philosophical. But my Cousin Wanda's grandson had an exhibition of paintings. The poor deluded boy isn't talented, not a bit. All the same I bought two of his paintings that are downstairs in the hall closet, shut off from all eyes.

Anyway, at the opening of the exhibition there was Lewis looking all forlorn. He had come because the boy was a distant cousin of his dead wife. Lewis leaped up from a bench when he got a glimpse of me and said, why, Lucy, I haven't seen you in donkey's years, and we stood there talking while everybody was going ooh and aah over the boy's paintings, and Lewis said he was hungry and I asked him to come on home with me and have a bite to eat.

I fixed a quick supper and Lewis ate like a starving man, and then we sat in the back parlor and talked about this and that, and about midnight he said, Lucy, I don't want to leave. This is the nicest feeling I've ever had, being here with you. I don't mean to be disrespectful to the dead, but there wasn't any love lost between Ramona and me. I'd like to stay on here forever.

Well, after that—after a man's revealed his innermost thoughts to you—you can't just show him the door. Besides, I couldn't put him out because it was beginning to snow, and in a little while the snow turned to sleet. He might have fallen and broken his neck going down the front steps and I'd have had that on my conscience the rest of my life.

Lewis, I said, it seems foolish at this stage of the game for me to worry about my reputation, but thank heaven Cousin Alice came down from Washington for the exhibition and is staying with me, and she can chaperon us until we can make things perfectly legal and aboveboard.

That's how it happened.

You don't plan things like that, I wanted to tell the girl. They happen in spite of you. So it's silly of you to ask me what the best way is to get a husband.

My silence hadn't bothered her a bit. She sort of closed one eye like somebody about to take aim with a rifle and asked: Exactly how many times have you been married?

Well, she had backed up. She was repeating herself. That was practically the same question she had asked me earlier. It had been put a little differently this time, that was all.

I certainly had no intention of telling her the truth, which was that I wasn't exactly sure myself. Sometimes my husbands become a little blurred and blended. Sometimes I have to sit down with pencil and paper and figure it out.

Anyhow, that's certainly no way to look at husbands—the exact number or the exact sequence.

My husbands were an exceptional bunch of men, if I do say so. And fine-looking, too. Even Art, who had a harelip. And they were all good providers. Rich and didn't mind spending their money—not like some rich people. Not that I needed money. Because Aunt Sallie Mae, for all Mama's suspicions, left me hers, and there was nothing spiteful about her stipulations. I could have the money when, as, and how I wanted it.

Anyway, I never have cared about money or what it could buy for me.

There's nothing much I can spend it on for myself. Jewelry doesn't suit me. My fingers are short and stubby and my hands are square—no need to call attention to them by wearing rings. Besides, rings bother me. I like to cook and rings get in the way. Necklaces choke me and earrings pinch. As for fur coats, mink or chinchilla or just plain squirrel—well, I don't like the idea of anything that has lived ending up draped around me.

So money personally means little to me. But it's nice to pass along. Nothing gives me greater pleasure, and there's not a husband of mine who hasn't ended up without having a clinic or a college library or a hospital wing or a research laboratory or something of the sort founded in his honor and named after him. Sometimes I've had to rob Peter to pay Paul. I mean, some of them have left more than others and once in a while I've had to take some of what one left me to pay on the endowment for another. But it all evened itself out.

Except for Buster. There was certainly a nice surplus where Buster was concerned. He lived the shortest time and left me the most money of any of my husbands. For every month I lived with him I inherited a million dollars. Five.

My silent reminiscing like that wasn't helping the girl with her St. Valentine's Day article. If I had been in anybody's house and the hostess was as taciturn as I was, I'd have excused myself and reached for the knob of the front door.

But, if anything, that young lady became even more impertinent.

Have you had a favorite among your husbands? she asked and her tongue flicked out like a snake's.

I was silent even when my husbands asked that question. Sometimes they would show a little jealousy for their predecessors and make unkind remarks. But naturally I did everything in my power to reassure whoever made a disparaging remark about another.

All my husbands have been fine men, I would say in such a case, but I do believe you're the finest of the lot. I said it whether I really thought so or not.

But I had nothing at all to say to that girl on the subject.

Yet if I ever got to the point of being forced to rank my husbands, I guess Luther would be very nearly at the bottom of the list. He was the only teetotaler in the bunch. I hadn't noticed how he felt about drink until after we were married —that's when things you've overlooked during courtship can confront you like a slap in the face. Luther would squirm when wine was served to guests during a meal, and his eyes looked up prayerfully toward heaven when anybody took a second glass. At least he restrained himself to the extent of not saying any word of reproach to a guest, but Mama said she always expected him to hand around some of those tracts that warn against the pitfalls that lie in wait for drunkards.

Poor man. He was run over by a beer truck.

The irony of it, Mama said. There's a lesson in it for us all. And it was broad daylight, she said, shaking her head, not even dark, so that we can't comfort ourselves that Luther didn't know what hit him.

Not long after Luther's unfortunate accident Matthew appeared—on tiptoe, you might say. He was awfully short and always stretched himself to look taller. He was terribly apologetic about his height. I'd ask you to marry me, Lucy, he said, but all your husbands have been over six feet tall. Height didn't enter into it, I told him, and it wasn't very long before Matthew and I were married.

He seemed to walk on tiptoe and I scrunched down, and still there was an awful gap between us, and he would go on about Napoleon almost conquering the world in spite of being short. I started wearing low-heeled shoes and walking hunched over, and Mama said, for God's sake, Baby, you can push tact too far. You never were beautiful but you had an air about you and no reigning queen ever had a more elegant walk, and here you are slumping. Your Aunt Francine was married to a midget, as you well know, but there wasn't any of this bending down and hunching over. She let him be his height and he let her be hers. So stop this foolishness.

But I couldn't. I still tried literally to meet Matthew more than halfway. And I had this feeling—well, why shouldn't I have it, seeing as how they had all died on me—that Matthew wasn't long for this world, and it was my duty to make him feel as important and as tall as I possibly could during the little time that was left to him.

Matthew died happy. I have every reason to believe it. But then, as Mama said, they all died happy.

Never again, Mama, I said. Never again. I feel like Typhoid Mary or somebody who brings doom on men's heads.

Never is a long time, Mama said.

And she was right. I married Hugh.

I think it was Hugh.

Two things I was proud of and am proud of. I never spoke a harsh word to any one of my husbands and I never did call one of them by another's name, and that took a lot of doing because after a while they just all sort of melted together in my mind.

After every loss, Homer was the greatest solace and comfort to me. Until he retired last year Homer was the Medical Examiner, and he was a childhood friend, though I never saw him except in his line of duty, you might say. It's the law here, and perhaps elsewhere, that if anyone dies unattended or from causes that aren't obvious, the Medical Examiner must be informed.

The first few times I had to call Homer I was chagrined. I felt apologetic, a little like calling the doctor up in the middle of the night when, however much the pain may be troubling you, you're afraid it's a false alarm and the doctor will hold it against you for disturbing his sleep.

But Homer always was jovial when I called him. I guess that's not the right word. Homer was reassuring, not jovial. Anytime, Lucy, anytime at all, he would say when I began to apologize for having to call him.

I think it was right after Sam died. Or was it Carl? It could have been George. Anyway, Homer was there reassuring me as always, and then this look of sorrow or regret clouded his features. It's a damned pity, Lucy, he said, you can't work me in somewhere or other. You weren't the prettiest little girl in the third grade, or the smartest, but damned if from the beginning there hasn't been something about you. I remember, he said, that when we were in the fourth grade I got so worked up over you that I didn't pass a single subject but arithmetic and had to take the whole term over. Of course you were promoted, so for the rest of my life you've been just out of my reach.

Why, Homer, I said, that's the sweetest thing anybody has ever said to me.

I had it in the back of my mind once the funeral was over and everything was on an even keel again that I'd ask Homer over for supper one night. But it seemed so calculating, as if I was taking him up on that sweet remark he had made about wishing I had worked him in somewhere among my husbands. So I decided against it.

Instead I married Beau Green.

There they go laughing again—Eliza and Lewis down in the kitchen. *My* kitchen.

It's funny that Eliza has turned up in my kitchen, acting very much at home, when she's the one and only person in this town I never have felt very friendly toward—at least, not since word got to me that she had said I snatched Beau Green right from under her nose.

That wasn't a nice thing for her to say. Besides, there wasn't a word of truth in it. I'd like to see the man that can be snatched from under anybody's nose unless he wanted to be.

Eliza was surely welcome to Beau Green if she had wanted him and if he had wanted her.

Why, I'd planned to take a trip around the world, already had my tickets and reservations, and had to put it off for good because Beau wouldn't budge any farther away from home than to go to Green River—named for his family—to fish. I really wanted to take that cruise—had my heart especially set on seeing the Taj Mahal by moonlight; but Beau kept on saying if I didn't marry him he would do something desperate, which I took to mean he'd kill himself or take to drink. So I canceled all those reservations and turned in all those tickets and married him.

Well, Eliza would certainly have been welcome to Beau.

I've already emphasized that I don't like to rank my husbands, but in many ways Beau was the least satisfactory one I ever had. It was his nature to be a killjoy—he had no sense of the joy of living and once he set his mind on something he went ahead with it, no matter if it pleased anybody else or not.

He knew good and well I didn't care for jewelry. But my preference didn't matter to Beau Green, not one bit. Here he came with this package and I opened it. I tried to muster all my politeness when I saw that it was a diamond. Darling, I said, you're sweet to give me a present, but this is a little bit big, isn't it?

It's thirty-seven carats, he said.

I felt like I ought to take it around on a sofa pillow instead of wearing it, but I did wear it twice and felt as conspicuous and as much of a showoff as if I'd been waving a peacock fan around and about.

It was and is my habit when I get upset with someone to go to my room and write my grievances down and get myself back in a good humor, just as I'm doing now because of that girl's questions; but sometimes it seemed like there wasn't enough paper in the world on which to write down my complaints against Beau.

Then I would blame myself. Beau was just being Beau. Like all God's creatures he was behaving the way he was made, and I felt so guilty that I decided I ought to do something for him to show I really loved and respected him, as deep in my heart I did.

So I decided to make him a cake by that elaborate recipe that had been in our family nobody is sure for how long. I took all one day to do the shopping for it. The next day I got up at five and stayed in the kitchen until late afternoon.

Well, Beau was a bit peckish when it came to eating the cake. Yet he had the sweetest tooth of any of my husbands.

Listen, darling, I said when he was mulish about eating it, I made this special for you—it's taken the best part of two days. I smiled at him and asked wouldn't he please at least taste it to please me. Really, I was put out when I thought of all the work that had gone into it. For one terrible second I wished it were a custard pie and I could throw it right in his face, like in one of those old Keystone comedies; and then I remembered that we were sworn to cherish each other, so I just put one arm around his shoulder and with my free hand I pushed the cake a little closer and said, Belle wants Beau to eat at least one small bite. Belle was a foolish pet name he sometimes called me because he thought it was clever for him to be Beau and for me to be Belle.

He looked sheepish and picked up his fork and I knew he was trying to please me, the way I had tried to please him by wearing that thirty-seven carat diamond twice.

Goodness, Belle, he said, when he swallowed his first mouthful, this is delicious.

Now, darling, you be careful, I said. That cake is rich.

Best thing I ever ate, he said, and groped around on the plate for the crumbs, and I said, darling, wouldn't you like a little coffee to wash it down?

He didn't answer, just sat there smiling. Then after a little he said he was feeling numb. I can't feel a thing in my feet, he said. I ran for the rubbing alcohol and pulled off his shoes and socks and started rubbing his feet, and there was a sort of spasm and his toes curled under, but nothing affected that smile on his face.

Homer, I said a little later—because of course I had to telephone him about Beau's death—what on earth is it? Could it be something he's eaten? And Homer said, what do you mean, something he's eaten? Of course not. You set the best table in the county. You're famous for your cooking. It couldn't be anything he's eaten. Don't be foolish, Lucy. He began to pat me on the shoulder and he said, I read a book about guilt and loss and it said the bereaved often hold themselves responsible for the deaths of their beloved ones. But I thought you had better sense than that, Lucy.

Homer was a little bit harsh with me that time.

Julius Babb settled Beau's estate. Beau left you a tidy sum all right, he said, and I wanted to say right back at him but didn't: not as tidy as most of the others left me.

Right then that young woman from the *Bulletin* repeated her last question.

Have you had a favorite among your husbands? Her tone was that of a prosecuting attorney and had nothing to do with a reporter interested in writing about love for St. Valentine's Day.

I had had enough of her and her questions. I dragged myself up to a sitting position in the bed. Listen here, young lady, I said. It looks as if I've gotten off on the wrong foot with you—and then we both laughed at the pun I had made.

The laughter put us both in a good humor and then I tried to explain that I had an unexpected caller downstairs who needed some attention, and that I really was willing to cooperate on the St. Valentine's Day article; but all those questions at first hearing had sort of stunned me. It was like taking an examination and finding all the questions a surprise. I told her if she would leave her list with me I'd mull over it, and she could come back tomorrow and I'd be prepared with my answers and be a little more presentable than I was now, wearing a rumpled wrapper and with my hair uncombed.

Well, she was as sweet as apple pie and handed over the list of questions and said she hoped that ten o'clock tomorrow morning would be fine; and I said, yes, it would.

There goes Eliza's laugh again. It's more of a caw than a laugh. I shouldn't think that. But it's been such a strange day, with that young reporter being here and Eliza showing up so early.

Come to think of it, Eliza has done very well for herself, as far as marrying goes. That reporter should ask Eliza some of those questions.

Mama was a charitable woman all her life and she lived to be eighty nine, but Eliza always rubbed Mama's skin the wrong way. To tell the truth, Eliza rubbed the skin of all the women in this town the wrong way. It's not right, Baby, Mama said, when other women have skimped and saved and cut corners all their lives and then when they're in their last sickness here comes Eliza getting her foot in the door just because she's a trained nurse. Then the next thing you hear, Eliza has married the widower and gets in one fell swoop what it took the dead wife a lifetime to accumulate.

That wasn't the most generous way in the world for Mama to put it, but I've heard it put much harsher by others. Mrs. Perkerson across the street, for one. Eliza is like a vulture, Mrs. Perkerson said. First she watches the wives die, then she marries, and then she watches the husbands die. Pretty soon it's widow's weeds for Eliza and a nice-sized bank account, not to mention some of the most valuable real estate in town.

Why, Mrs. Perkerson said the last time I saw her, I know that Lois Eubanks McIntyre is turning in her grave thinking of Eliza inheriting that big estate, with gardens copied after the Villa d'Este. And they tell you nursing is hard work.

I hadn't seen Eliza in some time. We were friendly enough, but not real friends, never had been, and I was especially hurt after hearing what she said about me taking Beau Green away from her. But we would stop and chat when we bumped into each other downtown, and then back off smiling and saying we must get together. But nothing ever came of it.

And then three weeks ago Eliza telephoned and I thought for sure somebody was dead. But, no, she was as sweet as magnolia blossoms and cooing as if we saw each other every day, and she invited me to come by that afternoon for a cup of tea or a glass of sherry. I asked her if there was anything special, and she said she didn't think there had to be any special reason for old friends to meet, but, yes, there was something special. She wanted me to see her gardens—of course they weren't her gardens, except by default, they were Lois Eubanks McIntyre's gardens—which she had opened for the Church Guild Benefit Tour and I hadn't come. So she wanted me to see them that afternoon.

It was all so sudden that she caught me off guard. I didn't want to go and there wasn't any reason for me to go, but for the life of me I couldn't think of an excuse not to go. And so I went.

The gardens really were beautiful. And I'm crazy about flowers.

Eliza gave me a personally guided tour. There were lots of paths and steep steps and unexpected turnings, and I was so delighted by the flowers that I foolishly didn't pay attention to my footing. I wasn't used to walking on so much gravel or going up and down uneven stone steps and Eliza didn't give me any warning.

Then all of a sudden, it was the strangest feeling, not as if I'd fallen but as if I'd been pushed, and there Eliza was leaning over me saying she could never forgive herself for not telling me about the broken step, and I was to lie right there and not move until the doctor could come, and what a pity it was that what she had wanted to be a treat for me had turned into a tragedy. Which was making a whole lot more out of it than need be because it was only a broken foot—not that it hasn't been inconvenient.

But Eliza has been fluttering around for three weeks saying that I should sue her as she carried liability insurance, and anyway it was lucky she was a nurse and could see that I got devoted attention. I don't need a nurse, but she has insisted on coming every day, and on some days several times; she seems to be popping in and out of the house like a cuckoo clock.

I had better get on with that reporter's questions.

Do you have a recipe for a happy marriage?

I've already told her I don't, and of course there's no such thing as a recipe for a happy marriage; but I could tell her this practice I have of working through my grievances and dissatisfactions by writing down what bothers me and then tearing up what I've written. For all I know it might work for somebody else, too.

I didn't hear Eliza coming up the stairs. It startled me when I looked up and saw her at my bedside. What if she discovered I was writing about her? What if she grabbed the notebook out of my hands and started to read it? There isn't a thing I could do to stop her.

But she just smiled and asked if I was ready for lunch and she hoped I'd worked up a good appetite. How on earth she thinks I could have worked up an appetite by lying in bed I don't know, but that's Eliza for you, and all she had fixed was canned soup and it wasn't hot.

All I wanted was just to blot everything out—that girl's questions, Eliza's presence in my home, my broken foot.

I would have thought that I couldn't have gone to sleep in a thousand years. But I was so drowsy that I couldn't even close the notebook, much less hide it under the covers.

I don't know what woke me up. It was pitch-dark, but dark comes so soon these winter days you can't tell whether it's early dark or midnight.

I felt refreshed after my long nap and equal to anything. I was ready to answer any question on that girl's list.

The notebook was still open beside me and I thought that if Eliza had been in here and had seen what I had written about her it served her right.

Then from the kitchen rose a wonderful smell and there was a lot of noise downstairs. Suddenly the back stairway and hall were flooded with light, and then Eliza and Lewis were at my door and they were grinning and saying they had a surprise for me. Then Lewis turned and picked up something from a table in the hall and brought it proudly toward me. I couldn't tell what it was. It was red and heart-shaped and had something white on top. At first I thought it might be a hat, and then I groped for my distance glasses, but even with them on I still couldn't tell what Lewis was carrying.

Lewis held out the tray. It's a St. Valentine's Day cake, he said, and Eliza said, we iced it and decorated it for you; then

Lewis tilted it gently and I saw L U C Y in wobbly letters spread all across the top.

I don't usually eat sweets. So their labor of love was lost on me. Then I thought how kind it was that they had gone to all that trouble, and I forgave them for messing up my kitchen and meddling with my recipes—or maybe they had just used a mix. Anyway, I felt I had to show my appreciation, and it certainly wouldn't kill me to eat some of their cake.

They watched me with such pride and delight as I ate the cake that I took a second piece. When I had finished they said it would be best for me to rest, and I asked them to take the cake and eat what they wanted, then wrap it in foil.

And now the whole house is quiet.

I never felt better in my life. I'm smiling a great big contented smile. It must look exactly like that last sweet smile on all my husbands' faces—except Luther who was run over by a beer truck.

I feel wonderful and so relaxed.

But I can hardly hold this pencil.

Goodness, it's

f
a
l
l
i
n
g

THE WAY IT LOOKS

by THOMAS WALSH

Walter Rafferty was just in the nick of time that night. Not only did he get a brief glimpse of what by all odds must have been the getaway car, but he also, because of instinctive professional habit, tucked it away in his mind with one or two very important details. About the driver, who had his head turned in the other direction, he was not so sure. Young, it seemed to him, average size, dark pullover sweater. But he was altogether positive about the car. So it was all in his mind a minute or so later on, every bit of it put together for him—the battered old jalopy, the driver, the time, the neighborhood, and the deed. Q.E.D.

About the car, anyone at all would have been dead certain. It was one of a kind. In make and color it was an old yellow Ford convertible, with a bold female nude posed like Diana the huntress as the radiator ornament. It had sportily glittering wheel covers; the right part of the windshield was cracked, and the front fender on Rafferty's side had been crumpled in noticeably. Racing out of the side street at about 55 miles an hour against a red light, the Ford cut off a taxicab that had to brake desperately, and then zoomed off even faster than 55 along Lexington Avenue.

Rafferty turned to look after it, his lips pursed. Crazy damned fool! But it was a rainy and wind-lashed autumn night; the taxicab, already occupied, was the only other vehicle to be seen at half-past two in the morning; so all Rafferty could do was watch the convertible race off into another side street two or three blocks farther along. The deeply humming, big-city silence drifted back, after which, just as Rafferty swung into his own street, a girl ran out onto the steps of a tall gray apartment building halfway along the block and began screaming and screaming . . .

"Prettiest girl you'd ever want to see, too," Rafferty explained perhaps a little bit too enthusiastically next morning to Inspector Birmingham. "A figure that would knock your eye out, kind of tall and elegant, you know; very dark and kind of dreamy blue eyes; and real blonde hair that comes all the way down to her shoulders."

"Dark and dreamy," Iron Mike grunted, without raising his eyes from some other report on his desk, but quite obviously not missing anything. "I see. I also see that she must have used them on you pretty good last night. I thought you were a married man, Rafferty. Is that right?"

"Well, sure," Rafferty said, at once innocently virtuous. "Of course. Don't think that I—"

"Then don't make me think," Iron Mike grunted. "What was she doing in the apartment-house vestibule at that hour of night? You asked her, didn't you?"

"Lives there," Rafferty said, teeth delicately together. Damned old buzzard! Always putting the knock on you, to show his authority. "On the fourth floor. And just coming home from a date, that's why. I couldn't quiet her down for about ten minutes, but I wouldn't say you could blame her. She saw the whole thing."

"Which was what?"

Damn it, give me a chance, Rafferty thought grimly, but did not utter, not to Iron Mike. Instead, he took a careful breath, composing himself, and trying to anticipate and maneuver around another of Inspector Birmingham's famous trap questions.

"The fellow she was out with had just dropped her off before the thing happened. She was unlocking the street door when she saw these two other people who have an apartment on the twelfth floor waiting for the elevator. Then she sees something else—this guy darting out from kind of a dark alcove near the back of the hall and pulling a knife on Tolliver. Tolliver grabs for him. They begin fighting. But the guy is knocked off balance by Tolliver, stumbles into Mrs. Tolliver, or else she into him, and stabs her right in the heart when his arm is jerked up. Then he knocks Miss Sanderson out of the way, runs out into the street, and jumps into his car."

"Wait a minute," Iron Mike put in, with a very brief upward look over his eyeglasses. "You mean the girl saw him do that?"

"Didn't have to," Rafferty said, just as curtly. "How else does it fit? I was coming home along Lexington Avenue from the subway station, and I saw him come out of that sidestreet like a bat out of hell. We got quite a break, Inspector. We'll locate that car, and when we do locate it we'll have the guy. This thing is open-and-shut."

"Is it?" Iron Mike said, pushing back in his swivel chair, placing both hands on the desk and studying Rafferty up and down with no favor. "Well, well, well. Very glad you told me, Rafferty. I wouldn't have suspected it myself. You mean that there couldn't have been two men—one fellow who ran out of the apartment vestibule after stabbing Mrs. Tolliver and vanished somewhere, and another one who just happened to drive by at that moment with maybe a few drinks in him, and in a bit of a hurry to get somewhere?"

"Well, sure," Rafferty had to admit. "There could have been two men. But what I figure—"

"Is usually and almost infallibly one hundred percent wrong," Iron Mike trumpeted. "Is this a husband-and-wife thing or isn't it? And what's the first thing we do—the very first thing, Rafferty—when a husband or wife is killed suddenly?"

"Check up on how they were getting along," Rafferty had to admit a bit smugly, ready for that, at any rate. "Find out if the whole thing was a put-up job, with one party trying to get rid of the other."

"And you checked that part out, of course?"

"You mean already?" Rafferty asked, pushing the pin a little himself now. "In just five or six hours? Well, not completely, Inspector. Now I'm just trying to tell you how it looked last night to me and the precinct men."

"You fellows are always *going* to do something you should have thought of first thing," Iron Mike gritted. "Every damned one of you. Well, don't be going to, Rafferty. Get busy on it right now, and do a little honest work for a change. Don't jump the gun and tell me what you think. Get me the facts. Haven't you learned yet in this job that the way it looks isn't necessarily the way it is? You know the car, you say, and you'd know the fellow who was driving it?"

"Pick it out of a million," Rafferty said. "The guy, too. But I never thought, until the Sanderson girl ran out on the stoop and began screaming—"

"Correct," Iron Mike said. "You never do think, somehow, or not in time, at any rate. Ah, you're brilliant, Rafferty. Got the whole thing open-and-shut already. But let me tell you what it signifies to me so far. Not a damn thing. Well, God help your poor brains. Send in Andy Bennett and Jack Kollecker to me. Then go out and find the car for yourself, since you're so positive about that angle. Go on, I tell you. What the hell are you waiting for? Attend to your work. Don't stand there looking at me with a face like a bad potato on you."

So Rafferty did get out, put properly in his place, and only when safely outside complained to Fat John Kollecker about the treatment he had received.

"The thing's staring you right in the face," he declared bitterly. "But not with that old buzzard. He just never gives you any credit at all. What could be any plainer than this setup? But he won't buy it from me, or not until he's run my tail into the ground to throw his weight around. Jump, jump, jump. But one day I just might shove it right back down his throat. What the hell is he trying to make out of this, anyway?"

Yet after that, under Iron Mike's explicit instructions, two roads were explored. Fat John and Andy Bennett pursued the husband-and-wife angle, and Rafferty went after the car harder than he had ever gone after anything in his life. Stupid, was he? Careless, slipshod, always ready to jump the gun, was he? Well, they'd see. Somebody would have to eat crow, but that somebody was not going to be Walter Rafferty.

So Rafferty scoured the neighborhood doggedly, twelve hours the first day, longer than that the second. He talked to children playing in the streets; he talked to people lounging on street corners; he talked to shopkeepers. And on the third morning, not knowing where to turn next—because who knew if the man who had killed Mrs. Tolliver even lived in the neighborhood?—he was standing on a streetcorner in almost savage despair when he saw the car for a second time.

But he only saw it out of the corner of his eye, for a brief second, as it whipped very fast again into the next sidestreet down from him. Rafferty had long legs, however, and Rafferty ran very fast, knocking people out of his way with no apology, and even jumping over two small boys who were playing marbles along the curb. It was no good. There were parked cars all along the street he wanted, but none of them was the yellow convertible. It had vanished.

There was no point walking into the street then, but Rafferty did, for no sensible reason, apart from Iron Mike. A bakery shop, a radio store, a church crowded in by tenements on both sides, a supermarket with a parking space—and in the parking space, when Rafferty glanced in, and almost unseeingly, the yellow convertible in the first spot off the street. Rafferty lit a cigarette, feeling just fine then, and took up position in a convenient doorway. He moved away from it only when two young men came out of the supermarket loaded with bags, and put them into the yellow convertible. One was a husky blond kid, who looked as if he didn't have a care in the world. The other, thin and very quick-moving, wore a pullover sweater and had haggard and wearily haunted dark eyes. He was the one who got into the convertible, and drove off. Rafferty let him go. There was no problem any more. Rafferty now had the license number.

"Hey, Bud," Rafferty called to the other boy, who was whistling his way back to the supermarket. "That fellow you were just talking to, in that yellow car. Looked something like a friend of mine, Jack Farrell. Is that his name?"

Of course it wasn't. But then Rafferty had the right name, Paul Kovacs, and a little further information. Paul Kovacs worked in the store as a delivery boy, and he had just started out on another round.

"Okay, made a mistake." Rafferty grinned, and from a corner drugstore, not to start tongues wagging, phoned the store manager. After that he had about everything he wanted. Paul Kovacs was 17 years old, and he had worked in the store for three months. It was a store that delivered, and two of the customers to whom it delivered were Mr. and Mrs. Edwin Tolliver.

"So it's the husband-and-wife thing, all right," Rafferty explained a bit later to Iron Mike. "I'd say this Tolliver tips the kid pretty good when he delivers the groceries, gets real friendly with him and sizes him up. Then when he's sure what kind he is, the kind of young punk that will do anything for a buck, he makes the proposition to him.

"Nothing to it, he probably coaxed the kid. Easy as pie. They'll fake a purse-snatching, making sure there's an outside witness around, this Miss Sanderson, and kill Mrs. Tolliver without anyone thinking twice about it. Tolliver will describe the wrong guy to me, which he did. Miss Sanderson described the kid pretty good, she's the honest witness, but Tolliver describes him all wrong, because he's the lying witness. I'd say he slipped the kid five hundred, or maybe a thousand, and the kid jumped at it. Easy money, all right, and now Tolliver and the kid think they've pulled it off on us."

"Maybe it is," Iron Mike admitted, rubbing his mouth petulantly. Of course, Rafferty thought. Always wants to tell *you* how it was, not you tell him. "But one question, Rafferty. How did they know that Miss Sanderson would come along right then and back up their story? She was only coming in through the street door when it all happened, you told me."

"They could have waited for her," Rafferty insisted, "or waited for anyone to show up. It's a glass door, and Tolliver must have seen her through it getting her keys out. Then he must have signaled the kid. 'Come on, come on. Right now. We're all set.' "

"And how about the elevator?" Iron Mike asked him, as if he hadn't heard. "Suppose it came down just then with three or four men inside and they grabbed this Paul Kovacs? Then they'd be taking a hell of a chance, Rafferty. No. It doesn't fit that way. And how could he keep his wife waiting and waiting for the elevator—waiting for the Sanderson girl to come in—when he didn't know she was even coming in?"

"Could have been something between him and the girl," Rafferty said, as if suddenly inspired. "I tell you she's a real knockout, Inspector, and they lived in the same house. Maybe that's it. Maybe they had something going between them."

"Maybe, maybe, maybe. Well, to hell with your maybes, Rafferty. I want the facts. And besides, it wasn't Tolliver running around on Mrs. Tolliver. Andy Burnett tells me it was the exact opposite. For quite a few years now Mrs. Tolliver has been running around on him. Three years ago she left him for another man, and he was damned fool enough to take her back after it. Just mad crazy about the woman, from what Andy found out."

"Then maybe dough," Rafferty thought up. "He could have had her insured for fifty or a hundred thousand dollars —or she might have had money of her own."

"Not a red cent," Iron Mike shot out curtly. "And no insurance, either. No, the money was all his, and he appears to have loved the woman. Which leaves us where?"

Rafferty could not say. Offer an angle, he was thinking bitterly, and the old buzzard ripped it to bits—and enjoyed doing it. Rafferty's lips curled.

"Wouldn't care to suggest anything at all," he snapped. "What the hell's the use?"

"I take it you mean with me," Iron Mike shot back, even

more curtly. "Well, in five or ten years, Rafferty, I might be able to make a competent and intelligent police officer out of you, but you aren't one yet, and don't think it. I tell you there's something else here that none of us have looked at yet in the right way. But now pick up the Kovacs boy, while Andy Burnett gets in touch with Tolliver and the Sanderson girl. If they both identify him for us, wonderful. If they don't, we'll have to trip him up one way or another out of his own mouth. Get on it."

So Rafferty did, with a convenient precinct man. They went back to the supermarket in a squad car and found Paul Kovacs in back of the store, unpacking pork and beans on one of the shelves. He knew at once what they wanted, without even asking them—a telltale sign. When the precinct man flashed his badge, Paul Kovacs only nodded silently—as if almost from relief, it seemed to Rafferty—and took off his apron.

On the way downtown the precinct man asked two or three questions, but Kovacs would not answer. Both hands were clasped between his knees, and there was something lost and hopeless in the way he kept watching them. Toward the end of their ride he suddenly made a low sound in the throat and covered his eyes.

Upstairs in the building there were two rooms with a panel of one-way glass between them. Rafferty and the others could see Paul Kovacs through that, but he could not see them. He stood with five other men in the lineup, second from the left, and stared straight ahead, wetting his lips. Iron Mike took charge.

"Now I want you to tell me," he instructed Tolliver and the Sanderson girl, "if either of you recognize one of the men on the other side of this window. If you do, go back into the hall outside and tell Andy Burnett which man it is. That's all. But everything has to be shipshape and regular here, with no hint of collusion. Take your time now. But don't talk to each other, don't even look at each other. Step up to the window, look at the men in line, make up your mind—and that's all. Do just what I've told you."

So they did, and Rafferty could see that the girl knew at

once. Her eyes touched Paul Kovacs, stopped on him—and she moved a fearful step or two back from the window. Tolliver, a tall thin man with a gaunt face and brooding dark eyes, showed nothing at all. One by one he looked at the men, taking the same time and care with each of them. After that he turned, still without any expression, and walked out to the hall.

"Think we got it all set," Andy Burnett boasted, hurrying in a few seconds later. "The girl identified Kovacs right off the bat, Inspector. Just positive, she told me. And one's enough, isn't it? All we need."

"You never have all you need," Iron Mike rasped. "And if you think that you do, with all these damned shyster lawyers around, you're nothing but a damned fool. Tolliver had just as good a look at the boy. Then why wouldn't he make the identification for us?"

"Told you before," Rafferty had to put in. He felt fine. "They're in it together, that's why. Tolliver's trying to cover up for him."

Iron Mike did not answer. He walked over to the open street window—it was a very humid day for October—and stared out of it while patting his hands irritably behind him. Finally he turned.

"Bring Kovacs in here," he directed then, "and bring Tolliver in here. And don't say a word, any of you, until I show that I want you to. For the present just keep your eyes open. I'll do whatever talking I think necessary."

At first, however, it seemed that no talking at all was necessary. There was perfect stillness in the room. Paul Kovacs did not look at Tolliver, but kept his eyes lowered. His lips had puffed out slightly. His expression, what Rafferty could see of it, was one of blind hate.

When Iron Mike finally spoke, at least a full minute later, he used an indifferent, completely disinterested tone of voice.

"Still no good?" he inquired of Tolliver. "You never saw this fellow before in your life? He isn't the man who murdered your wife the other night?"

"No, he isn't," Tolliver said, also evenly. "Nothing like him. He's not the man."

"Then that's a very queer thing," Iron Mike said, pursing his lips for a moment. "From what I understand, he's been delivering groceries to your apartment for five or six months now. But still, you never saw him before—not last Friday night, and not anywhere?"

"That's right," Tolliver said, turning his eyes slowly to Iron Mike and keeping them there. And now there was no mistaking the blind hatred in Paul Kovacs. He looked up at Tolliver, lips contracting, both hands clenched. Andy Burnett and Rafferty moved an unobtrusive step closer to him.

Tolliver said, "I'm a nine-to-five man at the office, Inspector, and I imagine the groceries are delivered sometime in the afternoon. He'd have dealt with Mrs. Tolliver, not with me."

"With Mrs. Tolliver," Iron Mike grunted. "Not with you. So that's it. Tell me something. Did you and Mrs. Tolliver have a good marriage? Were there no problems or difficulties at all between you?"

"Not even the slightest," Tolliver said. "Helen and I—"

"Damned liar," the boy said, his body shaking as if in the grip of a high wind. "Stinking damned liar. She hated your guts—and you know it!"

Still without looking back at the boy, Tolliver took a handkerchief out of his pocket and dabbed his lips calmly.

"Oh?" And Iron Mike turned to regard Paul Kovacs. "You know that for a fact, Paul?"

"I know it and he knows it," Paul Kovacs gritted. "Lousy rotten skunk. He never treated her right. He—"

It was beginning to come then, and Rafferty got a slight movement of the left eyebrow from Iron Mike.

"Now come on, come on," Rafferty ordered. "You'd better start looking out for yourself, kid. We know how and why it all happened Friday night. We know how the whole thing was set up, so don't be stupid enough to deny it. If you do, you know what will happen? You're going to be all the way up the creek, you little punk, and without a paddle. You'd better start talking."

"That's right, lad," Iron Mike warned seriously—the avuncular touch. "The girl identified you. Rafferty here can identify you, and identify your car. You killed Mrs. Tolliver Friday night and we all know it. Now tell us why."

Paul Kovacs darted his eyes around the room desperately; but no help. Tolliver and Iron Mike faced him from the other side of the table. On his right stood Andy Burnett, and on his left, Walter Rafferty.

"Now don't let them fool you," Tolliver said, still icily calm and composed. "They know nothing at all. They're only guessing. If you keep your mouth shut now, and don't answer even one question until your lawyer gets here, which is your constitutional right—"

"Yeah?" Rafferty grated at him, to shut that off. "We know nothing at all, hah? Then tell me this. You didn't describe this kid to me Friday night. You lied about him, saying he was about forty years old, and maybe a Puerto Rican. And you lied about what a happy marriage you and your wife had. She left you three times that we know of, and last time she lived eleven months with another guy. When she finally came back to you, you beat her up—and that's a matter of police record. So don't you just stand there and try to tell us—"

"Which didn't matter at all," Tolliver replied with the same rigid calmness of tone. "The thing that did matter was that I loved Helen, and Helen loved me."

"Never," the boy whispered. "Never, you rotten lying—"

He was very quick. He tried to get over the table at Tolliver, but Rafferty and Andy Burnett, already alerted, were quicker. They caught him between them and threw him back, where he crouched down at the open window. He was like a child there, Rafferty saw. He was actually sobbing.

"Never," he screamed at Tolliver. "Never *you.* She loved me, she loved me, she loved me!"

"So that's it," Rafferty heard Iron Mike murmur. "The whole bunch of us have been looking at the thing backwards. We all—stop him, Rafferty! Grab him! Get his legs!"

But that time Rafferty had no chance. Paul Kovacs had lurched back into the open window, the blinding tears still in his eyes, and as Rafferty lunged he kicked himself out of the window. For a moment he seemed to float lazily, spread-eagled on empty air. Then, in about half an instant, he seemed to dwindle down and away with fantastic and inconceivable speed. It was eight stories down, and at the last instant Rafferty pulled his head back into the room, not to see.

"So all right." A shaken Rafferty tried to defend himself a minute or so later down on the pavement. "What the hell did you expect me to think, when Tolliver kept lying and lying the way he did? He saw the kid Friday night even closer up than Miss Sanderson, and he wouldn't admit it. He described somebody else to me right out of his head. I don't know why. I can't even guess, Inspector. He just had to put the kid up to it, didn't he?"

Iron Mike was looking down at a shapeless something or other between them that was all covered over by a dirty old tarpaulin. He had a very curious expression on his face, for Iron Mike.

"I think he lied to you," he said slowly, "because he loved the woman. Oh, I know, I know. After the way she'd treated him? But some day you'll find out there are times when that doesn't matter at all, Rafferty—and it didn't with that fellow. And maybe, despite all her flings, he was the only man who really mattered to her. That's why she tried to protect him Friday night by pushing herself in between him and the boy.

"She knew right away what was up, and she knew who caused it—herself. So at the end your friend Tolliver tried in turn to protect her, by keeping another little escapade of the woman's out of public knowledge. She did her best to protect him, and he did his best after the thing happened to protect her. That's why he lied to you. Despite everything, he still loved the woman, Rafferty."

"Some love," Rafferty growled. "Whatever it was, he sure bollixed everything up anyway. Because how it looked to me—"

"How it looks to Mr. Rafferty," Iron Mike advised, "isn't always and necessarily the way it is. I'd remember that.

What went on between Mrs. Tolliver and the poor silly young lad here, I don't know, and I don't care to know. Very probably nothing at all. She might have only been keeping her hand in with Paul Kovacs by turning his head with her cunning tricks and her beguiling manners.

"But what probably started out as a joke to her soon became dead-earnest to the boy here, or so I'd say. How old was he? Seventeen, was it? And at that age—well, just think back to what he screamed at us upstairs a few minutes ago. 'She loved me, she loved me, she loved me!' Which showed that he believed what he said, all right. A boy his age was simply no match for her."

"Then maybe she put him up to it," Rafferty urged. "Led him on little by little until he agreed to kill the husband for her. Until she got him so worked up and excited—"

"God save your poor head," Iron Mike answered to that. "If that was the case, why did she push herself in between them Friday night? No, no. I don't think she had any idea of what the boy had made up his mind to do until that moment. She might even have tried to break it off with him, but he wouldn't have it. She had got more than she bargained for. Paul Kovacs alone must have decided that if only the husband stood in the way of true love, then the husband had to go.

"It wasn't Tolliver's idea, Rafferty, and it wasn't Mrs. Tolliver's. But take a boy seventeen years old, and in love for the first time in his life, probably, and anything can happen. He's as likely to go hog wild as not. There's the only answer to this whole dirty mess for you, and remember it next time. When I was a young fellow like him, just starting to feel my oats, I rode down in the elevator one day with a girl who lived in the same apartment house. And by God—"

"What?" Rafferty put in, intrigued by such unexpected human frailty in Iron Mike. "You mean she was a real knockout, Inspector, like that Miss Sanderson?"

"Oh, I suppose," Iron Mike admitted, eyes still fixed on the old tarp under them. "But I can't even remember now what she looked like. I was just sixteen or seventeen, Rafferty, and there was the whiff of her perfume around me and the brush of her right arm against mine—half a second—when she was pressed back in the car by some other people. Now I'm a damned happily married man with a fine family—but however it was, whatever it was, all I can say—and only half a second, mind you—is that even now I find myself thinking of that damned woman almost every day of my life. Seventeen, Rafferty, is a very bad age. May God rest his poor silly boy's soul."